PRAISE FOR STEPHEN LEATHER

'A writer at the top of his game'
Sunday Express

'A master of the thriller genre'
Irish Times

'Let Spider draw you into his web, you won't regret it'
The Sun

'The sheer impetus of his storytelling is damned hard to resist'
Daily Express

'High-adrenaline plotting'
Sunday Express

'Written with panache, and a fine ear for dialogue, Leather manages the collision between the real and the occult with exceptional skill, adding a superb time-shift twist at the end'
Daily Mail on *Nightmare*

'A wicked read'
Anthony Horowitz on *Nightfall*

'He has the uncanny knack of producing plots that are all too real'
Daily Mail

'In brisk newsman's style he explores complex contemporary issues while keeping the action fast and bloody'
Economist

'Stephen Leather is one of our most prolific and successful crime writers ... A disturbing, blood-chilling read from a writer at the top of his game'
Sunday Express on *Midnight*

'He has the uncanny knack of producing plots that are all too real, and this is no exception. It is the authenticity of this plot that grasps the imagination and never lets it go'
Daily Mail on *First Response*

Standing Strong

Also by Stephen Leather

Pay Off
The Fireman
Hungry Ghost
The Chinaman
The Vets
The Long Shot
The Birthday Girl
The Double Tap
The Solitary Man
The Tunnel Rats
The Bombmaker
The Stretch
Tango One
The Eyewitness
Penalties
Takedown
The Shout
The Bag Carrier
Plausible Deniability
Last Man Standing
Rogue Warrior
The Runner
Breakout
The Hunting
Desperate Measures
Standing Alone
The Chase
Still Standing
Triggers

Spider Shepherd: SAS thrillers:
The Sandpit
Moving Targets
Drop Zone
Russian Roulette
Baltic Black Ops

Spider Shepherd thrillers:
Hard Landing
Soft Target
Cold Kill
Hot Blood
Dead Men
Live Fire
Rough Justice
Fair Game
False Friends
True Colours
White Lies
Black Ops
Dark Forces
Light Touch
Tall Order
Short Range
Slow Burn
Fast Track
Dirty War
Clean Kill
First Strike

Jack Nightingale supernatural thrillers:
Nightfall
Midnight
Nightmare
Nightshade
Lastnight
San Francisco Night
New York Night
Tennessee Night
New Orleans Night
Las Vegas Night
Rio Grande Night

Standing Strong

A Matt Standing Thriller

Stephen Leather

Copyright © 2024 by Stephen Leather
The right of Stephen Leather to be identified as the author of this work has been asserted by him in accordance with the Copyright, Designs and Patents Act 1988.

All characters in this publication are fictitious and any resemblance to real persons, living or dead, is purely coincidental.

TABLE OF CONTENTS

Chapter 1 · 1
Chapter 2 · 9
Chapter 3 · 17
Chapter 4 · 29
Chapter 5 · 34
Chapter 6 · 37
Chapter 7 · 41
Chapter 8 · 48
Chapter 9 · 53
Chapter 10 · 55
Chapter 11 · 60
Chapter 12 · 73
Chapter 13 · 80
Chapter 14 · 87
Chapter 15 · 103
Chapter 16 · 107
Chapter 17 · 114
Chapter 18 · 121
Chapter 19 · 132
Chapter 20 · 146
Chapter 21 · 159
Chapter 22 · 167
Chapter 23 · 176
Chapter 24 · 179
Chapter 25 · 188

Chapter 26 · 202
Chapter 27 · 208

About the Author · 213
First Strike · 215

Chapter 1

HEREFORD, FEBRUARY 2022

Matt Standing had jogged just over five miles in desert fatigues and boots, with a packed Bergen on his back and a carbine in his hand. He looked at his watch, a black Casio G-Shock. It had taken him an hour and a quarter, which was pretty good going, but his work out had been across the relatively flat terrain of the SAS's Stirling Lines barracks at Credenhill. Carrying that amount of weight across the desert would be a whole different ball game. Not that Standing was heading out to the Middle East any time soon, but nothing was set in stone so he was determined to stay match fit. He took a deep breath and exhaled slowly. He was sweating and his fatigues under his armpits were as damp as his hair, but he had promised to run at least eight miles before calling it a day.

He pulled a canteen from his belt and took a swig. As he wiped his mouth with the back of his hand he saw movement in a grey SUV parked next to the admin building. The car belonged to Tom 'Bash' Macleod, an SAS veteran with more than seven years' active service behind him. Standing hadn't seen the car arrive so Macleod must have been sitting there for some time. Standing clipped his canteen back onto his belt.

Even by SAS standards Macleod was short - just five foot three - but he was a formidable soldier. Fitter than almost all of his fellow troopers, he was focussed, ruthlessly efficient, iron-hard and equally lethal with weapons or in unarmed combat. His major weakness was a short fuse that had became legendary in the Regiment. His turned down mouth and habitual expression of a bulldog chewing a wasp had initially earned him the nickname of 'Grumps', but his height must have put one of his patrol-mates in mind of the seven dwarves because he then christened him 'Bashful'. Soon shortened to 'Bash', it had become his permanent nickname.

As Standing walked towards the SUV, he realised that Macleod had his hands on top of the steering wheel, and in his right hand he had a gun. It was an all-black Colt Cobra .38 Special, a lightweight, aluminium-framed short-barrelled revolver that was perfect for concealed carry. Standing frowned. There was no way that Macleod had a legitimate reason for having the weapon in his car. As Standing watched, Macleod slowly raised the gun and placed the end of the barrel against his temple.

'Bash!' shouted Standing, breaking into a sprint. Macleod was staring straight ahead through the windscreen. The gun was shaking in his hand, either from tension or the weight. 'Bash!' Standing shouted again, but the man showed no sign of hearing him. The gun jerked in Macleod's hand but there was no explosion, in fact no sound or reaction at all. Macleod continued to stare through the windscreen.

Standing reached the SUV and banged on the window with the flat of his hand. Macleod flinched. His finger was still on the trigger of the gun.

'Open the bloody window, Bash!' Standing shouted.

Macleod nodded and pressed the button to lower the window.

'Get your finger off the trigger, now!'

Macleod looked at the gun as if seeing it for the first time. He slid his finger off the trigger and Standing reached in and took the gun from him. 'Where did you get this from?' he asked.

'The armoury.'

'Why?'

'I told them I wanted to do some concealed carry exercises.'

'I mean why did you put it to your head and pull the trigger?' said Standing. 'I saw what you did. What the hell are you playing at?'

'Sarge, it's not what it looks like,' said Macleod.

'Bollocks, I saw you put it to your head and pull the trigger.'

'If I was serious about killing myself, I'd have put more rounds in.'

'What are you talking about, Bash?'

Macleod nodded at the gun. 'Look for yourself.'

Standing clicked the cylinder release button and flicked out the cylinder. There was only one round chambered, and it would have gone off if the trigger had been pulled again. Standing shook his hand to flick the cylinder back into place and stuck the gun in his belt. 'So what, you're playing some sick version of Russian Roulette, is that it?'

Macleod grimaced. 'You wouldn't understand.'

'Yeah, well I'm going to have to understand, because there's no way I'm going into combat with a man who has a death wish.'

Macleod opened his mouth to speak, but then shook his head, clearly lost for words.

'Get out of the car, Bash. We need to talk.'

'Just leave me alone, Sarge. This is none of your business.'

'Get out of the car now, or you can pack up your gear and go back to your unit.'

Macleod glared at Standing, his jaw set tight, then he nodded and climbed out. Standing took him along to the Sergeants' Mess, dropping off his gear on the way. The mess was almost empty, with a civilian barman in a white jacket standing behind the bar. Standing pointed Macleod towards a corner table and asked the barman for whisky. 'A good one,' said Standing. 'A single malt.'

The barman reached for a bottle of Laphroaig. 'Single or double?'

Standing held out his hand. 'The bottle. Two glasses. And an ice bucket.'

The barman used a scoop to fill a stainless steel bucket with ice and Standing carried everything over to the table. Macleod stared through the window as Standing sat down opposite him. Standing had been in D Squadron with Macleod for the best part of six months, and Standing knew a fair bit about the man's background. Macleod had grown up in Muirhouse, one of the most deprived areas of the otherwise genteel city of Edinburgh. With an alcoholic mother and a father who had walked out when his son was still in nappies, it was almost inevitable that he would have drifted into crime. He joined the local street gang and had stopped going to school by the time he was thirteen. He acquired a formidable reputation in fights with rival gangs and by the age of seventeen, he already had a criminal record including twelve months in 'juvie' - the Young Offenders' Institution at Polmont near Falkirk - for assault. When he was again arrested after yet another street brawl, he was given a final warning by the magistrate to mend his ways or face a long custodial sentence if he appeared in court again. A few days later he chanced on two soldiers setting up an Army recruitment stand in the street. One of the soldiers had been in the young offenders' institution with Macleod and after being reassured that his criminal conviction was not a barrier to joining the Army, he found himself signing up. His fighting skills and toughness were not in doubt but his fitness levels were nowhere near the level required, making basic training the hardest thing he had ever done, but he gritted his teeth, toughed it out and came through it near the top of his group. He joined the Paras and then followed the well-trodden path to SAS Selection. His endurance, determination and guts were unbreakable and although one SAS NCO expressed reservations about his temperament, he passed Selection at the first attempt and then joined D Squadron.

One thing that Standing knew about Macleod was that he had a short fuse and had already been RTUed once from the Regiment for flattening a young officer on attachment to the SAS. RTU - Returned To Unit - was often permanent, but Macleod's fighting skills were such that, after serving a two year banishment with the Paras, he was allowed to retake Selection and rejoin the Regiment, although he was warned that any further incident would lead to his permanent dismissal. Standing's own past issues with anger management made him more sympathetic than most to Macleod. While serving with the Paras, Standing had lost his stripes after assaulting an officer and after joining the SAS, he had punched one officer so hard that he broke his nose and cracked his jaw for him. That again cost him the stripes he had only recently regained. His phenomenal soldiering skills had saved him from an immediate Return To Unit but he had been forced to undergo anger management therapy at the insistence of his CO, Colonel Davies.

Standing poured generous slugs of Laphroaig into the glasses and handed one to Macleod. Macleod wrinkled his nose, then clinked his glass against Standing's before downing the whisky in several gulps. Standing did the same, then refilled both glasses. 'So what's the story, Bash?' he asked. 'Why the death wish?'

'It's not that, Sarge.' said Macleod. 'In fact, it's the opposite. I was trying to feel…alive, I guess. Trying to feel something. I just feel…' He shrugged. 'I can't explain it.'

'You're going to have to, Bash. I saw you put a gun to your head and pull the trigger.'

Macleod shrugged again. 'Six to one odds,' he said. 'We've gone into combat facing worse odds than that.'

'Five to one,' said Standing. 'One round and five empty chambers. You've done this before?'

'A few times.'

'Bloody hell, Bash, five to one is lot less acceptable if you keep doing it.'

'That was the third time.'

'And you get a kick out of it, is that it?'

'Not a kick, no. But I get a surge of adrenaline, I feel alive. It's been months since I saw any action. All this training is doing my head in.'

'Train hard, fight easy, you know that, Bash.'

'I'm not a rookie, Sarge.'

'Nobody enjoys training. I spent the afternoon running around the camp with a full Bergen and it wasn't for fun, I can tell you that. But it has to be done. There's more to this than an adrenaline surge. There has to be.'

Macleod drained his glass and Standing refilled it. Macleod used his fingers to drop in two cubes of ice and he swirled the glass around. 'I don't want to talk about it, Sarge.'

'I hear you. But your career is on the line here, Bash.'

Macleod sneered at him. 'You're gonna grass me up, is that it? Yeah, well snitches get stitches, remember that.'

Standing grinned. 'Think you can take me, Bash?'

'I'd give it a good try.'

'Yeah, you would. But you'd still end up on your back with a broken nose. Or worse.'

Macleod put down his glass and sighed. 'I'm sorry, Sarge. I know you've got my best interests at heart.'

'I do, Bash. You've got a problem and unless you talk about it, that problem, whatever it is, will just get worse. I don't want to have to tell the CO what happened, but if you're putting the Regiment at risk I won't have any choice. You say you don't have a death wish, but putting a gun to your head and pulling the trigger isn't normal behaviour.'

'Like I said, I wanted to feel something. Anything.'

'And trying to kill yourself makes you feel something?'

Macleod fixed his eyes on Standing. 'It does, yes.'

'Is that why you keep punching officers? To feel something?'

Macleod laughed. 'I punch Ruperts because they sometimes need punching.'

Standing grinned. 'Amen to that.'

They clinked their glasses and drank again.

'Have you done other stuff like this?' asked Standing as he poured more whisky. 'Things that put you at risk?'

Macleod sipped his whisky and nodded. 'Yeah. I guess.'

'You guess? Or you know?'

Macleod sighed. 'A month or so back I went out on the live fire area of the PATA range.'

'You did what now?'

The small size of Pontrilas Army Training Area and the proximity of civilian houses outside the wire, meant that the ranges there were not used for artillery or mortars because of their wide potential killing zone, so nothing heavier than grenades was fired there, but it was still a live fire area. At PATA, SAS men could not only carry out the relentless practice with their weapons that saw them fire literally thousands of rounds in training, but they could also take part in exercises simulating infiltrations, storming targets, casevacs and other manoeuvres under the heaviest enemy fire. In those exercises, to simulate actual combat as closely as possible, torrents of live rounds would be passing inches over the heads of the participants.

'The range was in use, but it was quiet over lunchtime. I found a dip in the ground and made myself comfortable in it. I watched the skylarks above until the firing started again. Rounds whizzing all around me. I stayed there until the siren signalled that it was over for the day. Then I went back to the barracks.'

'And how did it make you feel?'

'At the time, yeah, I felt alive. But afterwards, I realised how stupid I was. I always do, after the event. The adrenaline dies down and the numbness returns.' He shrugged. 'My life.'

'You know we've got an exercise over at PATA tomorrow?'

Macleod nodded. 'Yeah, I know.'

'I'm serious, Bash. If there's any chance of our people being at risk, you need to stay away.'

'I'll be fine, Sarge. I never put anyone else at risk, I swear.'

Standing took a long pull on his whisky. 'You told me about your mum, her drinking and all. Did she have similar issues?'

'Did she play Russian Roulette? Nah.'

'But she drank, you told me that. I know they say that alcoholism is a disease, but often it can be a symptom of another problem.'

Macleod's eyes narrowed. 'You think it's genetic, my mother was sick in the head and so am I?'

'Bash, I went through a shed load of therapy to deal with my own anger management issues,' said Standing. 'I explored a lot of avenues.'

Macleod drained his glass. 'I never knew my dad. Not really. Mum always said he used to knock her around. Put her in hospital several times, she said.'

Standing poured more whisky for him.

'Never got my father's side of the story, obviously. But even after he'd gone, mum was never really right. She had ups and downs, for no rhyme or reason. Up one minute, down the next.'

'Bipolar?'

'They didn't call it bipolar back then. But yeah, that was probably it.'

'And when she was down, she drank?'

'Nah, the opposite. When she was up she'd reach for the bottle. Vodka when we were kids but she graduated to wine as she got older. She had happy pills for the depression. Mother's little helper.' He frowned. 'You think I'm bipolar?'

'I'm not an expert, Bash. Maybe you need to see one?'

'If they say I've got mental health issues, I'm out.'

Standing shook his head. 'That's not true. We're in the SAS, mate. We're trained to fight and kill. If we were normal, there's no way we could do the jobs we're tasked with. If we were all touchy-feely there's no way we could look someone in the eye and pull the trigger.'

'Aye, we're a bunch of psychopaths and no mistake,' said Macleod. He clinked his glass against Standing's. 'Here's to psychos.'

They both drank.

'Are you going to tell the CO, Sarge?'

'No mate. But I need you to promise me that you won't be playing Russian Roulette again any time soon.'

'I can do that.'

'And you need to see a therapist. I can give you some names.'

'Can't I just talk to you?'

'Bash, I'm not an expert. I can show you a few techniques to control your temper, but this other thing, your death wish or your bipolar tendencies, that's out of my league. You need to talk to someone experienced in the field. I'll give you some names.'

'But the Regiment won't know?'

'They won't hear it from me, Bash. You have my word.'

Chapter 2

Standing had been put in charge of safety protocols for a series of hostage rescue exercises at PATA: the Pontrilas Army Training Area, in the Welsh borders, twenty miles from the SAS base at Credenhill. It was not designated as a Special Forces training area and in theory was available to any army unit that wanted to train there, but in practice anyone enquiring about its availability on any date in any year from here to eternity, would always be told 'I'm afraid it's already been booked on that date.' Standing was doing the heavy lifting on the exercise, but he was under the command of a young officer, Lieutenant Peregrine Balfour, 'Perry' to his friends, though that did not include any of the SAS officers, NCOs and men he was serving with. In the past junior officers serving with the SAS had to come from another regiment, do Selection and then serve for no more than three years with the Regiment before returning to their former unit. However, the MoD, perhaps hoping to impose a greater sense of military discipline on the frequently unruly men of the SAS, who served in a Regiment in which only the NCOs and other ranks were permanent members and officers were merely passing through, had now imposed a new system. In its wisdom, the MoD had now decreed that men like Balfour could join the SAS straight from Sandhurst on what was described as 'Officer's Direct Entry'. Known as 'Special Forces Officers', they were no longer subject to the previous three-year rule, and once they were in the Regiment, they could build their military careers within it. Most of the existing SAS officers didn't like the system at all and the trogs all hated it, because the direct entry men had never passed Selection nor had any background in Special Forces.

Although Balfour had now been with the SAS for two years, his previous duties had been confined to training and admin, and he was desperate to make a good impression on his superiors, not just in Hereford but in the MoD as well. He was less concerned about the impression he made on Standing and the troopers and had a habit of addressing them curtly, as if he was a schoolmaster and they were unruly pupils.

PATA was a former munitions depot served by a now dismantled railway line. A public road, the C1221 Elm Green Road, cut right through the middle of the site but MoD attempts to close or divert it had always been rejected by the council after furious complaints from locals who would have to make a detour of several miles if that happened. As a result, the site had two separate entrance gates on either side of the road, and the access points to other parts of the site were all screened from public view by fences and tarpaulins, though the constant sound of shots and explosions would have left no one in any doubt about what was going on behind them. Any car, cyclist or pedestrian passing along the road was subject to close scrutiny by MoD police and anyone coming to a halt there would be challenged and either rapidly moved on or detained while their identity was established and the records and databases of the police and the intelligence services checked for any red flags against their names.

A wooded hill divided the open fields to the west of PATA from the firing ranges on the eastern side. Those included 'Building 1011' - the Indoor Weapons Range - and a separate building for Close Quarter Battle training, a function once performed by the Killing House in the old SAS camp in Hereford.

There was also a sniper range and various buildings and pieces of special equipment scattered across the site, enabling the SAS to train for almost any conceivable scenario in counter-terrorism. The fuselage of a passenger jet helped prepare for aircraft hijackings, and in case a train was targeted, there were redundant railway carriages which could be completely blacked out to simulate a hijacked train in a tunnel, including the Channel Tunnel, or a Tube train on the London Underground.

There were buildings mimicking those found in different parts of the world where the Regiment was already operating or was likely to be doing so in the future. They ranged from the terraced houses and blocks of flats that had originally simulated buildings in Northern Ireland, to the kind of flat-roofed, mud-brick buildings found in Afghanistan and right across the Middle East, though the effects of the prevailing weather in the Welsh borders meant that the mud-bricks had to be repaired regularly and completely replaced every couple of years. Every building functioned as a separate firing range and every room within each building was also treated as a separate range. That system meant that, providing troopers stayed within their demarcation zone, snipers and assault teams could practise live firing, but it was dependent on absolutely rigid control.

The exercises were partly for the SAS to demonstrate the effectiveness of a new carbine that was being offered to the Ministry of Defence by an American manufacturer. The name had been withheld from the SAS and there were no markings on the weapons. It was similar to the M4 but with a shorter barrel and a double-stacked magazine. The SAS had put the gun through its paces on the ranges at Credenhill, and hadn't been impressed. It was lightweight and came with very low recoil, but the double-stacked magazine kept jamming. The idea was that magazines wouldn't have to be changed so often during combat, but a jammed magazine could make life very difficult. Standing had conveyed the reservations of his troopers to Lieutenant Balfour but the officer had just shrugged and suggested that they simply dispose of any magazines that had proven to be faulty.

There were three exercises in total - a plane scenario, a Tube train scenario, and a building that had been fitted out as a supermarket. Standing had been made the designated Exercise Safety Officer for the hostage rescue exercise, and it was being watched by observers from all the branches of the security services involved, including the MoD, the regular Army, hostage negotiators, police, fire and ambulance crews. Two representatives of the carbine manufacturer - slick guys in expensive suits - were also there. They were well groomed with loud, braying laughs and they always stayed close to the MoD officials.

The first two exercises were straightforward and ones the SAS troopers had carried out dozens of times.

The plane was fitted out with several dozen shop dummies, and the hostage takers were also mannequins. But the places of the hostages were taken by SAS troopers, adding a bit more realism to the situation. The troopers were to go through the front and rear doors, using flashbangs and the new carbines, and live ammunition.

In his role as Safety Officer, Standing had a bank of screens in front of him showing the view from CCTV cameras in every part of the ranges and from within every individual firing range. As Standing checked the video feeds from the plane he realised that Macleod was playing the part of one of the hostages and had taken it upon himself to wear a long flowery print dress and a shoulder length blonde wig. 'Bash, what are you playing at?' Standing asked over the radio.

'Getting in touch with my feminine side, Sarge,' said Macleod.

The exercise went perfectly, with two four-men teams entering at the same time and taking out the hostage-taking mannequins with rapid-fire double taps. The observers were standing fifty yards away from the plane behind a bullet-proof glass shield, with a bank of monitors similar to the ones that Standing was looking at. They applauded enthusiastically when the exercise was over and the SAS troopers came out of the aircraft, but Lieutenant Balfour gave Macleod a frosty look.

The second exercise involved another two four-man teams breaching a Tube carriage in which there were half a dozen passengers, played by SAS troopers, and a single dummy, this one wearing a suicide vest. One of the teams created a diversion while the other moved in from the side of the carriage. This time Macleod was leading the inserting team, thankfully having replaced his dress and wig with body armour and a Kevlar helmet.

The observers were once again watching behind a bullet-proof glass screen but Standing followed the exercise on another bank of monitors, further away from the carriage. Speed was of the essence when dealing with a suicide bomber - the aim was to neutralise the threat as quickly as possible, ideally with a head shot. In the real world, a round smashing into a vest loaded with explosives could end up ruining everybody's day.

Macleod led the team in, his carbine at the ready, but instead of taking the head shot he ran forward, upended the carbine, and slammed the stock against the dummy's head. The head flew off and clattered along the floor of the carriage. The observers frowned in confusion as Macleod and his team left the carriage. The SAS troopers who had been playing the part of passengers were laughing uproariously,

As the troopers left the carriage, they were confronted by the lieutenant who was clearly unhappy at what had happened. Standing hurried over and the officer was still berating Macleod, who was taking the abuse with gritted teeth.

'You think this is funny, Macleod,' spluttered the officer,

Macleod held up his carbine. 'What's funny is this pile of shit you gave us. It jammed. Right as I went for a head shot. If that had happened in a live situation me and my team would have been blown to pieces.'

'Someone else could have taken the shot,' said Balfour.

'How, you fucking moron? We were in single file moving down the carriage. What was I supposed to do. Take a seat? Have you ever been in a hostage situation? Have you?'

Balfour prodded Macleod in the chest. 'Don't you dare talk to me like that!' he hissed.

Macleod glared at the officer and raised his carbine as if he was preparing to smash the butt against the lieutenant's chin. Standing reached them just in time to grab the gun and he took it from Macleod. 'I'll get this checked out, you grab yourself another weapon.'

Macleod looked as if he was going to argue, but Standing silenced him with a steely glare. Macleod walked away, shaking his head.

'Did you hear what he called me?' said Balfour.

'Heat of the moment, Sir,' said Standing. 'I did warn you that the troops are not happy with these guns. They've been jamming all week.'

'We can discuss this later,' said Balfour. 'But make it clear to Macleod that if he doesn't treat me with some respect, there'll be consequences.'

'I will, Sir,' said Standing.

'Make sure that you do,' said Balfour, before turning his back on Standing and walking over to the observers.

The third exercise was in a large metal-sided building that had been fitted out as a supermarket, with tills and rows of shelves, many of which were packed with cardboard boxes. As it was a live fire exercise there was no way the observers could be safely inside the building and so they would watch on monitors outside. Tea, coffee, soft drinks and several plates of sandwiches had been provided for the visitors.

This time there would be three four-man teams against a simulated MTA, a marauding terrorist attack with multiple attackers using machetes. The attackers were in the form of ten dummies with machetes duct taped to the hands. Half a dozen troopers dressed in civilian clothing would be moving around, playing the part of panicking bystanders. It was always useful for the troopers to get some insight in how it felt to be a civilian under fire. But it was a dangerous situation for everyone and Standing was on full alert as he gave the go-ahead for the exercise to begin.

There were two ways in to the building, a front entrance with glass sliding doors, and a back way through a box-filled store room. Two teams were to move in through the main entrance, while a four-man team led by Macleod would come in the back way. The aim of the exercise was to identify and neutralise the attackers without any members of the public getting hurt.

The area was covered by half a dozen cameras and Standing's eyes flicked between the monitors as the SAS teams moved in. The two teams entered through the main entrance and immediately began taking out the targets. The SAS 'civilians' ran to the rear of the shop, shouting and screaming, clearly enjoying the role-playing just a little too much.

Macleod emerged from the store room, with three troopers tucked in behind him. He took out one of the dummies with a head shot and planted a second round in the dummy's chest a fraction of a second later. Standing nodded his approval at the perfect shooting.

Macleod's team fanned out. There were shots being fired all around the store now, double taps that often were so close together that they could be mistaken for single shots.

Macleod took aim at another dummy and pulled the trigger. There were so many shots being fired that Standing didn't hear Macleod's shot, but then Macleod straightened up and began cursing. His gun had clearly jammed. The rest of his team continued to fan out, firing as they moved, but Macleod stormed towards the main entrance, oblivious to the rounds whizzing around him.

Standing yelled 'Stop! Stop! Stop!' so that everything immediately ground to a halt. He jogged over to the front entrance and got there just as Macleod emerged into the open air, his cheeks flushed and his eyes wide. 'Calm the fuck down, Bash,' he said.

'Fucking gun jammed again, Sarge. This is fucking madness.'

'I hear you, but you need to calm down. You could have been hit yourself just then, storming out like you did.'

'Sarge, if we ever use one of these guns in combat, someone is going to die.'

Standing couldn't help but smile. 'That's sort of the point, isn't it?'

Macleod glared at him. 'You know what I mean. How are we expected to work with guns that keep jamming?'

'We're not, and hopefully one of the results of these exercises is that the powers that be will realise the weapon is a non-starter. But that's no reason to lose your rag, especially when live rounds are flying about. Doesn't help my record as a safety officer if a trooper gets shot in the head.'

Macleod held up the carbine. 'No one's going to get shot with this piece of shit,' he said, and threw it to the ground, just as Lieutenant Balfour walked up.

'What the hell is going on, Sergeant?' he snapped at Standing.

'We've had another weapon malfunction, Sir, so I thought it safest to call a halt to the exercise,' said Standing.

'Was that before Macleod decided to put his own life and the lives of others in danger?'

'I thought it better to bring the exercise to a close, Sir,' said Standing, avoiding the question.

Balfour glared at Macleod. 'And pick that weapon up now,' he said.

'Pick it up yourself,' snarled Macleod.

'What did you say?' shouted the lieutenant. All the observers were looking in their direction now.

'Bash, you need to calm down,' said Standing. 'I understand your unhappiness but there's a time and a place.'

Macleod sneered at Standing, then turned and walked away.

'Don't you dare walk away from me, Macleod!' shouted Balfour. 'I'll see you in the glasshouse for this!'

Macleod gave him the finger without looking back and Balfour stamped his foot in frustration.

'Sir, Macleod has been under a lot of pressure recently,' said Standing.

'That goes with the job, Sergeant. And if he can't stand the heat then he needs to get the hell out of the kitchen.' He pointed at Macleod, who had removed his Kevlar helmet and thrown it to the ground. 'That man is on the way out, you have my word on that.'

Standing opened his mouth to reply but realised that there was nothing he could say that would change the lieutenant's mind.

Chapter 3

Later that day, the lieutenant made a formal complaint to Colonel Davies and the CO summoned the three of them - Balfour, Macleod and Standing - to his office. Balfour spent the best part of fifteen minutes berating Macleod and arguing that the man had no place in the SAS. Macleod took the barrage of abuse in silence, though most of the time he had his jaw and his fists clenched. Standing kept catching his eye and trying to give him a reassuring nod, but Macleod didn't seem to notice and kept staring at a spot on the wall behind the Colonel's head.

Eventually Balfour ran out of steam and stood ramrod straight, his chest rising and falling.

The Colonel nodded. 'Step outside, Macleod,' he said.

'What, I don't get to give my side of the story?' said Macleod.

The Colonel flashed him an icy look. 'Outside. Now.'

Macleod realised he had overstepped the mark and he nodded. 'Sorry, Boss. My bad.'

'Yes, very much your bad,' said the Colonel. 'Go.'

Macleod saluted, which was clearly ironic because in the SAS men never saluted their officers. He didn't wait for the salute to be returned, but spun on his heels and marched out of the office, his feet stamping on the ground with every step. Standing had to fight not to grin. Macleod really was pushing his luck.

The Colonel waited until Macleod had closed the door behind him before waving to Balfour and Standing to sit on the two chairs facing his desk.

'The man is a loose cannon,' said Balfour. 'He…'

The Colonel raised a hand to silence the lieutenant. 'I understand your frustration, Perry. I do. But with our staffing levels the way they are, I'm reluctant to start throwing experienced troopers on the scrap heap. We've a major op coming up that I can't tell you about yet, but we'll need all hands to the pumps. Having said that, Macleod needs to be punished, and he will be.'

'So he'll be charged with insubordination?' asked Balfour.

'You understand how discipline works in the SAS?' said the Colonel. 'Most crimes and misdemeanours are dealt with by 'VCs' - Voluntary Contributions - even though there's nothing voluntary about them. If an SAS man screws up in some way, I can examine the crime and the circumstances that led to it and then usually say something like 'Right, a month's pay,' and if the trooper pays it without argument, that's the end of the matter and nothing goes on his record. However, if he doesn't pay, then it automatically becomes a Form 252 and is added to his permanent record.'

'He needs to be charged, Sir. He put his own life, and the lives of others, at risk by his actions.'

'I hear you, lieutenant. But as you know, as soon as a formal charge is laid, there is a process that has to be followed. The accused is marched in, evidence presented and the accuser - you in this case - is allowed to speak. At the end the accused will be asked by me if he accepts the punishment. And I think that we both know Macleod well enough to be sure that the answer will be "No". At that point he can ask for "Redress of Grievance" and can also demand a court martial. Until that point, he can only be represented by military lawyers, who we must assume are likely to be sympathetic to the requirements of military discipline and the structure of command, but if the case goes to a court martial, it passes out of the army's hands and Macleod can insist on a civilian lawyer. And once that happens, the whole business of the reliability of these new guns will be brought up in open court. That means it will be picked up by the Press and we know that the MoD wouldn't be happy about that, would they?'

The lieutenant nodded slowly. 'No, they wouldn't.'

'So it's best all round if we handle this internally, don't you agree?'

Balfour sighed and nodded. Standing was, as always, impressed with the Colonel's way of handling dissent. The Colonel had painted Balfour into a corner and there was no way out.

'Excellent, so we are in agreement,' said the Colonel. 'Thank you so much for bringing this to my attention, it will most definitely be acted upon, and now if you don't mind I need to thrash out the details of Macleod's punishment with Sergeant Standing.'

Balfour stood up and began to salute before stopping himself and leaving the office.

The Colonel sighed and sat back in his chair. 'Bash just gets worse, doesn't he, Matt?'

'Not really, Boss. The old Bash would probably have taken a swing at the lieutenant. The fact that he didn't shows that he's making progress.'

'He was lucky that Balfour's main concern is to work his way up the MoD's promotion ladder while seeing as little combat as possible. His time here is a stepping stone to greater things, he knows that and we know it. And if the lack of reliability of this new gun gets out, it'll be blamed on him. So Macleod caught a break. But he's running out of lives, Matt. I'll read him the riot act and explain how close he came to being RTUd, but you need to talk to him, too.'

'I will do, Boss.'

'I've made every allowance for Bash over the years,' said the Colonel 'He's a bloody good soldier. I'd hate to lose him because he is a huge asset in combat situations but he is also a considerable liability when he's back at base between ops. In short, he's a ticking time-bomb and if he can't get his anger under control, I'm going to have to RTU him.' He gave Standing a shrewd look. 'You've had your own anger management issues in the past, and I've been impressed with the way you've knuckled down and dealt with them. So, what I'd like is for you to take Bash under your wing and try to help him deal with his own issues. Find a tactful way to phrase it obviously or it may trigger another nuclear explosion from him, but for god's sake explain to him that he's in the last chance saloon, and if he can't or won't find better ways to deal with his anger, he's going to be gone.' He paused. 'Can you do that for me?'

Standing nodded. 'I can try, Boss, but I can't guarantee he'll listen.'

'You're his last chance, Matt. So do your best.'

Standing thanked the Colonel and left the office. He found Macleod in the gym, stripping off his fatigues. 'Thought I'd go for a run, Sarge,' said Macleod. 'Burn off some of the nervous energy.'

'Are you okay?' asked Standing.

Macleod shrugged. 'I've been better.'

'Would a drink help?'

Macleod gave a brief smile. 'It might. It certainly couldn't hurt.'

'Let's get changed then I'll call a cab.'

'I can drive, Sarge.'

Standing shook his head. 'We're going to be doing some heavy drinking, Bash. Neither of us are getting behind the wheel.'

Standing chose a pub down by the river outside Hereford, well away from the normal SAS haunts. Even at half past three in the afternoon it wasn't as quiet as he had hoped because a group of four young men were occupying one end of the bar. They'd obviously been there since lunchtime and were getting increasingly rowdy as the drink took effect. Standing bought a couple of pints and he and Macleod settled themselves at a corner table at the other end of the bar. Without even being aware that they were doing so, both men sat with their backs to the wall, facing towards the door to the street. It was one of the unwritten SOPs of SAS men always to be in a position to see approaching danger so that, if necessary, it could be met head on. Special Forces called it the 'Point of Domination', the place from which you were able to dominate and exercise control over the entrances and exits from the room.

They had only been chatting for a few moments when there was a crash from the bar as one of the young men dropped his pint on the tiled floor, sending glass fragments flying and spraying beer in all directions, including some froth which landed on Macleod's jacket. As the barmaid hurried out from behind the bar with a dustpan and brush, the man just said, 'When you've cleared that up, get us another pint, will you darling?'

He looked up and intercepted a stare from Macleod, who had stood up and was using a handkerchief to wipe the beer off his jacket.

'What's your problem, Short-arse?' the bloke said, glaring at him. He was well-built and a head taller than Macleod, not that the size of their potential adversaries had ever been a concern for SAS men.

'I was just thinking that it's a shame your parents never taught you some manners,' Macleod said, his voice dangerously quiet.

'Well, why don't you come over here and try and teach me some then, you haggis-munching dwarf?' the yob said, as his mates fanned out to either side of him.

Standing rested a warning hand on Macleod's forearm. 'Easy, Bash,' he said, quietly. 'You're already in enough trouble for one day. We're here for a quiet pint and a chat, not a ruck with a bunch of morons.' He raised his voice. 'We don't want trouble boys, let's all just relax and enjoy ourselves, eh?'

'Yeah? Well then best your mate sits down and shuts the fuck up,' the yob said, eyeballing Macleod again.

Standing kept up the insistent pressure on Macleod's forearm until he resumed his seat.

The barmaid was holding up her phone. 'I'm gonna call the police if you don't behave yourselves,' she said.

One of the other yobs scowled at her. 'No need to get your knickers in a twist, darling. Nobody's making trouble.' He glanced at his mate, who was still staring at Macleod. 'Leave it Tel,' he said. 'They're not worth it.' He dropped his voice and murmured something to the one called Tel, who smiled and nodded, giving Macleod one last hard stare before turning back to his mates.

Standing was thoughtful as he watched them. 'I'm not sure we've heard the last of that,' he said, 'but we'll cross that bridge when we come to it and meanwhile, well done mate. Believe me, I know what it must have taken, not to walk over there and take that yob and his mates apart at the seams. Anyway at least we can have that quiet chat now. Or we can as soon as you buy me another pint, anyway.'

Macleod drained the rest of his pint in one gulp and headed for the bar.

'So look,' Standing said, when Macleod came back with the beers. 'I'm not your shrink or your father confessor, or anything like that, but I've had - I still have - anger management issues of my own, so perhaps I understand more than most what it's like for you. The shrinks I saw mainly said that my own problems are mostly because I lose patience with people who screw up and then instead of acknowledging it they deny it or try and cover for it with bluster and bullshit.'

'Ruperts,' said Macleod scornfully. 'We'd be so much better off without them.'

'Yeah, but in my case, it isn't just officers that set me off. It can be anyone. Anywhere. Anytime.' He paused. 'But impatience doesn't really cover it, because it's more like sheer blind fury with me. I can go from nought to a hundred in the blink of an eye, and I've decked people for practically nothing, sometimes without even thinking about it.'

'So how did you sort it?' Macleod said. 'Assuming that you did, that is.'

'Well, I needed help and none of us like to admit to that do we? But in this case, it's true, though the Boss had to hold a pistol to my head before I'd agree to do it. I must confess that I didn't take kindly to seeing a therapist at first and I probably wouldn't have gone except saying "No" wasn't an option. The Boss made it very clear to me that it was that or an RTU, and although I went in not really expecting anything to come from it, I've got to admit that the therapy really helped me. It hasn't made my anger issues disappear altogether of course, but it has given me some strategies to deal with it and, never say never, but so far it seems to be working.'

'Maybe you could teach me some?'

'Sure, I can do that. I use something called square breathing. You breathe in slowly, and count to four. Then you hold your breath for four seconds. Then you exhale for four seconds. Then you hold it for four seconds. Repeat until you feel centred.'

'Bit like counting to ten, and that never works for me.'

'It's the controlled breathing that does the trick,' said Standing. 'That and the fact that you have to concentrate on the count.' He shrugged. 'But you need an expert on the case, Bash. You've got the same anger management issues that I had, but your death wish is something else.'

'It's not a death wish, Sarge.'

'Bash, you stood up and walked through a hail of bullets.'

'The guys know what they're doing. I was never in any danger.'

'You were, Bash. I saw the whole thing on the monitors. You walked past two targets. You could easily have been hit.'

'Nah. The guys are pros. There's no such thing as collateral damage with us, you know that.'

'You could have died, Bash. And from the look on your face, you couldn't have cared less. If that's not a death wish, I don't know what is.' He took another pull on his pint. 'Anyway, the Boss is on your side. That's why you're sitting here chatting to me rather than heading out of Credenhill in the back of a three-tonner, being returned to your unit. But if you get on the wrong side of another officer again, even the Boss won't be able to save you.'

'So he's asked you to be my minder? Robin to my Batman. Jiminy Cricket to my Pinocchio? Tonto to my Lone Ranger?'

Standing laughed. 'More like a sounding board.' He paused. 'So when did your anger issues start or have you always had them?'

'No, I've not always had them,' Macleod said. 'Even though I did have the classic forces rough-arse background.'

'Yeah, I know you had it rough as a kid.'

Macleod forced a smile. 'Yeah, I had more than my share of scraps growing up, and plenty of run-ins with the Polis in my teens before I finally wised up and joined the Army. But I never felt the sheer blind fury I get now until after I'd started active service with the Regiment.' He broke off, staring into space, but Standing did not break the silence, leaving Macleod to wrestle with his demons until he felt ready to speak again. 'My patrol was on an op in Helmand,' Macleod said at last. 'I was point man and we were moving past a village, well a hamlet really, just three or four mud-brick houses. You've been in Afghanistan, you know the kind of places.'

Standing nodded. Yeah, he knew. It had amazed him the way that people could exist with next to no resources in places where survival wasn't just a skill, it was an art form honed through generations of endurance.

'We passed a woman in a burqa sitting outside the door of her house with two small boys playing in the dirt in front of her. One of the guys kept her covered while we searched the house, though I wasn't expecting any issues; what kind of woman would put her own kids in the firing line? We were moving on to the next house when the IED detonated. It had been buried right where the kids were playing. You're always alert for disturbed ground, right? But I'd assumed it was the kids' play that had scuffed it up. The woman and the kids were vapourised. Two of my patrol mates were killed instantly - there wasn't enough left of one to even scrape up and put in a body bag - and the other one, a guy we called Taters, had his leg and his balls blown off. He was between me and the IED so I only got some shrapnel wounds to my back and left arm. I've still got enough shrapnel in me to set off the security alarms every time I go through an airport security scanner.'

He took another long pull on his pint. 'Two Taliban fighters had detonated the IED remotely and the blast had exposed the end of the command wire. I could see the direction of it, running across the field to a low wall a couple of hundred yards away. I didn't call in air support; I was going to take care of those bastards myself. The blast had blown me off my feet, so I wormed my way into a patch of dead ground and then lay there waiting for them to come and admire their handiwork. There were two of them, an old guy with the hennaed hair of a Haji who'd done the pilgrimage to Mecca, and a boy with a wispy beard who might have been his son or his grandson, not that I cared either way. He was laughing as they approached and so eager to see the bodies that he was running ahead of the other guy. I double-tapped him and then emptied the rest of the magazine into the old guy. I called in a medivac and managed to get a tourniquet on what was left of Taters' leg and put a wound dressing on his groin. He was still conscious and I was going to give him a syrette of morphine but he shook his head. "Has it blown my balls off?" he asked and he could see from the look on my face what the answer was. Before I could stop him, he'd put the muzzle of his AK under his chin and fired a burst through the top of his head. There hasn't been a day since then when I don't ask myself why my mates got killed, while the one who fucked up - me - survived. And I still keep asking myself as well, did that woman know? Was she so terrified of the Taliban or so eager for martyrdom that she was willing to let her kids be slaughtered? Or were they even her kids at all?'

There was a long silence. 'Mate, I can't imagine what you went through and what you're still going through now,' Standing said eventually. 'And I don't have any glib solutions. But the one thing I do know is that your patrol mates would not have wanted your own life to be blighted by what happened that day. From what you've told me, I honestly don't think you did fuck up, but even if you did, we all make mistakes, and yes, sometimes they have awful consequences. I've had my share of screw-ups along the way but if it happens, like the man said, all you can do is get back up and keep fighting one more round. If you don't, or if you take it out on one of your own side - no matter how incompetent or irritating he might be - rather than the enemy, it's almost like you're giving the Taliban another win.'

'Yeah, you're right,' said Macleod. He forced a smile. 'Thanks, Sarge.'

Standing grinned. 'You'll not be thanking me tomorrow when you find out that the price of getting Balfour off your back was for you to lose a month's pay.'

Macleod winced but then shrugged his shoulders. 'You know what, it was cheap at twice the price…though if I'd known it was going to cost me that much, I'd have taken a proper swing at him.'

As Standing and Macleod were finishing their pints and getting ready to leave, the yobs at the bar also drank up and then headed out of the door, the one called Tel giving Macleod one last hostile look as he did so. Standing's fighting instincts rarely let him down and he was sure that the yobs were planning to lie in wait outside somewhere, ready to give them a kicking. It wasn't a thought that caused him any concern but he was trying to think of a way to keep Macleod out of it. If it all went tits up and the police got involved, it might be the final straw for Macleod's SAS career, whereas Standing was confident he could smooth over any problems it might cause for himself, if they should arise. 'Tell you what,' he said, wanting to allow the yobs time to think better of it and go home. 'Let's have a short for the road. Single malt?'

He ordered a couple of large ones and while Macleod was in the Gents, Standing took the opportunity to phone for a taxi. When it arrived, he drained the last of his whisky and followed Macleod outside, waiting until he'd got into the cab before saying, 'Actually, you know what? I think I'm going to walk.'

Macleod did a double-take. 'Back to PATA?'

'Yeah, it's a nice stroll along the riverbank most of the way.'

'All right, I'll come with,' Macleod said, starting to get out of the taxi.

'No, you're alright mate. If you don't mind, I could do with a bit of time to myself - thinking time - so I'll just see you back there.'

Macleod hesitated, then shrugged. 'Okay, if you're sure.' He sat down and pulled the door shut.

As Standing watched the taxi drive out of sight, he noted a movement behind the hedge at the side of the car park. Smiling to himself, he took the path down to the river bank, and began following it upstream, apparently sauntering along without a care in the world, although out of the corner of his eye he kept a close watch on the four figures who were hurrying ahead of him along the road running parallel to the path.

A couple of anglers were taking advantage of the long summer evening, standing in the shallows of the river eight or ten feet below him as they were casting flies, fishing for the trout that were keeping station in the faster-flowing current near the far bank. Fifty yards further on, in the shadows of the far side of the bridge that carried the road over the river, Standing saw the brief glow of a cigarette end that was swiftly extinguished as it was tossed into the water. His skin prickled and although there was no outward change in his demeanour, he felt the jolt as he went into full fight or flight mode and adrenalin began coursing through his system. The path narrowed as it passed under the bridge, and at that point was barely wide enough for two people to pass abreast, making it perfect for what he needed. He stopped just short of it and called out, 'Come on then, this is what you've been waiting for, isn't it? My mate's not here, so you'll just have to make do with me.'

The four yobs emerged from the shadows and two of them: Tel, the one who had smashed the glass and given Macleod a mouthful, and the one who had muttered something to him in the pub, began advancing towards Standing while the other two, unable to flank them because of the narrowness of the path, had to hang back and wait their turn. Tel had a motorbike chain in his hand and began swinging it as they closed on Standing. The other yob had armed himself with a piece of wooden rail he'd broken off the fence at the side of the road.

In a heartbeat Standing had assessed the relative threats of the two men and their weapons, and without conscious thought had already worked out his first moves. He feinted towards the one carrying the piece of wood, and as the one called Tel saw what he thought was his chance and took a stride forward, whirling the bike chain over his head, Standing ducked underneath it. He heard the whistle as it passed close enough to his head to part his hair, and then, as he straightened, he broke Tel's nose with a single blow from the heel of his hand. A fountain of blood spurted from the yob's nose and, blinded by the tears that had started to his eyes, Tel was effectively defenceless as Standing gave him a boot to the side of his knee that crumpled his leg underneath him and pitched him into the river.

Even before Tel had hit the water, Standing had smashed his elbow into the side of the other yob's head, then followed up with a knee to the groin, doubling him up in agony. As the yob gasped for breath, Standing grabbed his hair and jerked his head down, as he brought his knee up again, smashing it into the man's face.

As the yob collapsed in a crumpled heap on the path, Standing stepped over him and advanced on the other two. One launched himself at him but was rewarded with a punch to the throat that stopped him in his tracks and another blow to the head that pole-axed him. He followed Tel into the river, leaving only one of the four still standing. 'Honest mate, we didn't mean nothing by it,' he said, his voice rising to a squeak of panic as he saw Standing closing in on him.

'I'm not your mate and it's a bit too late to think of that now,' Standing said, burying his fist deep in the yob's solar plexus. As he measured another punch for the coup de grace, the yob threw himself into the river before Standing could put him there and began frantically splashing his way towards the far bank. On the way he passed his mate Tel, who was floundering in the middle of the river with a look of blind panic etched on his face.

'Help! I can't swim!' Tel shouted from the water, still well out of reach of the bank and coughing and spluttering as he flailed his arms around him.

'Best hope you're a quick learner then,' said Standing. He walked away without a backward look.

Chapter 4

Early the following morning, Standing was called in by Colonel Davies and 'warned off' for an op. The men were given only a couple of hours to gather their personal kit and say their farewells, before going into isolation from everyone. That included not just friends and family but even fellow SAS soldiers who were not part of the team for the op. While others hurried to catch a few words, hugs and kisses with their families, wives and girlfriends, Standing had no one to say his farewells to. His mother had died years before after being stabbed to death by his father, who was serving a life sentence in prison for the killing. Having lost both parents, his only other close relative, his sister, eight years his junior, had been fostered with a family who made it clear to Standing that he was not welcome at their door and even took out a restraining order to keep him away from her. In a trademark burst of furious anger, Standing had then gone around and punched the foster father and he had joined the Army mainly to avoid going to jail for the assault. His last family tie was broken when his sister died from a heroin overdose. Standing avenged her death by finding and killing the man who had supplied her with the drugs, but ever since then he had found himself completely alone in the world. In the forces and particularly in the SAS, his patrol mates became as much of a family as he had ever had, but even among them, he remained something of a loner. He was unmarried and although he was never short of female company, none of his girlfriends had ever been invited to share his life, only his bed.

Colonel Davies sent him to an immediate briefing with an MI6 officer. She was a woman of indeterminate middle-age, late forties or early fifties he guessed, with greying hair, cut short, and eyes so dark brown they looked almost black in poor light, framed by a pair of thin, wire-framed glasses. She stood up as Standing entered and extended her hand. Her grip as she shook hands with him was surprisingly firm. 'Sergeant Standing, how do you do? I'm Agnes Day.' She paused, noting the brief flicker of a smile that Standing hastily suppressed, before adding, 'and I'm already wearisomely familiar with all the Catholic jokes, thank you.' Standing frowned. He had absolutely no idea what she was talking about.

She smiled at his confusion. 'Agnus Dei is the Latin for Lamb of God.' She spelled it out for him to make absolutely sure that he understood. Also Agnes of Rome was a Christian martyr who was made a saint. January 21st is St Agnes Day.'

Standing forced a smile. 'I'm not really religious,' he said. 'Anyway, pleased to meet you, My friends call me Matt.'

'I don't think it's necessary for us to be on first-name terms. I'd prefer to keep things a little more formal, Sergeant Standing. It helps to maintain the boundaries.'

'I wouldn't have thought you'd have needed any help in maintaining those, Ms Day,' he said. 'Or is it Mrs?'

She shook her head. 'It's Ms.'

Standing grinned. 'Ms it is,' he said. 'Now, which bungled SIS op would you like the guys and me to step in and salvage for you this time?'

Her expression became glacial. 'I know the SAS like to think that every op that goes wrong is the fault of the SIS and every one that succeeds is entirely down to you, but…'

'And there's no shortage of supporting evidence for both of those propositions,' Standing said.

She showed a brief flash of irritation at the interruption but swiftly masked it. 'But as I was about to say, I think you'll find that any op is more likely to succeed when we work as a team. After all, we are all on the same side, are we not? Now, if we can continue?

You'll be aware, I'm sure, of growing concerns about Russian military activity on the borders of Ukraine. Under the pretext of routine manoeuvres, a huge Russian build-up of men and war materiel is already taking place. And every source of intel - humint and sigint - is pointing to the same conclusion: a fresh Russian invasion of Ukraine is being planned and is going to happen.'

'When? How long have we got?' Standing said.

She spread her hands. 'We think we have three or four weeks, maybe a little more.' There was a bottle of water on a table by the window and she drank some before continuing. 'They are also not only massing on their own border with Ukraine but on the Belarusian one too. That gives them a short, direct line for a blitzkrieg attack into Ukraine, theoretically enabling them to achieve the objective of smashing through to Kyiv, deposing its government and installing a puppet regime, before we in the West can marshal the resources, political, diplomatic, economic and military, to prevent it. So the first essential is obviously to blunt that Russian offensive by helping Ukrainian forces to slow down and repel any Russian tank columns advancing into Ukraine. It's a task that will be made even more difficult by the inevitable Russian air superiority over the outnumbered and outdated Ukrainian air force. The Ukrainian ground troops will certainly fight back and we believe that they are a capable conventional force but they need an effective anti-aircraft and anti-tank capability which they don't currently possess and that is something that we, and of course the US, can provide.'

She took another drink of water. 'Which is where you and your comrades come in. The crucial factor in equipping the Ukrainians to repel Russian tank columns will be a new and ultra secret weapon. Developed by BAE Systems, it's nicknamed Thor after the Norse god and it is a far more sophisticated version of the FGM-148 Javelin anti-tank missiles in NATO's current armoury that you are probably already well-used to handling in training and combat. The Thor fires laser-guided, air-exploding, anti-tank missiles fitted with microchip locator beacons. Once fired, the missile flies up to

5,000 feet, far above the Javelin's 150 metre height-ceiling, which of course puts it out of range of almost any ground fire. It identifies the target of choice by any or all of magnetic field, laser sighting and radio transmissions, making it pretty much immune to any Russian counter-measures and then, descending again at a speed of Mach 2, its warhead attacks through the top of the armoured fighting vehicle's turret, where, as you know, the armour is thinnest.'

'Well it sounds like a very bright and shiny new toy,' Standing said, when Ms Day had finished her briefing. 'When do we get our hands on it and when do we go?

'Immediately and with the minimum of delay respectively,' she said. 'I have arranged for you and your team to become part of a composite group, already put together by the Ministry of Defence Weapons Sales Department that is taking Thor missiles to Larkhill for field trials. There you will be joined by a small contingent of Ukrainian troops, who will train in the use of the weapon alongside you. As soon as possible after that, accompanied by the Ukrainians, you will then deploy to forward areas of Ukraine between the capital, Kyiv, and the border with Belarus where, if our intel is correct you will soon be able to test the effectiveness of the Thor system under real battlefield conditions.'

Standing grimaced. 'I don't really see myself as a trainer,' he said. 'Apart from anything else and all due modesty aside, it's a waste of my fighting skills if I'm not deployed in a more active role when the shot and shell start flying.'

'Don't worry, Sergeant Standing, I'm sure there will be more than enough combat for everyone before we get through with this. But whether you approve or not is pretty much irrelevant, it's not your place to decide where and in what role you will serve. The priority is to get the Ukrainians up to speed with the Thor missile system as soon as possible.'

'And at what point do we stop nursemaiding the Ukrainians?' Standing was finding it difficult to hide his annoyance and had already begun taking deep breaths to calm himself down.

Her expression again showed her distaste at his choice of phrase. 'As soon as they have mastered the weapon so that they can not only operate it themselves, but teach other Ukrainian soldiers how to do so, you will be redeployed to areas more suited to your own particular specialist skills. However, I cannot emphasise enough how vital it is that neither Thor launchers nor intact Thor missiles ever find their way into Russian hands. This is cutting edge technology and we know from previous bitter experience that, no matter how crude their own technology and electronics may sometimes be, the Russians are more than capable of reverse engineering any new NATO technology that falls into their hands, or even worse, devising counter-measures that might render the weapon almost useless. The launchers are fitted with concealed personal locator beacons, enabling them to be individually tracked, and the missiles have a built-in, self-destruct system; once launched, even if they fail to impact a target, they will detonate. Your job is to make sure that the Russians have no opportunity to capture any part of the system, and if your firing position is threatened with being over-run, your first responsibility is not to the Ukrainians, nor even to your own comrades. If you cannot exfiltrate with the Thor system you will be using, you must ensure its complete and utter destruction.' She closed her briefing file with a snap. 'Questions?'

Standing shook his head. 'None at all. A pleasure to do business with you Ms Day.'

She gave him a quizzical look. 'I'm afraid I am not blessed with a sense of irony, Sergeant Standing, so I always take comments at face value.' She smiled without warmth. 'Anyway, I wish you the best of luck. Though from what I've heard, I doubt you'll need it.'

'I'll take that a compliment,' said Standing.

She smiled coldly. 'I was just stating a fact, Sergeant.'

Chapter 5

By the time Standing had called his team together and brought them up to date, a Chinook was waiting, its rotors slowly turning, ready to transfer them to the Larkhill Garrison and School of Artillery. At its closest point the Larkhill Garrison was only a mile and a half from Stonehenge. It overlooked almost 40,000 hectares of Salisbury Plain that was used for artillery live fire drills. All military firing ranges have a safety template covering the types of weapons and ordnance that can be used there, but because of their huge size, the ranges at Larkhill could accommodate almost every weapon in the MoD armoury, including air-launched missiles. So many shells had been fired there since it was first established as an artillery range way back in the late 1800s that it was estimated that a quarter of a million unexploded rounds were still buried in its vast acreage.

On arrival at Larkhill, they discovered that a number of other green army officers and men had also been attached to the group. In addition to a senior officer who was nominally in charge, there were a couple of junior officers and a Guards warrant officer. They were supported not only by the SAS contingent, but by various admin and support staff. The officers and the warrant officer were happy to be along for the ride, both in Britain and when the team deployed to Eastern Europe, but it was clear that they had no intention of going any farther towards the potential battlefields than Poland; only Standing's SAS team was designated to take the weapons to the front line inside the combat zone of Ukraine.

The SAS group was eight-strong. In addition to Standing and Macleod, there was Grant 'Banger' Parker, who had been given his nickname because he was the patrol's explosives expert. As a kid in the days before terrorists' home-made bombs had given sodium chlorate a bad name, Parker had loved making up improvised explosives using household chemicals or the gunpowder from fireworks he'd emptied out, and then blowing up everything from tree stumps to live frogs. After joining the Army and later passing SAS Selection, he was at last given the chance to be the demolition expert he'd always wanted to be, but he had other valuable skills too, for he was also a trained sniper and a black belt in Shotokan karate.

The other members of the team included the patrol medic, Karl 'Cowpat' Williams, a powerfully built six-footer with a strong West Country accent. A farmer's son, he had begun training as a vet but abandoned it to enlist, saying that, on reflection, he'd much rather have his hands on a weapon than up a cow's arse. The equally strapping Terry Ireland, inevitably nicknamed 'Paddy' even though he came from Norfolk, was a linguist who spoke fluent Russian. The signaller, Ricky 'Mustard' Coleman, was the oldest member of the group with a receding hairline as proof of that. He had come late to SAS Selection and was already in his mid-thirties, even though he had only been serving with the Regiment for five years.

The last two members of the group, Norman Connor and Brian Perkins, had grown up in the same declining rust-belt town in the West Midlands. Although they weren't related and had not even known each other before passing Selection, they were so physically alike - short and stocky with round, guileless faces framed by mops of unruly brown hair - and even sounded the same, with identical thick Black Country accents, that they had initially been nicknamed 'Tweedledum' and 'Tweedledee'. However, since three-syllable nicknames were a bridge too far for some SAS troopers, those were rapidly shortened to 'Dum' and 'Dee' instead, although behind their backs, Williams had been known to voice the opinion that 'Dumb' and 'Dumber' would have been even more appropriate. Nicknames were not just the typical armed forces piss-taking but a means of disguising their identities; no SAS man would ever use his own or a patrol mate's real name when on ops.

A small group of mainly young, keen Ukrainian army conscripts most of whom had been recruited from university for their technological skills, were also attached to the patrol to provide local knowledge and language capabilities, and also to learn to operate the missiles. Although intensely patriotic, the thought of dying in battle, even for their country, clearly terrified all of them. Their boss, the Ukrainian liaison officer, Major Volodymyr Sukut, was a fluent English speaker with barely a trace of an accent. A senior officer in his late fifties, a lifetime soldier, he said, first with the Red Army in the days when Ukraine was part of the Soviet Union and now in the Ukrainian army. With a temper as sharp as his features, he was disliked by his fellow Ukrainians and instinctively distrusted by Standing. 'Pleased to meet you Vladimir,' he had said at their first meeting.

'Not Vladimir. That is the Russian version. I'm Ukrainian and my name is Volodymyr.'

'Tell you what,' Standing said. 'I'll just call you Sukut.'

Sukut's deputy, Captain Pavlo Jankiv, looked to be a year or two younger and had similar military experience but was an altogether more warm and user-friendly character, with a genial expression and a broad smile. He was soon given the nickname 'Goodno' by the SAS men, since after almost every sentence in his slightly laboured English, Jankiv would add 'Is good, no?' It was probably inevitable that the nickname they chose for Major Sukut was 'Suckit' and they smiled among themselves whenever he tried to correct their pronunciation.

Chapter 6

Along with everyone else, the Russian invasion of Ukraine had caught the SAS language school by surprise. Foot soldiers in the Regiment instinctively distrusted local interpreters, feeling probably rightly, that anything the interpreter told them would have an added twist which benefited the interpreter. Tasked with providing Ukrainian linguists fast and finding that there was no Ukrainian language app that they could draw on, the language school tutors fell back on a tried and tested formula. When the course was assembled each attendee was given thirty words a day to learn using flash cards. The following morning was spent learning grammar, conjugation of verbs and construction of sentences, while in the afternoon a Ukrainian woman spent time conversing with the group. She had come to England after marrying a Wiltshire businessman and had been a mother and home-maker in a village near Salisbury ever since. She had little in common with the rough and ready soldiers she was tutoring but her enthusiasm and that of the participants in the language training produced immediate results, despite Standing's cynical comment that 'If I ever want to bake a Ukrainian sponge cake, I can now buy the ingredients from any shop in Kyiv and I'll even know the gas mark setting for the oven as well'.

Standing spent much of his downtime at Larkhill with the younger Ukrainian conscripts, improving his language skills by trying to learn the language as it was spoken on the street. He became close to a young man and woman, Dudik and Lipka, both still in their late teens, and obviously an item. When he asked their opinion of Major Sukut, their reply was *'Ne duzhe mylyy cholovik'* - not a very nice man.

Training the Ukrainians in the use of the new weapon and the tactics to ensure it was deployed to maximum effect began at once. The additional propellant needed to boost the Thor to 5,000 feet and the powerful warhead it carried, made it weigh in at 35 kilograms, far heavier than the 22-kg Javelin anti-tank missile - the standard NATO anti-tank weapon that had already been supplied in limited quantities to the Ukrainian forces. However, it was still man-portable and SAS men were well used to carrying even heavier loads on punishing route marches over rough terrain. They were now about to find out whether the Ukrainians were equally capable of delivering the weapon to where it was needed and operating it once they got there.

Standing first led the Ukrainians, each carrying a Thor launcher and missile or the equivalent weight in a Bergen, on a gruelling forced march along one of the rough tracks on the perimeter of Larkhill. Only when they had covered twenty miles, leaving some of the Ukrainians close to exhaustion, did the firing practice begin. A couple of derelict cars, obtained from a vehicle dismantler and scrap metal yard on the outskirts of Salisbury, had been towed into position, half a mile apart. With the red flags flying and a siren sounding to warn visitors not to stray off the public footpaths that passed close to the ranges, Standing talked the Ukrainians through the Thor system, and simulated a missile launch. 'If you've handled a Javelin launcher, you'll realise that the Thor is not that different,' said Standing. 'The one unbreakable rule is to fire in sequence, not simultaneously. If two missiles are launched simultaneously they will both go for the target emitting the largest electronic or magnetic signature, which will not only result in overkill of that target but potentially allow the target time to fire its own weapons or take evasive action. Right, since these missiles cost well over £50,000 a pop, and there is as yet only a limited supply, most of you will be simulating a launch like I did, but two lucky lads will get the chance to fire one for real. Suckit? Who do you want to nominate?'

'How many times do I have to tell you? It is Sukut.'

'Duly noted,' Standing said, with the ghost of a wink to Macleod, standing next to him.

In the event Sukut and Jankiv pulled rank and fired the two missiles themselves. Sukut went first. There was a low whine from the electronics as he first put it in stand-by mode. When he pressed the firing button there was a flash that seared the grass behind him as the launcher sent the missile roaring upwards in a steep, near-vertical climb. At the top of its arc, a warhead separated and arrowed in on one of the derelict cars, which disappeared in a blinding flash, leaving only fragments of bodywork fluttering down like autumn leaves. Jankiv went next and destroyed the other scrap car, and after the other ranks had all simulated a launch, Standing marched them back to the administrative area and gave them the rest of the day off.

Larkhill's directing staff and instructors had all been watching through binoculars as the Ukrainians practised the missile launches and when Standing and Macleod wandered into the bar in the Sergeants' Mess that evening, they found it packed with them joking about how bad the Ukrainians were. They took special delight in taking the piss out of the young, vulnerable Ukrainian couple.

Standing took them to task for it and Macleod joined in, shouting at the most senior man in the room, an overweight Lieutenant-Colonel with an alcohol-blossomed nose. Macleod looked like he was ready to take it even further when he clenched his fist and took a step towards the officer.

'Bash!' hissed Standing.

Macleod looked over at Standing. His lips were curled back in a snarl and he was breathing like a bull at stud. He locked eyes with Standing, then took a deep breath and let it out slowly. He nodded at Standing, then relaxed his fist into a 'cheery-bye' wave of the hand before turning and walking out of the Mess.

Standing found him outside, taking a series of deep breaths. 'A definite improvement there,' Standing said with a grin. 'No officers were filled in or even touched.'

Macleod winked at him. 'Yeah, so far so good, but like the alcoholics say, let's take it one day at a time. Thanks, Sarge.'

Even though Macleod had brought his anger under control, the irate Lieutenant-Colonel reported the incident to the Head Shed at Hereford, demanding 'disciplinary action', and Macleod duly received a bollocking from Colonel Davies down the line from Pontrilas for blowing his fuse. However, as Macleod said to Standing after breaking the connection, 'I've had so many bollockings from him that you can tell his heart's just not in it any more. He started chewing me out but then ran out of steam about halfway through and just said, "Well, you know the rest, don't you?" and hung up on me!'

'He knows you're trying,' said Standing. 'Like you said, one day at a time.'

Chapter 7

By the end of the next day, contrary to the opinions of the Larkhill directing staff, the training with the Ukrainians had gone well enough that, after consulting with the rest of the team, Standing told Colonel Davies that they were now ready to deploy to Ukraine.

At their final briefing, as part of their SOPs, every SAS X Squadron patrol member was routinely issued with a personal 'CommsPad'. The size of a mini-iPad, it transmitted and received audio and text messages, automatically encrypting and decrypting every message, and frequency hopping during its operation. The pad was also a PLB - Personal Locator Beacon - and worked between individuals, with a preset function to copy every message back to the SAS Head Shed, based in the Operations Room in Pontrilas, Hereford, although Standing, ever the loner, routinely disabled that function whenever he was on an op.

They made the fifty mile journey from Larkhill to RAF Brize Norton in a Chinook. By now the mission had been given the grandiose title of 'Operation Odin'. The code name allowed them to discuss their task and indent for equipment without disclosing any of the operation's finer details. Arriving at one of the air cargo hangars at Brize, Standing was surprised to see how much equipment they had already accumulated, courtesy of their attached green army officers. Apart from the Thor missiles, the rest was mostly gear to make the base staff's life comfortable in Poland while Standing and the team were doing the real work in Ukraine. It even included a couple of Land Rovers for the base staff to use as runabouts.

They flew out of Brize Norton on a C-17 Globemaster, and even with their base staff's considerable accumulation of kit, all the personnel and equipment took up barely a quarter of the aircraft's vast capacity. They landed at an airfield in Central Poland, set in the heart of the flatlands of the Polish plains with a belt of scrubby woodland surrounding the airfield and the buildings of the base. They deployed first to the ordnance park adjoining the airfield, an enormous storage facility left over from the days of the Cold War. The base had been home to squadrons of Soviet bombers in those days and the ordnance park was an old Warsaw Pact ammo store, built to house weapons and ammunition, including tactical nuclear weapons, to supply the Red Army in the event of the Cold War ever turning red hot. The facility still had hundreds of round-topped, bomb-proof storage shelters, some with underground accommodation and living quarters inside them. Each of the shelters had an identifying number but many of these had been worn away and the road signs between them had long ago been chopped up and used as firewood.

The airfield next to the facility was busy with a constant stream of fighters from the Polish Air Force taking off to fly combat air patrols to deter the Russian Air Force from any incursions into Polish air space. There was also a constant stream of cargo aircraft landing and taking off. The aircraft were Russian-built but they were now in use to bring in military supplies from the former Soviet satellite states throughout Eastern Europe that were now allies of Poland and Ukraine against Russia.

'They've clearly been getting the same intel as us,' Macleod said, as he watched the cargo being unloaded from a Lithuanian air force plane.

'Yeah,' Standing said, 'but I'm guessing most of the equipment they're bringing will be so old that it will be well past its sell-by date and about as much use to the Ukrainian Armed Forces as a consignment of pea-shooters.'

As soon as the Globemaster landed, it had quickly been unloaded, with everything dumped at the end of the runway. Sukut set off to find out to which area they had been allocated. Standing was picking up a bad vibe from the Ukrainian so he took his two young Ukrainian acolytes on a recce.

When the two parties arrived back, Sukut told Major Taggart the number painted on the roof of the bunker he said they had been given but Standing contradicted him at once, giving the Major the number of a different location. Sukut argued and when Taggart sided with Standing, he stormed off.

'What was that all about?' asked Taggart.

'I just have a bad feeling about him,' said Standing. 'It doesn't really matter which bunker we're in, but when Sukut is so insistent about going to one in particular and so furious when I suggested a different one, it gets me wondering why. Maybe it's nothing, but if he is a wrong 'un and he's setting us up, being somewhere other than the place they're expecting us to be will make their job a little harder. Anyway, just in case, I suggest we stay on the very highest alert level until we get sorted and get the missiles out of here.'

Major Taggart agreed and began issuing orders to heighten security.

Standing lost no time in procuring a fleet of Gaz-66 light trucks. They were old but usually reliable vehicles, and he had used them on previous operations in Afghanistan. He recruited a team of local mechanics to modify the vehicles, by adding fuel tanks cannibalised from much larger Ural-375 trucks to increase their range. On his instructions the mechanics also strengthened the chassis and cut holes in the roofs of the cabs so that RPD belt-fed 7.62mm light machine guns could be fitted there for defence. An old Russian weapon, out of production since the 1960s, it was nonetheless reliable and still in use and widely available throughout the former Soviet bloc, Asia and Africa.

While the final preparations were continuing, the combat troops, both SAS and Ukrainian, had immediately gone into a state of fifty percent alert readiness, doing four hour stags on guard duty with an SAS trooper and a Ukrainian allocated to each position. Everyone took their turn and when not on stag they remained fully clothed and booted, sleeping fitfully on top of their sleeping bags, and eating and drinking close to their guard positions, with weapons and equipment ready for instant action.

In the early hours of the following night, Standing was on stag on the roof of the bunker with Dudik. They were lying full length behind a low wall of sandbags, which not only offered protection against enemy fire but also shielded them from the unseasonably bitter easterly wind that felt like it was blowing all the way from Siberia.

Looking through the passive night goggles he was wearing, Dudik whispered how nice it was to see fireflies in this part of Poland. Standing, instantly alert, swung his binoculars to where Dudik was pointing.

As Dudik had said, flickers of light could be seen flitting among the trees flanking the site, but Standing recognised what he was seeing at once, and it was not the local wildlife. 'Those aren't fireflies,' he said. 'They're fluorescent patches being used as ID tags on camouflage uniforms. We're under attack.'

He immediately pressed the stand-to button on his communications pad to alert the rest of his team. A moment later all the bunker lights, inside and outside, suddenly flashed on and off. There could not have been a more obvious target designator if a neon arrow had been pointing down at the bunker. If the attackers had previously been uncertain of the location of their target, they were now in no doubt and bursts of automatic fire shattered the night air. It was swiftly answered by the defenders around the bunker, the rate of fire increasing as the remaining men, jerked awake by the stand-to signal, stumbled from the bunker and took up firing positions.

Standing was loosing off short, aimed bursts, targeting the muzzle flashes of the attackers' weapons, but firing and rolling between bursts, so that his head and shoulders never broke the line of the sandbags in the same place twice. Each time he had fired and dropped back into cover before any enemies could target him.

Dudik,was new to the game and although he kept up a rapid rate of fire, he was understandably slower to pick his target and bring his weapon to bear and he was also reappearing in the same firing position. Among the rate of automatic fire from the enemy, Standing detected a different sound, the whipcrack of single rounds. There was a 'Thwock!' as one struck the sandbag parapet to his right, and he reached out and dragged Dudik back down as he was about to rise and fire again.

'Sniper fire!' Standing said, shouting to make himself heard above the thunder of gunfire. 'You've got to move between bursts like we taught you, then fire and drop, or you're going to have a hole drilled through your forehead.'

Dudik blanched but followed Standing's orders.

Using his binoculars and squinting through a gap in the sandbag wall in front of him, Standing ignored the multiple muzzle-flashes from automatic weapons for the moment, scanning the margins of the woods and beyond for the single flash of sniper rifles. As they fired again, he glimpsed a muzzle-flash and as it faded the faint glint of light from the metal legs of the bipod mount of a sniper rifle. It was positioned on a low rise set back from the edge of the tree line, behind the other attackers. A second flash showed there was another sniper lying prone nearby, about ten metres from the first. He spoke into his comms. 'Paddy, two snipers, on a low rise 700 metres East-North-East. Got them?'

A heartbeat later, Standing saw Ireland bring a black cylinder up to his shoulder. There was a micro pause as he took aim and then a blast and a searing tongue of flame shot out of the back of the RPG launcher. A flash of light streaked through the darkness and the low mound erupted as the rocket-propelled grenade blasted into it, unleashing a storm of shrapnel that shredded the darkness around it. Neither sniper fired again.

'Nice one, Paddy,' said Standing. 'Two birds with one stone.'

Having lost the element of surprise, the attackers were making little progress, unable to cross the open ground separating the tree-line from the bunker without exposing themselves to the lethal fire of the SAS squad. After unleashing a final blitz of fire to cover their retreat, the demoralised survivors of the attack melted away among the trees.

The last echoes of the battle were a series of single shots from among the trees and Standing already suspected what they would find when he sent out Connor, Perkins, Coleman and Macleod on a patrol to search the wood for survivors and clear any remaining attackers. No-one living remained there; all the wounded casualties had been despatched with a single shot to the head.

'Dead men tell no tales,' Standing said, when the patrol returned and reported in.

'You're right about that,' Macleod said. 'We searched every single body. There was nothing on any of them, no dog-tags, no ID, no wallets, no personal mementoes, not even any currency - Polish or otherwise.'

Standing flashed him a thin smile. 'No surprises there,' he said. 'We may be still on Polish soil but I'd be very surprised if the men attacking us were Polish. I'd bet good money that they're Russians.'

During the after-action post mortem, Standing tried without success to identify who had signalled to the attackers by switching the lights on and off. The two Ukrainian officers, Major Sukut and Captain Jankiv, both claimed to have been sleeping at the time the attack began and no one could contradict them. Everyone else was questioned but all were also either asleep or were able to give a convincing account of their whereabouts and movements at the time of the attack.

Standing remained unconvinced by Sukut and was determined to keep an even closer watch on him from then on. As the men filed out of the briefing room, Jankiv approached him. 'Could I have a word with you, in private?' he asked.

Standing nodded. 'Go ahead,' he said, 'there's no-one else but us here now.'

Jankiv hesitated. 'I hope you won't think me disloyal, but…' He paused. 'I have some concerns about Major Sukut. There is nothing I can quite put my finger on, but there have been one or two puzzling incidents both when we were in the UK and now here. Sometimes he has disappeared without warning and can not be found anywhere on the base. If I ask him where he has been when he comes back, he avoids the question, or tells me something I know is not true, or says it is none of my business and orders me to attend to my own affairs.' He gave a helpless shrug. 'Maybe there is some perfectly innocent explanation.'

'Maybe,' Standing said, 'but for now, just keep your eyes and ears open and let me know if anything else happens. Okay?'

Jankiv nodded. 'You won't challenge him directly about it, will you? If he finds out I've been talking to you about him, it will not go well for me.'

Standing smiled. 'Relax, I'll not say anything but I'll be keeping an eye on him, too.'

Chapter 8

Later that morning the convoy of fully-loaded Gaz-66 trucks left the base and headed east. They drove through a landscape of empty arable fields, thick woods and forests of birch and pine, passing only the occasional isolated and often impoverished-looking village. It took several hours to reach the Ukrainian border at the crossing point Agnes Day had briefed them to use. A queue of trucks with a handful of cars among them was waiting to pass the border control point. The line of vehicles stretched back over a mile from the border and the glacial pace at which it was moving suggested that the border guards were being unusually thorough in checking the drivers' documents, or the bureaucracy was even more labyrinthine than usual in an ex-Soviet state. However, Ms Day's preparations had been meticulous and Standing knew that a senior Ukrainian government official would be waiting at the border point to usher them through. They accordingly pulled out and swept past the queue of vehicles, intercepting more than a few hostile glares from the trapped drivers that they overtook, before cutting in right at the head of the queue.

Standing's group were on maximum alert as they got closer to the border. They held their weapons at the ready, in case their secrecy had been breached, either inadvertently or deliberately. The tentacles of the FSB reached deep into all Russia's neighbouring states, and what intelligence-gathering, communications intercepts and old-fashioned espionage could not achieve, bribery and blackmail often could, so Standing was in no doubt that their op could be compromised at any time. However, on this occasion at least there were no problems or signs of compromise and after the briefest of pauses, during which cartons of American cigarettes and a few fifty dollar bills were distributed among the border guards, they almost fell over themselves to raise the barrier and wave the convoy through into Ukraine, even saluting as they drove by.

Standing called a brief halt a few kilometres further on, at a Ukrainian military facility that had been made available to them as a temporary base. They refuelled there and left some reserve stores of fuel, food and ammunition for future use, but then moved on again straight away. A few miles further on they pulled off the road into an area of cleared forest, still littered with the bulldozed stumps and brushwood left behind by a logging company. They remained there throughout the rest of the daylight hours, waiting for darkness before deploying to their intended area of operations.

Just after dawn the following day, Standing and his group were travelling across the Ukrainian grasslands north-east of Kyiv with the Thor missiles, loosely covered with tarpaulins, on the back of the Gaz trucks. Standing and Macleod were in the lead vehicle with the other SAS men spread out two to a vehicle in the other four trucks, with the Ukrainians distributed among them.

As they drove on, Standing saw a black speck in the sky due east of them, and behind it another and another, all swelling rapidly in size as they approached. A group of six Russian Cub aircraft, similar in size and profile to the Western military's Hercules transport aircraft, were flying low and line astern, coming from the direction of Kursk beyond the Russian border. As the gap to them shrank, the planes began climbing sharply before levelling out at about 5000 feet.

Macleod stood up on the passenger seat, poked his head out through the hole cut in the roof of the cab and brought the 7.62mm machine gun fixed to the roof to bear. Glancing behind him, Standing could see that the others were also manning their machine guns, though with their weapons having a maximum range of 1000 metres they could not remotely threaten the Cubs while they were flying at their current height.

The pilots of the Cubs began firing off anti-missile flares in anticipation of ground fire as they began rapidly off-loading their cargo. To Standing's surprise, a drogue parachute was deployed from the lead aircraft followed by an armoured fighting vehicle suspended from four enormous chutes. As it dropped, it came within range of the machine guns, which set up a deadly chatter. The old Russian design of the weapons included no provision for semi-automatic fire, but Macleod and the others fired off short-bursts, with the tracer rounds stitching patterns across the sky before intersecting on the AFV.

The smoke and flames from anti-missile flares were adding to the chaos and confusion caused by the bursts of ground fire. The pilot of the last Cub in the line panicked, and desperate to escape the danger from the ground fire, tried to climb too steeply, stalled his aircraft and with no air-room to recover, it crashed to the ground and erupted in flames, immolating not only the entire crew of the aircraft but also that of the AFV it had been carrying.

Another Cub, dropped its AFV. Buffeted by the slipstream, the AFV twisted at an angle, breaking free of one of its chutes. The remaining chutes were nowhere near strong enough to hold the weight of the AFV on their own, and as ground fire from the SAS machine guns sliced through yet another chute, the AFV dropped like a stone, burying itself in the ground, almost certainly killing the unfortunate troops trapped inside.

Having discharged their cargo, the surviving Cub aircraft turned for home, dropping back down to low-level as they flew out of range of Standing's group. Although two Russian AFVs had been destroyed, four had made it safely to earth. As soon as they hit the ground, with gouts of thick black diesel smoke belching from their straining diesel engines, the AFVs had begun roaring towards the convoy of Gaz trucks. Standing immediately identified them as BMD-4s, vehicles issued to Russian Guards' Airborne Infantry Units, the equivalent of Britain's Paras. They were formidable fighting vehicles, armed with a 100 mm gun, a 30 mm coaxial auto-cannon and a 7.62 coaxial machine gun, mounted to fire along a parallel axis to the cannon.

There had been no time to deploy the Thors before the Cubs were overhead, but Standing and the SAS gunners in the other three trucks had now ripped off the tarpaulins covering the missiles and were readying themselves to launch them, even as heavy incoming fire from the BMDs began to rake the Gaz column.

Standing was the first to be ready to launch a missile and he sent one streaking skywards, but he caught a flash of light out of the corner of his eye as Sukut launched his missile simultaneously.

The two missiles shrank to almost invisible black specks in the sky, before locking on to their targets and beginning to descend at hypersonic speed. Homing unerringly on the target, the two missiles streaked down in tandem and crashed through the turret of the same BMD. The double impact of the missiles struck with a force that literally blew the vehicle apart, vapourising its occupants in a micro-second. As the BMD erupted in a ball of fire, Ireland launched a third Thor missile that destroyed a second vehicle.

Meanwhile auto-cannon fire from one of the other BMDs raked the Gaz truck with Connor and Perkins, and the two young Ukrainians, Dudik and Lipka, aboard, from one end to the other. A round pierced the fuel tank and as fuel sprayed out and ignited, wreathing the truck in flames Connor and Perkins shouted at Dudik and Lipka to get out before they dived over the side, through the wall of flame. They rolled over a couple of times before coming to a halt, flattening themselves to the ground and and burying their faces in the dirt as the Gaz, with nearly full fuel tanks and thousands of rounds of ammunition aboard, blew apart.

Both SAS troopers had facial burns and singed hair and eyebrows, but were otherwise unhurt, but Dudik and Lipka had been too slow and were caught in the blast.

The drivers of the remaining BMDs had screeched to a halt as they took in the fate of the others, and they and the paratroops they were carrying scrambled out and put as much distance between themselves and their vehicles as they could before the next salvo of Thor missiles obliterated them.

Even though they were now fighting on foot, the Russian paratroops showed no sign of wanting to retreat and the ferocious rate of fire from their AKs, machine guns and RPGs kept the SAS and the Ukrainians pinned down. Another Gaz had now been disabled as a torrent of rounds chewed through its engine compartment and cab. Small groups of Russian paratroopers were also advancing on either flank, threatening to expose the SAS team to a deadly cross-fire.

Standing cut apart one of the paratroopers as he sprinted across a gap from one patch of cover to the next and put a shot through the face of another one, an inch below the rim of his steel helmet, as he rose to hurl a grenade. As always when he was in combat, time seemed to slow to a crawl.

Macleod and the others were also exacting a toll on the Russians, but two more of the Ukrainians had now gone down badly wounded and the situation for the SAS and their allies was looking increasingly desperate when, out of nowhere, a Hind helicopter gunship, battle-worn, with rust-patches all over its fuselage and showing no markings of any kind, roared in from the west and began targeting the Russian paratroops. It unleashed an avalanche of fire from its Gatling gun and auto-cannon, and, exposed in open ground with virtually no cover, dozens of the Russians were slaughtered in the Hind's initial pass.

As it swung round to make another strafing run, the surviving paratroopers began to flee. Several more were killed as they ran for their lives and only a handful were left alive by the time the Hind's gunner stopped firing.

When the battle was over, incandescent with rage that Sukut had ignored the golden rule never to fire the Thor missiles simultaneously, Standing stormed over to the Ukrainian officer. Sukut tried to wave it away. 'Better to hit a target twice than not at all, is it not?' he said and walked away.

As Standing turned on his heel, fighting down a wave of rising anger, he caught a questioning look from Jankiv, but he merely shrugged in response. There was nothing he could say. But one thing was for sure - Sukut was not to be trusted, on any level.

Chapter 9

With the battlefield clear and the enemy neutralised, the Hind circled, landed and switched off its engines. When the pilot emerged from her cockpit, she turned out to be an American woman in her thirties, a pretty brunette with hazel eyes and a half-smile on her lips. Her crewman and gun-operator was tall and powerfully built. He nodded to the SAS men. 'Name's Earl,' he said.

'Nice shooting, Earl,' said Standing. 'We owe you one.'

Earl threw him a mock salute. 'All part of the service,' he said.

Standing walked over to the pilot, who was checking the fuselage of the heli for battle damage. 'We owe you big time,' Standing said to her. 'We were under some heavy pressure until you came riding out of the sunset.' He checked his watch. 'Actually, make that riding out of the sunrise.'

She smiled. 'All in a day's work, but it certainly looked like a bit of a shit-storm down here. Anyway, before we ride off back into the sunrise, we can load your wounded and take them to the nearest field hospital and we can drop your captives off too, in a place where they'll be sure of a warm welcome.'

Standing continued chatting with her while the Ukrainians helped Earl to get their wounded comrades aboard and then loaded the Russian captives. Once the Russians were on board, they cable-tied their ankles as well, just to make sure that they couldn't try to escape before the heli took off or attempt to overpower the crewman in flight,

'So how come you just happened to be cruising over the Ukrainian grasslands, just now?' he said to the pilot.

Her smile broadened. 'Well, I fly this crate on behalf of a civilian contracting company which operates around here, among other places. We provide air support to engineering projects in remote, high risk areas around the globe, using Russian aircraft liberated from the war in Iraq. The main transport is done by a Hip supply helicopter, which I also sometimes fly, but they have several Hinds like these as well that are used for smaller loads but a few are also kept in reserve in case any situations ever turn violent, requiring a hot extraction of all personnel.'

Standing gave a non-committal nod. He could recognise a cover story when he heard one and he was pretty sure that the 'civilian contractor' was a front for the CIA, while the helis were used to fly deniable black ops as part of the US Government's never ending 'war on terror' in what sometimes seemed like about half of the countries in the Third World. The aircrew serving on such ops were almost always time-served veterans from US Special Forces, usually looking to prolong their careers while seeking further excitement and a few more adrenaline rushes in the process.

'And you ended up in Ukraine because…?' he said to her.

She shrugged. 'I guess we sort of wandered here from somewhere further north.' She paused. 'Oh, and in case you're interested, the name's Lisa.'

'I'm very interested. I'm Matt.'

'Good to meet you,' she said. She flashed him a smile, then turned and strolled off towards the heli, the swing of her hips now even more pronounced.

A few moments later the engines fired up, the rotors ground into action, accelerating swiftly to a blur, and the Hind rose into the air and swung back towards the south-west.

Chapter 10

When Standing checked in with the Colonel for an update on a secure line, he was told that the latest intel garnered by MI6 and GCHQ was that while some Russian artillery were shelling Ukrainian towns near Kharkiv and Donetsk, and their forces had fought a few skirmishes close to the existing front lines, a full-scale invasion had still not yet begun. 'The SIS believe these preliminary attacks are diversions,' Colonel Davies said, 'designed to tie up Ukrainian reserves and prevent them strengthening their defences in the Chernihiv region north of Kyiv where we expect the main hammer blow to fall.'

'I don't suppose Six have any intel or any theories about how half a dozen Russian Cub aircraft with AFVs aboard just happened to be crossing the Ukrainian border on a course to intercept us, do they?' asked Standing. 'Call me paranoid if you like but it's almost as if they knew we were coming.'

'They've not flagged up anything,' the Colonel said. 'I'd say it was a coincidence except I don't really believe in those. Not in combat situations anyway.'

'Nor me,' Standing said. 'I can't help wondering if one of our Ukrainian friends is somehow finding a way to pass on some intel about our movements and plans, but unless and until we get something more solid to act on, I guess all we can do is stay vigilant.'

Having studied the mapping, Standing and his patrol mates were unanimous that although the Russian offensive when it came would be a multi-pronged one, targeting Kyiv from three or four different directions, one of the most obvious routes for a Russian lightning assault on the capital would be by crossing the Belarusian border close to its southernmost point. The Russian column could then skirt the northern edge of the national park and strike the E95 road south of the city of Chernihiv. From there, the dual carriageway ran arrow-straight into the heart of Kyiv. Even if the Ukrainians mined the road, the terrain flanking it for most of the way was classic tank country, enabling the invaders to simply by-pass the road and advance parallel to it.

Using one of the Gaz trucks, Standing and Macleod followed the road from Kyiv right to the outskirts of the city of Chernihiv and then chose the best available location for their killing ground: a point where the dual carriageway passed through a forest of old growth oak and beech trees, their trunks so massive that even Russian tanks and bulldozers would have great difficulty in carving an alternative route, were the road itself to be blocked by destroyed and burning vehicles. Standing and his SAS team at once began setting up a Forward Operating Base, establishing firing positions around the killing ground and deploying their Ukrainian troops into them.

Although the earlier attack by the armoured fighting vehicles carried in Cub transports had not been the signal for the full-scale Russian invasion to begin, Standing and his group did not have to wait long. At dawn two days later, on 24 February, Russian armoured columns crashed across the border onto Ukrainian territory. Even while Putin's officials in Moscow were still issuing flat denials of any plans to attack, Russian tanks were churning through Ukrainian soil and Russian aircraft were bombing Kyiv and Ukraine's other cities. They attacked on four fronts: in the east towards Kharkiv, in the south-east from The Donbas, in the south from Crimea and in the north from Belarus towards Kyiv, the 'blitzkrieg' attack that MI6 had predicted. An official statement, some hours later, claimed that Russia's 'special military operation' - the word 'invasion' was not to be uttered by Kremlin spokesmen or TV presenters and newsreaders under any circumstances - was purely to 'de-militarise and de-Nazify' Ukraine. The aim was allegedly to prevent any further attacks on Russian speaking citizens, or the 'humiliation and genocide' that Putin's propagandists insisted were taking place in Ukraine on a massive scale. Had anyone asked them for their opinion, Standing and Macleod would have been only too happy to give their comments offering a rather different view of what was going on, though it would inevitably have contained far too many obscenities to be broadcastable.

Any hopes or expectations that the Russian generals might have harboured about their forces making a lightning sweep through Ukraine to the heart of Kyiv were demolished within hours of the start of the invasion. As the columns of Russian armoured fighting vehicles continued to pour across the border from Belarus, the first ones were already beginning to suffer massive losses.

Standing's teams were already in position around their chosen killing ground when the full scale invasion began. The Russian approach was heralded by the distant thunder of tank engines, the sight of clouds of black smoke belching from their engines and the crash of projectiles as they blew apart buildings that might offer cover to Ukrainian forces. Aircraft and Hind helicopter gunships flew top cover above the column, ready to put down barrages of fire on any resistance, but even before the columns of armoured vehicles reached Standing's chosen killing ground, the numbers of aircraft above them began to be depleted as Ukrainian troops with SAS men acting as advisers, operating in two or three-man groups from prepared positions in deep cover, began launching Stinger missiles at the invaders.

The Stingers, so devastating against Russian helicopters in Afghanistan, proved equally effective now. Although the countermeasures used by helicopters had been improved in the intervening years, the Stingers had also been substantially upgraded and the result was the same: a succession of Hind helis were shot down in flames. Several of the surviving pilots were quick to take the most effective evasive action: turning for home, leaving the armoured column dangerously exposed.

The lead tank entered the old-growth oak wood that Standing and his patrol-mates had chosen and they allowed it to pass through the wood almost to its southern fringe before launching the first Thor missile. Soaring to 500 feet in the blink of an eye, its warhead then arrowed down into the top of the tank, blasting through the armour-plate and detonating right inside it. White-hot flames burst from its gun ports and a dense pall of black smoke formed above it, while the noise of its ammunition detonating inside continued long after its engine had fallen silent. A second Thor had already been launched, destroying the next tank in line, while a third missile, fired by an SAS/Ukrainian team positioned at the northern end of the wood, wiped out one of the last armoured vehicles in the column.

Once they had used the Thor missiles to knock out the tanks spearheading the advance and the rear-most vehicle, the column was forced to come to a juddering halt, unable to advance or retreat. More Thor missiles, Javelins, RPGs and other anti-tank weapons then wrought havoc among the remaining vehicles until a scrapheap of wrecked, smoke-blackened tanks and other armoured vehicles stretched back for a mile. Russian troops who had somehow survived the infernos that consumed their vehicles were then engaged with ground fire. The SAS men's accuracy and prodigious rate of fire, augmented by the storm of rounds from the Ukrainians, convinced the Russians that they were facing a regiment rather than a few patrols, and as their casualties mounted, they began to retreat. Before long most had simply turned and run away, abandoning their surviving comrades to their fate.

The SAS teams and their Ukrainian allies had stopped the Russian advance on that route in its tracks but two other Russian spearheads made more rapid progress, one to the north-west of Kyiv even reaching the outskirts of the city before being repelled in ferocious fighting. Helped by further fusillades of Thor, Javelin and Stinger missiles, wreaking havoc among the Russian armour and the ground-attack aircraft and helis, the Ukrainians then launched counter-offensives that drove the Russians back. The withdrawal turned into a full-scale retreat and then something closer to a rout, with the demoralised Russian troops leaving a trail of abandoned, burned out vehicles and mounds of dead bodies behind them as they fled back over the Belarusian frontier.

Chapter 11

When Standing carried out the routine post-action roll-call in their own battle area, to check for dead, wounded and missing in action, he realised that both Sukut and the Ukrainian infantryman he had been fighting alongside were missing. Standing made for the firing positions they had been occupying at the start of the battle to search for them. As he approached the hollow from which the two men had been using a Thor missile launcher to attack the enemy's armoured fighting vehicles, he could see no immediate trace of Sukut, even though there were no shell or bomb craters in the area around the hollow, nor any sign that the position had come under heavy enemy fire. Unfortunately the infantryman had obviously been hit, because he was sprawled on his front, unmoving, in the mud at the bottom of the hollow. As Standing moved closer, he could see that there was no need to check for a pulse; the infantryman's head was turned towards him and half of his face had been blown away. Sukut's whereabouts remained unknown but there was no sign of any bloodstains to suggest he had been badly wounded.

Standing was about to turn away when he realised that the wound in the infantryman's face was an exit wound, even though he must have been facing the enemy when he died. There was also no sign of the Thor missile launcher that they had been using. With a growing feeling of unease, Standing slithered down the side of the hollow and turned the dead man's body over with his boot. A neat round hole had been drilled in the back of his head. From its size, it had been made not with a round from a Russian AK or machine-gun but with a 9 mm round from a weapon like the Makarov pistol that Sukut and Jankiv both carried. When Standing looked closer, he could even see powder-burns around the wound, showing that the fatal shot had been fired from very close range.

He climbed back out of the hollow and ran to each of the Ukrainian firing positions in turn, asking the same question, even though he already knew what the answer would be. 'Where's Sukut? Have you seen him?'

All that greeted him were blank looks.

Standing sank to his haunches and for a moment he gave himself up to his anger, furious with himself that, despite the instinctive dislike and suspicion he had felt for Sukut since his first encounter with him, he had taken no action and had allowed him to continue to be part of the team. Now Sukut had gone missing and even worse, he had taken the Thor missile launcher that he had been using with him, perhaps seeing it as his passport to climbing higher on the slippery pole of promotion and position in Russia. It would benefit the Russian war effort either by enabling their scientists to reverse engineer the missile system and produce their own version or by allowing them to devise counter-measures to neutralise the threat it posed. That would also enhance Sukut's own personal prospects enormously.

Standing remained motionless, lost in thought for a few moments longer, then got to his feet and began walking swiftly towards Macleod, who was checking the wounded and organising a patrol and a stag rota.

There was no point in wasting further time on self-recrimination. Standing now had to do what he could to minimise the damage. 'Sukut's a Russian agent,' he said. 'He shot his comrade in the back of the head with his pistol and now he's done a runner with a Thor launcher. I'm leaving you in charge. I'm going after him, I have to get that Thor back before he can hand it over to the Russians.'

'How are you going to do that?' Macleod said. 'You've no idea where he's gone.'

'There's a PLB concealed in the launcher. Give me your CommsPad and I'll have no problem in tracking him, and however fast he runs, he won't outpace me.'

'Are you sure we aren't better off calling in an airstrike?' Macleod said. 'Even if he doesn't link up with any more Russian forces, it's not many miles to the border with Belarus, and he's got a head start on you.'

'All the more reason to get moving,' Standing said. 'And we can't guarantee an air strike will destroy Sukut or the missile, whereas I can be sure of it. Give me your CommsPad and all your spare magazines for the AK, it'll save me some time not having to go back to the truck.'

'Is that all the weaponry you're taking?'

'That and some Willie Pete grenades,' he said, using the nickname coined by US forces for white phosphorous. They could be used to create a dense choking smokescreen, but they could also inflict fatal wounds on a target, scattering incandescent fragments burning at a temperature of up to 2,500 degrees Celsius that stuck to clothing or exposed skin and were then almost impossible to extinguish as they burned through flesh and bone like paper.

As he was making his final preparations, Macleod was getting ready as well. 'You'll need a wingman,' he said. 'I'll come with.'

Standing shook his head. 'No, you stay here and get these guys' heads straight again. The Russians'll be back sooner or later and they need to be ready for them. And anyway, Sukut was my screw up. I had made up my mind from the start that there was something not quite right about him, but even though I was half-convinced that he was a wrong 'un, I just decided to keep a close watch on him, until I was sure one way or the other. Well, as what happened today showed, it wasn't anywhere near a close enough watch. So, my screw up, my job to take care of the problem that I created, and I'll be doing it alone.'

Macleod looked as if he was about to argue, then read Standing's expression and thought better of it. 'If you change your mind, you know where I am,' he said.

Standing grinned. 'Just don't deck any officers while I'm away,' he said.

Standing moved off, heading past the wrecked armoured vehicles, with his rifle tracking the path of his gaze in case any wounded or hidden Russian soldiers had been missed by his patrol-mates and the Ukrainians as they carried out their post action sweep through the battlefield. He moved quickly along the destroyed Russian column, passing a succession of blackened and burned out tanks, armoured vehicles and troop transporters. Smoke was still rising from many of them and the air was heavy with a horrible stench, a cocktail of diesel fuel, gunsmoke, sulphur and scorched flesh.

As he moved north towards the Belarusian border he was following a trail of discarded backpacks, radios, helmets, uniforms and rifles, thrown away by panic-stricken Russian conscripts, some as young as eighteen, as they fled the inferno of flames and explosions, and the lethal shards of metal from their devastated vehicles.

Assured by their commanders that they would be doing little more than parading through a defenceless Ukraine to be acclaimed as liberators by the grateful citizens of Kyiv, they had now discovered - too late - not only the truth behind those fictions but also the terrible reality of modern warfare. The traumatised survivors were now streaming back across the border and some of them, having thrown away their weapons, would not stop fleeing until they had reached their homes, hundreds or even thousands of miles away.

However, unless they stood in his way, Standing had zero interest in their fate. His only focus was on the blinking cursor on the CommsPad in his hand showing the location of the Thor missile that Sukut had taken and was aiming to hand to his Russian paymasters. The cursor showed that he was heading due north, avoiding the main road and working his way through the arable land and patches of woodland flanking it. That, coupled with his age and the weight of the loaded missile launcher he was carrying, made for slow progress. By keeping to the road, Standing could travel much faster, but he was also exposed to the threat of Russian patrols and the fighter-bombers, ground-attack aircraft and Hind heli-gunships, which with complete air superiority despite the attrition by the Ukrainian air defences, the Russians were still using in repeated sorties to batter the Ukrainian ground positions around Kyiv.

Every time Standing saw or heard an approaching aircraft he flattened himself in the dirt, worming his way into the thin cover of the verges at the side of the road and remained motionless, hoping that the pilots and spotters would either fail to see him or take him for just another of the multitude of dead bodies littering the road. As soon as the threat had passed overhead, he hauled himself to his feet and moved on. Ever-watchful, his gaze never still as he scanned the surrounding terrain for any semblance of a threat, his pace was apparently unhurried but his relentless stride was covering the ground fast enough to be rapidly closing on his target. The signal from the PLB was now coming from an area of woodland about a kilometre to the north-east of him and about ten kilometres short of the border with Belarus, but it did not appear to be moving. He left the road, working his way through a patch of marshy ground, his silent footsteps barely disturbing the pools of muddy water as he made his way across it.

Checking the CommsPad again, he was puzzled to see that the flashing cursor showing the location of the PLB had still not moved at all since he had last looked at it. That suggested two possibilities to him; either Sukut had paused to rest or to lie in wait, ready to ambush any pursuers, or he had found the PLB in the Thor missile and removed it before heading on towards the border. If the latter were the case, Standing's chances of overhauling Sukut and retrieving the missile had just nose-dived. He mentally scanned his other options but could see no alternative to pushing on to the location of the PLB. Every instinct was screaming at him to press on at top speed and overhaul his prey before he reached the border, but he knew that haste would only ensure his own death if Sukut was lying in wait.

He crept forward, using every scrap of cover to conceal himself from any watcher. When he neared the wood where the PLB was located, he first circled right around it so that he would be approaching it from the north, the opposite direction to the one Sukut would be expecting.

Standing began advancing towards the wood, moving at a snail's pace. He kept inching forward through the scrub and rough grasses until he reached the outer belt of trees that formed the wood. As he did so, he spotted tracks: partial boot-prints in the patches of moss and soft mud among the leaf mould and debris of the woodland floor. The line of the boot-prints showed that the person who had made them had come through the wood and was now walking north over the rough grassland that Standing himself had just crossed.

The tracks looked recent but even though the ground was very soft, the boot-prints did not look as deeply impressed as they ought to have been if made by a man carrying a heavy load like the Thor launcher, so there was nothing to confirm that they had been made by Sukut. There must have been plenty of farmers and foresters as well as soldiers from one side or the other in this area recently and the steady signal from the PLB showed that it remained motionless in the heart of the wood.

He moved on. As he worked his way through the trees and around the dense undergrowth in areas where wind-blown, felled or fallen trees had allowed sufficient light to reach the floor of the wood, he moved even slower, with even greater caution. At each step as he paused with his foot just above the ground, and swept it silently from side to side, brushing aside any twigs and dry leaves that might have given him away by their noise if he had trodden on them. It was agonisingly slow progress but the alternative was to risk a bullet in the guts.

When he was within a hundred metres of the PLB signal, he lowered himself full-length and began to belly-crawl forward, halting every couple of metres to listen intently for any sound and then cautiously raising his head to peer into the trees and foliage ahead for any unexpected shape or movement. Each time he then lowered himself and wormed forward a little further. At last, he reached the edge of a patch of open ground that would be difficult, if not impossible to cross unseen by a watcher in hiding beyond it among the dense clumps of brambles surrounding the trunk of an ancient oak tree. The oak had been struck by lightning in some past storm, but had remained standing, its split and blackened trunk still somehow supporting the thick boughs and branches extending from it.

He pulled the CommsPad out of the front of his jacket where he had stashed it and checked the signal again. The cursor remained unmoving and showed that the PLB concealed in the Thor missile launcher was now no more than fifty metres away. Standing remained motionless for several minutes, still with the barrel of his AK extended in front of him, ready to loose off a double-tap at the least sign of a threat. He stared intently at the brambles and undergrowth surrounding the tree, trying - as every SAS man learned in the jungle phase of training - to look through the screen of foliage rather than at the surface layer, seeking out the glint of light on the barrel of a weapon behind it, or any hint of movement, or a dark shape or outline that might be a man lying in wait.

He could still see nothing but the leaves and stems of the oak and the brambles around it until, as the breeze rustling through the wood stirred the foliage for an instant, he caught sight of the glint of metal close to the trunk of the tree. He frowned. There was no sign of movement. He thought about lobbing a grenade into the area, but rejected the idea almost at once. If Sukut was lying in wait, the trunk of the oak tree might well protect him from the blast and the attendant shrapnel. He decided that stealth remained his best option and he had just begun to creep forward again when a fresh gust of wind once more stirred the foliage and revealed enough of a glimpse of the metal object to show that it was not the barrel of Sukut's AK-47 or Makarov pistol, but the launcher of the Thor missile, concealed among the brambles around the base of the tree.

Standing was sure that there was no figure next to it and whipped his head around, searching for Sukut's hiding place, but as he glanced back at the missile, he realised there was a third possibility that until now he had not even considered. Much older, and much less fit than the SAS man pursuing him, Sukut might well have become exhausted from struggling through the woods and across rough open ground, carrying the 35 kilogram dead weight of the Thor missile and its launcher. Knowing that he was still several kilometres short of the border, he must have hidden the launcher in the undergrowth, using the lightning-split tree as a marker, and had now hurried on towards the frontier, planning to return with a Russian escort to protect him and help him carry his load the rest of the way. The boot prints Standing had found at the edge of the wood must indeed have been made by Sukut as he hurried away.

Standing estimated that, tired as he was, it would have taken Sukut less than two hours to reach the border, and assuming that he had lost no time in persuading the Russian troops guarding the border of the urgency of his mission, he would be returning with his escort in an armoured fighting vehicle or a heli much quicker than that. Standing's only focus now was on whether to simply take the launcher and its missile and retrace his steps to his comrades, or to set a trap for Sukut and the Russians when they came to retrieve it. But before he could emerge from cover and force his way through the brambles to retrieve the Thor missile launcher, above the persistent buzzing of the wood-flies circling above his head he heard a different noise. It swelled rapidly to a deafening roar: the thundering engine and rhythmic rattling of the rotors of an Mi-24 Hind heli gunship, the 'flying tank' as Soviet pilots had christened it. It was flying fast and low as it approached, but slowed and rose slightly before going into a hover above the clearing at the edge of the wood. The downwash from its rotors lashed the undergrowth around Standing, as the heli descended and the pilot set it down in the clearing.

Standing wormed his way back into the undergrowth and took up a firing position behind the rotting trunk of a fallen beech tree. From there he could command the part of the path by which Sukut and his escort would have to retrace his steps through the wood and also the open ground which they would have to cross to reach the Thor missile among the brambles by the oak tree.

He checked his AK, made sure his spare magazines were instantly accessible when he needed to change them, and placed two of his white phosphorous grenades behind the trunk to his right, close enough that he could grab and throw them in a heartbeat if needed. Then he settled down to wait.

The minutes dragged by. Standing cursed himself for not grabbing the Thor launcher the instant he realised that Sukut had hidden it. If he'd had it to hand, he could already have made a fireball of the Hind as it hovered, incinerating Sukut and everyone else aboard. The first priority now was to deal with Sukut and whatever ground troops the heli had been carrying. After that he would have to deal with the threat posed by the Hind itself. He had one substantial advantage; he was certain that neither the crew of the Hind nor the ground troops aboard it would have been able to spot him as it approached and landed. For the moment he would keep them ignorant of his presence. He kept his head down while he smeared his face with mud so that the whiteness of his exposed skin would not give him away.

Although its primary role was as a heli-gunship, Standing knew that the Hind could also carry up to eight soldiers as well, but he was hoping that the Russians had sent no more than a small patrol with Sukut for what would have seemed like a straightforward and relatively risk-free op. The Hind's engine was still rumbling and the pilot had kept the rotors turning, ready for a fast lift-off once the Thor system had been retrieved. Standing heard the thud as the loading ramp dropped and the clatter of boots as a group of soldiers scrambled out. He raised his head a little, peering through the fronds of a fern growing out of the rotting beech trunk, and saw Sukut with an escort of four soldiers in Spetsnaz camouflage uniforms fanning out to either side of him.

Standing pulled the pin from a WP grenade, lobbed it towards the Russians and followed it with another, arcing higher and thrown with more power to target the two on the other side of Sukut. He flattened himself behind the trunk as there was a double-blast, the second a beat behind, as if it was an echo of the first.

The disadvantage of using white phosphorous grenades was that they created a dense cloud of white smoke which made it impossible to see anything until it cleared, but the screams he heard told him that at least some of the Russians had been hit by the deadly shards of shrapnel and fiercely burning 'Willie Pete'. The smokescreen hid him from the gunner of the Hind, as Standing fired a series of short bursts into the heart of the smoke-cloud, then flattened himself again, changing magazines as he did so. He heard the whine of the Hind's turbines accelerate to a thunder and the rotors chopped at the air as it rose, the downwash dispersing the clouds of white phosphorous smoke in an instant.

Standing saw one of the Spetsnaz crouching, weapon at the ready, peering towards him through the rapidly-diminishing smoke but before the Russian could let off a round, Standing had double-tapped him, blowing a hole through his chest and putting another round through his throat as he fell backwards. Standing rolled sideways a few feet, in case any of the Russians were targeting the muzzle-flash from his first burst, and fired again at another Spetsnaz soldier who went down in a halo of blood.

He could also see another bloodied and burned body on the ground that must have borne the full impact of one of the grenades but there was no sign as yet of the other two men. In any case his main concern now was not whichever of Sukut and his Spetsnaz escort were still alive, but the gunner in the Hind who was now bringing the heli's formidable weaponry to bear.

The fallen tree trunk might have hidden Standing from the ground troops but it would do nothing to conceal him from the heli that was now rising through the air and was almost directly overhead of him. As he heard the rattle of a Gatling gun and rounds began chewing at the ground around him, he pulled another WP grenade from his webbing and lobbed it onto the edge of the open area he had to cross. As soon as he heard the detonation, he burst from cover even as the fragments of burning phosphorous were still falling to the ground, each with a trail of thick, white, phosphorous pentoxide smoke behind it.

Sprinting flat out, he plunged into the dense cloud of smoke, ignoring the acrid stink and the irritation in his eyes, nose and lungs. He knew those effects were temporary and was just praying that the pall of smoke would give him enough cover to reach the Thor before the downwash from the Hind's rotors blew the smoke away again. He ran towards the blackened shape of the oak tree, visible above the smoke cloud, and forced his way through the brambles, heedless of the barbed thorns tearing at his clothes and flesh. As he snatched up the Thor launcher, the Hind's gunner unleashed a fresh torrent of rounds from the Gatling gun through the thinning haze of smoke. Standing hurled himself behind the trunk of the tree as bullets smashed into the other side of it, tearing off chunks of bark and wood and filling the air with a blizzard of needle sharp splinters.

Standing knew that if he was to silence the heli's guns before they also tore him to shreds, he had to strike fast. He feinted to break left away from the tree, showing himself for an instant and then ducking back into the cover of the trunk as the Hind's gunner swung his guns to cover that move and then dived into the undergrowth on the opposite side, scrambling forward a few more yards on his hands and knees and then rolling onto his back and bringing the Thor launcher up to his shoulder. He hit the trigger. He had only one missile, one chance. The 'soft launch' of the missile, ejecting it to a safe distance from the firer before the main rocket motor ignited, should have made it harder for the Hind gunner to spot him. However, that was in theory and in practice, even as the Thor's motor roared into life and the missile disappeared skywards in a blur of smoke and flame, the gunner had brought his weapon to bear again and rounds were once more smashing into the ground within inches of Standing. He tossed another WP grenade - his last - and threw himself to one side, away from the blast, diving, rolling and diving again. Praying that the smoke cloud was hiding his track, he disappeared into a tangle of undergrowth that fought him all the way, with more bramble thorns tearing at his face and arms as he tried to force his way through.

He heard a fresh burst of fire thrash at the undergrowth behind him, and burst out of that feeble cover, sprinting towards another old oak tree that might shield him. He heard the Hind banking round to give the gunner a clearer shot at him, and cursed for it felt like an eternity since he had launched the missile.

The pilot of the Hind had seen the missile and began pumping out chaff and flares, but the Thor's guidance systems had been designed to ignore brief, intense bursts of flame and the metallic 'chatter' of chaff, focussing instead on the near-constant heat of a vehicle's or heli's exhaust and the heavy metal, magnetic signature of the target's armoured bodywork that no amount of chaff could conceal. Arrowing down almost faster than the eye could track it, the missile struck the Hind, which disappeared inside a starburst of fire. In seconds it disintegrated in mid-air, the remains spiralling down and crashing with a shock that shook the earth beneath Standing, as shards of twisted metal and splintered rotor blades scythed through the air. One twisted chunk of armour plate struck the blackened oak tree and completed the destruction that the lightning had begun, sending it crashing to the ground.

Standing didn't waste time reflecting on his close call. Crouching, dodging and weaving to throw off any enemy fire, he made his way back to the clearing where the remnants of the white phosphorous grenades were still burning and giving off smoke, which, with the downwash no longer disturbing it, was clinging to the woodland floor like ground mist.

A round smacked into a tree-branch inches from his head and he dived to the ground, worming his way through the cover. He fired a short burst at the place where he had seen the muzzle flash before diving and rolling again as answering fire tore through the place where he had just been.

Peering through the clumps of coarse grasses towards the area from where the fire had been coming, he saw a sapling bend and then spring back into place as someone brushed against it. He cradled his AK, gaze fixed on that point, waiting for the unseen man to reveal himself. He had to wait for no more than a few seconds before a rounded dark shape rose to break the line of the scrub and grasses around the sapling. Standing's AK spat once, twice, drilling two holes through the forehead of the Russian soldier no more than an inch below the brim of his steel helmet.

Four men were now dead and only one remained unaccounted for. Standing moved forward with ultra-caution, his gaze raking the ground ahead and to either side of him. He passed the bodies of each of the fallen Russians in turn, putting a round into the head of those who were not already undeniably dead. Only Sukut now remained and as Standing moved on he saw a figure sprawled in the long grass at the edge of the clearing and heard a low moan from him. As he approached, he could smell the stench of burning flesh.

Sukut had obviously been within the blast zone of the second WP grenade that Standing had thrown. A piece of shrapnel had almost severed his right arm at the wrist and he had been showered with fragments of burning phosphorous, which had eaten their way remorselessly through the flesh of his torso, face and arms. Standing's face showed no trace of pity as he kicked Sukut's AK away and reached down to take the Makarov from the holster at his waist. There was a mute appeal in Sukut's eye but Standing ignored it. He turned and walked across the clearing to pick up the Thor launcher from behind the tree trunk. When he glanced back, he saw that, despite the agony from his wounds, Sukut was dragging himself across the grass and reaching for the AK that Standing had kicked away.

Standing turned, brought up his own AK and put a round through Sukut's skull. He walked back, retrieved the other AK and slung it over his shoulder, then picked up the Thor launcher and moved off without another backward look.

Chapter 12

By the time Standing got back to the wood where they had ambushed the armoured column, Macleod and the others had reorganised the Ukrainians and set up a system of stags and patrols to give early warning of any fresh Russian incursions or infiltrations by ground troops.

As Standing handed the CommsPad back, Macleod nodded at the Thor launcher he had slung across his shoulder. 'Any problems getting that back?'

'None that I couldn't handle, no.'

'And Sukut?'

'Will not be returning to Russia to a hero's welcome. In fact, he won't be returning at all. Right. Next steps. Any word from the Boss or Secret Squirrel yet?'

'No, I guess they'll be too busy trying to keep on top of everything that's going on, to be bothering us as well. Every unit commander, field agent, Int officer and spook in the universe must be on their case, trying to find out what the hell's been happening.'

In the days that followed the initial battles, the Ukrainian armed forces, vastly out-numbered in personnel, artillery, armoured vehicles, aircraft, missiles - in fact every facet of modern military power - were slowly pushed back while the Ukrainian government made increasingly desperate pleas for Western military support and weapons.

'What are they waiting for?' Macleod said to Standing as they contrasted the desperate situation they were seeing on the battlefields with the slowness or downright resistance among the West's leaders to ship significant supplies of weaponry to Ukraine.

'They're afraid of poking the Russian bear,' Standing said. 'Which is pretty stupid because although it does a lot of growling, if you call its bluff, it runs out to be pretty toothless.'

'It's a shame NATO's leaders aren't a bit more like Zelenskiy.'

Standing nodded. 'Yeah, he's got some pretty big balls on him. Did you hear what he told the US when they tried to get him to flee Kyiv and offered him transport out of there? He turned them down flat, saying 'The fight is here in Kyiv; I need ammunition, not a ride.'

Macleod grinned. 'He was a comedian before he got into politics, wasn't he? And he's still got an eye for a good one-liner.'

Although one arm of the Russian invasion force had even reached the outskirts of Kyiv at one stage, there was a very high rate of attrition among their tanks and aircraft as the Thor missiles, Javelins and Stingers continued to reap a deadly harvest. The Ukrainian forces fighting in defence of their homeland were also having increasing success against the poorly motivated, trained and equipped Russian conscript invaders and as their casualties and losses of equipment mounted, the enemy advances began to slow, and then halt altogether. The front lines then began to inch back the other way as Ukrainian counter-offensives started to gather pace.

When Standing carried out his next debriefing over the secure comms link to Hereford, he found that Colonel Davies was flanked by Agnes Day from MI6 and a general that Standing did not recognise. 'There is still one hell of a long way to go,' Standing said. 'But for the moment at least, it looks like we've got the Russians on the run. We need a re-supp pronto though. We've fired off all the initial batch of Thor missiles. They've proven their worth but now we're out.'

'And we're all delighted with the results,' the general said, in a voice that sounded cured by long years of whisky and cigars in the Officers' Mess and the gentlemen's clubs of Pall Mall. 'Our sincere congratulations to you and your men. News of the weapon's success has travelled fast, courtesy of the MoD's Weapons Sales

Department, and we've already negotiated sales to Saudi Arabia, Oman, The Emirates, Australia and half a dozen other friendly nations. It's given a real boost to the prestige of HMG, and even more importantly, to our balance of payments. However, BAE have not yet geared up to full production and we have only limited stocks to meet the surge in demand, so I'm afraid you and your friends in Ukraine are going to have to take your place in the queue.'

'What?!' Standing said, momentarily lost for words and feeling the familiar drum-beat of the vein in his temple as his anger flared. 'With all due respect, General,' Standing said, 'none of the "friendly nations" you mention are currently facing the remotest threat of invasion. The need is greatest here in Ukraine and that's where the priority should be.'

The general's voice took on a noticeably colder tone. 'I hardly think a sergeant, even one as experienced and decorated as you, Sergeant Standing, is in any position to be telling Her Majesty's Government what its priorities should be. We are all professional soldiers and our job is to carry out the orders we are given, not to question them when they don't suit us. Ukraine will continue to receive shipments of weapons and ammunition from our existing stocks and when supply issues have been resolved, no doubt more Thor missiles will be among those shipments, but for the moment you and the Ukrainian armed forces will have to deal with the Russian threat by other means.' He glanced at his watch, a chronometer that probably cost at least twice Standing's annual salary. 'And now, unless there is anything further?'

'Sir, we need those weapons here. Now. This isn't an exercise, it's the real thing. The Ukrainians need our help and support and they need it now.'

'Matt, the general has made his position clear,' said Colonel Davies.

'And his position is plain wrong,' said Standing.

The general opened his mouth to reply but the connection went dead. Colonel Davies had probably cut the link to save any further argument. It was probably the right thing to do, Standing realised. Pissing off a general wasn't going to change the situation.

Standing relayed the gist of the conversation to Macleod and the others. 'Well,' Macleod said, showing unusual restraint. 'You can't be too surprised. After all, snatching defeat from the jaws of victory is an MoD speciality.'

An hour later, Colonel Davies was back on the secure line, still with Agnes Day alongside him. 'I'm sorry about that, Matt,' said the Colonel. 'I hope you know that if it was my decision, every Thor in the country would be on the first available aircraft out to you, but the armchair warriors took over the asylum long ago, and keeping the oil sheikhs supplied with shiny new toys is evidently still a higher priority than helping a nation fighting a war of survival.'

'So what's our next move?' Standing asked. 'The Ukrainians are up to speed with the Thor system and ready to train their own people now, always assuming they ever get any more missiles, and me, Bash and the rest of the boys are just going to be sitting around here like one-legged men at an arse-kicking party. So are you planning on recalling us any time soon?'

'No, we need you to keep training the Ukrainians. They've just formed a new elite SF unit - the Artan Unit - and your input there will help to make them special forces in more than just name. President Zelenskiy is apparently also very keen on the idea of forming civilian groups on both sides of the new front lines to carry out asymmetric warfare: sabotage and other disruptive actions that will tie down Russian troops and damage their morale.'

'We're a Sabre Squadron, Boss. We're fighters not teachers. Isn't that kind of task better suited to some of our own training teams?'

'It would be, were they not flat out on training tasks for our allies. The Saudis, the Kuwaitis, Omanis and all the others don't just want our weapons like Thor missiles, they want their own special forces to be up to SAS standard too. That may or may not ever happen of course, but the MoD's sales teams is selling the dream and there is no shortage of takers in the Middle East and beyond.' He paused studying Standing's expression. 'Hang tough there for a few more weeks and then,' he gave a sideways glance at Agnes Day as he said it, 'with the input of the SIS, we'll see if we can't find you something more interesting to do.'

For the next few weeks as the fighting on the battlefront ebbed and flowed, Standing and his SAS team were everywhere. They put in several sessions working with the new Ukrainian Artan Group, training them in advanced weapons and tactics. Then, leading by example, Standing, Macleod, Williams and their demolitions expert, Parker, joined up with eight Ukrainian Special Forces to put the training into practice in a series of covert ops against enemy targets behind enemy lines.

As well as intelligence gathering, they carried out a number of targeted assassinations that killed four Russian generals and seriously wounded another one. Those attacks not only disrupted the Russian chain of command but also caused hundreds of Russian elite troops, who could have been fighting on the battlefront, to be diverted to strengthen the protection around Russia's surviving front line generals.

As the fighting moved further from the capital, Standing's team also began training groups of civilians in guerrilla warfare. Thousands of them, too old, too young or too frail to join the Regular Army had volunteered to join what the Ukrainians were calling Territorial Defence Units and Standing and his SAS comrades trained many of those units in the basics of grass-roots urban warfare.

They showed them how to make Molotov cocktails and improvised explosive devices using a crude explosive mix of fertiliser and diesel with bits of scrap metal, nails, screws, nuts and bolts for shrapnel. They helped them build 'Czech hedgehogs' - tank and armoured vehicle obstacles - out of lengths of steel beams, welded or bolted together to form a three dimensional X-shape. They also made fake artillery and mortars out of old drainpipes and pieces of bodywork from wrecked or worn-out vehicles that they scavenged from scrap yards. They then sited them in fields and woods, covering them with enough branches and netting to suggest an attempt at camouflaging them. Having spotted them in surveillance flights, the Russians then wasted their own fire power trying to bomb and shell those locations instead of attacking the much better concealed genuine mortars and artillery pieces nearby.

The most able men and women among the groups of civilians were formed into increasingly well-trained guerrilla bands and, operating from the thick woods and forests in the north and east of the country, they began ambushing and harassing Russian troops in the areas occupied by the Russians in the first invasion. Standing and his team also urged the civilians to carry out even more low-level and homespun sabotage of the Russian war effort near the front lines and in the occupied areas, like disrupting their transport by digging up roadways at narrow choke-points, or blocking them with makeshift barriers. To avoid the possibility of being ambushed while trying to move or demolish the obstacles, the occupants of Russian military vehicles would always wait until enough additional soldiers had arrived to secure the area before the barriers could be removed or the holes in the road filled in again.

The Ukrainian civilians also removed or changed all road and street signs in their areas, causing more chaos for the drivers of Russian military vehicles, particularly as no soldier below the rank of lieutenant was ever issued with a map. That was a hangover from the Soviet era when other ranks were not given maps, reflecting the fear of the Soviet authorities that, given half a chance, many of their conscript troops would simply use the maps to help them defect to the West. In those days traffic marshals had to be deployed at every road junction just to show troop convoys which way to go, and the prime task of the SAS Sabre Squadrons, if ever the Cold War flared up into the white heat of actual combat, was to infiltrate behind enemy lines in East Germany and assassinate every Warsaw Pact traffic marshal they could find. That alone would probably have been enough to bring any attempt by the Soviet bloc to invade Western Europe to a grinding halt, since without maps or marshals, no one would have had the faintest idea which way to go.

Using social media, Ukrainian civilians also formed a spy network that covered the country. They reported on Russian troop movements via Telegram and a Ukrainian government app that had previously been used only for uploading documents to support applications for driving licences or medical treatments. Russian forces responded with ever increasing brutality, raiding homes to confiscate smartphones and computers, and subjecting people to forced detention, beatings and even rape, but as in any asymmetric conflict, such reprisals against civilians only succeeded in generating further recruits for the guerrilla bands.

Chapter 13

After the Russians and Ukrainians fought each other to a near-standstill, Standing and his SAS men began operating with a roving brief and a largely free hand, and with Thor missiles now unobtainable and even Javelins in very short supply, Standing gathered the commanders of half a dozen Ukrainian infantry units together and demonstrated a much more low-tech way of neutralising Russian AFVs. 'The Russian army's preferred modus operandi is always to stay inside their armoured fighting vehicles and use them as guard posts while they try to fight a mobile war,' he said. 'We need to discourage them from doing that and even if there are no missiles or even RPGs to hand, we can use different tactics against them. All you need is one of these and one of these-' He held up a steel wrecking bar and a fragmentation grenade. 'Vision from inside AFVs, through the firing slit and observation ports is very limited, which is why they tend to travel with one of the troopers sticking his head out of the hatch. So the first thing to do is to persuade him of the wisdom of ducking down and whenever you encounter a potentially vulnerable Russian AFV, all it will take is for your artillery to fire a diversionary barrage. That will encourage all the troops inside the AFV to keep their heads well down. All you've got to do then is approach the AFV from one of its blind spots, clamber up the vehicle and onto its turret. Even if the Russians have taken the wise precaution of closing the hatch, the catches that lock it are one of an AFV's weakest points and ten seconds work with the wrecking bar will snap them off. Open the hatch far enough to drop a grenade inside, push the hatch back down until you hear a bang, and

Hey presto! you've got an AFV full of dead Russians. Once you've removed the bodies, providing the grenade hasn't damaged the controls, you can even use the AFV to get back to base, but be sure to warn your comrades you're coming, otherwise you may find yourselves being attacked by your own side. You can even go lower tech if you want and use Molotov cocktails if you've run out of grenades. Drop one in as before and then jump down off the AFV and shoot anyone trying to escape the flames by climbing out of the hatch.'

Bored with their lack of recent action, and not content with telling the Ukrainians how to do it, Standing and Macleod also decided to give them a practical demonstration as well. As they were preparing themselves and checking their kit, Macleod gave a low whistle as he saw the gloves that Standing was pulling on. Almost all Special Forces wore some kind of gloves on ops, but most SAS men used the supple, black leather gloves that were standard issue for infantry soldiers. They were padded across the knuckles to protect them from scraping against walls and other hard surfaces, but many SAS men, including Macleod, unpicked the stitching, replaced the padding with a pair of knuckledusters and then sewed them up again. If it came to unarmed, hand to hand fighting, the knuckledusters usually ensured that the argument was settled with one blow. Standing also had a pair of knuckledusters in his gloves but they were not the usual black leather gloves, but the beautiful and much-coveted green chamois leather gloves issued to air crew. They protected the hands but were also sensitive enough for aircrew to feel the switches and levers in their cockpits through them.

'Bloody hell, Sarge,' Macleod said, as he caught sight of them. 'Where did you get the aircrew gloves from? I've been after a pair for ages but they're as rare as rocking horse shit and I've not been able to get my hands on any.'

Standing smiled. 'I got mine the way most people do - I pinched them when an RAF aircrewman wasn't looking. In fact, I had to do it twice, because one of the other guys pinched my first pair from me, so I nicked another pair.' He grinned. 'Just in case you're thinking of trying the same trick on me, I watch them like a hawk whenever they're not on my hands!'

They went into the front lines with one of the Ukrainian infantry patrols and saw two Russian AFVs, BTR-80 troop carriers, in the edge of a belt of woodland, using the tree-line as top cover and firing bursts from their General Purpose Machine guns to pin down Ukrainian troops who were trying to advance. The BTR's twin front hatches were both closed, with the driver and gunner and any troops inside keeping themselves clear of any Ukrainian counter-fire.

Macleod grinned at Standing. 'One each, Sarge, just the way we like it.'

'Yep, let's just clear some of the debris and then we'll get to it,' Standing said. Six Russian infantrymen were crouching behind the nearest AFV, using it as a shield. As Standing watched, one of the Russians raised his head long enough to loose off an unaimed burst in the general direction of the Ukrainian forces, but otherwise they were keeping their heads down. Carrying Russian-made RPG-7s grenade launchers as well as their AK-47s, Standing and Macleod worked their way round to a position even closer to the Russian front line but at right angles to the soldiers hiding behind the AFV. When they were in position, Standing gave Macleod a thumbs up and said, 'On a count of three: One. Two. Three!'

Jets of flame shot out of the back of the RPG-7s as they launched with a roar. The anti-personnel, fragmentation projectiles blasted into the middle of the group of soldiers and, erupting simultaneously, wiped out the entire group. The two SAS men were already putting distance between themselves and the launch site of the RPGs, diving into cover and wriggling away through the undergrowth as one of the AFVs fired bursts from its machine-gun at the position that Standing and Macleod had just vacated.

Back where the Ukrainian patrol was waiting in firing positions, they handed their RPGs to two of the soldiers. 'Hold your fire until we're clear of the AFVs,' Standing said. 'After that, if anyone puts their head out of the hatch, blow it off.' He glanced at Macleod. 'Ready?'

Standing Strong

'Ready as I'll ever be,' he said.

'Then let's do it. I'll take right, you take left.'

As the AFVs' machine guns began to chatter again, directing fire at the Ukrainian forces away to their left, both men burst from cover, keeping low to the ground as they sprinted across the grass, making for the rear corner of their chosen AFVs, a line that kept them hidden from the firing slit at the front and away from the observation ports on either side. Standing took off from a few feet away, vaulting up on to the rear armour of the vehicle and scrambling onto the turret. He immediately realised that the Russian operating the 7.62mm machine gun projecting from the front of the turret was almost certainly an untrained conscript, because he clearly did not understand the first principles of operating the weapon. Machine guns generate a fearsome amount of heat when fired and originally all of them had been water-cooled but ever since the development of the GPMG - General Purpose Machine Gun - all of them were now air-cooled. That required fire discipline from the men using them. In combat the barrels rapidly heated to dangerous levels. All machine guns had a spare barrel and it was quick and easy to swap them, allowing the original one to cool, but if you could not do so for whatever reason, you had to use whatever came to hand - water, snow, oil, your own urine - to cool the barrel down. If you didn't you could get what soldiers called 'a cook off', when the machine gun was so hot that a round entering the chamber would fire whether or not the machine gunner was pressing the trigger.

Given that the gun fired at 600 rounds a minute, ten rounds a second, you would then get a 'runaway gun' which would continue to fire until it had fired off every round in its magazine or belt. The only way to stop it was to remove the magazine or break the belt and since the belts were flexible that was usually easier said than done. The finishing touch for inexperienced gunners would come if a squib load - a defective round - was fired. When the next round hit it before leaving the barrel, a bulge would result, leaving the barrel looking like a snake that had swallowed a rat. That was what had clearly just happened here, for the barrel was red hot but also now bulging in the middle, even though the gun was continuing to rattle on like a runaway train, until at last it fell silent as the torrent of rounds came to an end

The sound of Standing's footsteps on the armoured top of the AFV may or may not have been detectable inside the vehicle above the thunder of the machine-gun, or even after it fell silent, but the Russians were soon left in no doubt that they were under attack.

The driver of the AFV gunned the engine and it lurched forward, almost throwing Standing from his perch on the turret, but he reached forward to grab the edge of the gun port for the machine gun. Touching the barrel itself, which was still red hot from the runaway firing would have burned through his gloves and blistered his hands in seconds. He braced his feet and used his other hand to ram the chisel-shaped point of the wrecking bar under the edge of the hatch.

As the vehicle slowed, with the driver seeking a way through the trees that had been shielding him but were now obstacles to evade, Standing used both hands and all his strength to force the handle of the wrecking bar down. With a protesting squeal, the steel locking bar of the hatch snapped off.

Standing grabbed a grenade from his harness, pulled the pin and jerked the hatch open, leaning well back to avoid any fire that might be directed up through the hatch. He tossed the grenade inside, let the hatch drop back down again and then jumped down and sprinted back towards the Ukrainian lines, ducking, dodging and weaving from side to side to throw off the aim of any Russians trying to target him.

From the corner of his eye, he saw Macleod also sprinting back from his target AFV and from behind him he heard the dull, muffled double thud of two fragmentation grenades detonating in rapid succession. In the same instant the AFVs' machine-guns both fell silent and the engines stalled, bringing the vehicles to a juddering halt. As he dived into cover, he heard the Ukrainian infantry opening up with their AKs and glancing back he saw a Russian soldier, his face already a mask of blood from shrapnel wounds, half-rise from the hatch of the nearest AFV as he tried to escape, and then fall back, cut apart by Ukrainian fire. No one else emerged from either vehicle.

The Ukrainians moved out of cover and began to advance up to and past the AFVs, while Standing and Macleod dropped back to the point a couple of hundred metres behind the line where a group of infantry officers had been watching the action through binoculars from a low hill.

'Convinced?' Standing said.

The senior officer nodded and grinned. 'Completely.'

Over the following weeks, the Ukrainian infantry adopted the tactics wholesale, using salvos from their artillery as diversions and to keep the enemy troops' heads down inside their vehicles before the Ukrainian soldiers clambered up on to the Russian AFVs and wiped out the men inside.

The Russians' heavy losses of men and AFVs had now forced them out of their vehicles and on to the ground, whereupon the Ukrainians changed tactics again and began attacking the exposed Russian troops with air burst long-range weapons. Follow-up attacks by the Ukrainian infantry and their SAS advisers continued to cause huge casualties and mass panic among the Russian conscripts, but a few groups of Russian soldiers put up far sterner resistance, often successfully resisting the Ukrainian attacks and even driving them back with counter-attacks of their own. Apparently indifferent to casualties, these Russian troops were heavily armed and, unlike the half-starved conscripts they fought alongside, appeared to be well-supplied with food and ammunition. After another ferocious fire-fight with the enemy, Standing and Macleod took a look at the bodies of some of their dead. A glance was enough to show that they were much older than the normal Russian conscript cannon-fodder. Their faces were often marked with the fading scars from old fist- and knife-fights and their bodies were almost all heavily tattooed. 'What do you reckon?' Macleod said as they stared at them.

'I don't know,' Standing said. 'The way they fight, they're certainly not frightened of combat but they're not very well organised, are they? In fact, they don't seem like regular soldiers at all to me. Mercenaries maybe? Wagner Group? Putin has been emptying the jails to replenish his front line troops and these boys definitely don't look like graduates of the Russian equivalent of Sandhurst or West Point.'

Macleod nodded. 'That would explain why they're pretty fearless in battle, because from what I've heard of Russian jails, death might even be preferable to going back there.'

'Nah, it's worse than that,' said Standing. 'From what I've heard, their own officers are under orders to shoot them if they take so much as one step backwards.'

'Fucking Ruperts,' said Macleod. 'They're the same the world over.'

'At least our Ruperts don't shoot us in the head if things go wrong,' said Standing.

'I know a few that would like to,' said Macleod.

Chapter 14

The heavy casualties the Russians had been suffering as the result of the Ukrainian use of air-burst weapons had now forced yet another reaction and another change of tactics as the Russian forces moved into the forests cloaking the lower slopes of the river valleys. That gave them top cover both against attack by Ukrainian aircraft and the air and satellite surveillance imagery that NATO was supplying to support Ukraine's war effort. They also began the hasty construction of a network of defensive trenches.

Russian forces had very little history of using trenches in the past, but the success of the new Ukrainian tactics had forced their engineers to begin digging an extensive network, spreading further and further along the front lines. The Russian engineers could excavate a trench in as little as a few minutes, using diggers like the buckets on JCBs but mounted on tank chassis, including a few that were even mounted on Russia's newest-model tanks, the sophisticated T-90s.

Having again observed their rapidly evolving battlefield tactics, Standing was ready to test the Russians' preparedness for the grim realities of trench warfare. When he arrived back at base from the front lines, with Macleod in tow, Standing immediately went to the Intelligence Centre, manned by personnel of the Intelligence Corps. They were not exactly beloved of most SAS men, who tended to see them as parasites, milking SAS ops for prestige and promotion by producing reports that played up their own contribution despite rarely providing the Sabre Squadrons with the intel that they needed to ensure the success of their ops. The nickname they had been given - 'Green Slime' - reflected both the cypress green colour of their berets and the contempt in which they were held by nearly all SAS men.

Ignoring the sign on the door reading 'Authorised Personnel Only', the two SAS men marched straight in. There were maps and charts on the walls, files and briefing documents on the tables, and half a dozen Intelligence Corps clerks sitting at laptops or talking into sat phones. Even though they always liked to big themselves up and called themselves 'Intelligence Officers', they were always just known as 'clerks'. Everyone looked busy and everything appeared absolutely neat and pristine, in fact a model of what a well-ordered operations room should be, providing you had the manpower and the time to keep it that way.

The Intelligence Officer, in his mid- to late-twenties with the two pips of a lieutenant on his shoulders, the accent a product of an English public school and the downy, apple cheeks of someone who'd only recently begun shaving, swivelled in his seat and glared at them. 'Can't you men read? The sign says Authorised Personnel Only. You can't just come barging in here like this. Get out and present yourselves properly.'

'Who the fuck do you think you're talking to?' snapped Macleod.

'What's your name soldier?' said the lieutenant, looking down his nose at Macleod. He was a good two inches taller than the SAS trooper and a dozen or so kilos heavier, but the extra weight came from fat and not muscle. But even if the officer had been built like an Olympic boxer, Macleod wouldn't have been intimidated. He walked up and stood just inches from the man, his eyes ice cold. 'My name is go fuck yourself,' he said. 'With a capital F.'

The Intelligence Officer stared at him open mouthed. 'Did you not hear what I just said? Get out.'

'We're here for intelligence but it's fucking obvious there's none of that on this room,' said Macleod.

'Easy, Bash,' said Standing, but Macleod's eyes were locked on the officer.

'Listen, pal,' Macleod shouted at the officer. 'In case you haven't realised, the reason you're here is not to arrange your pens in neat rows and push papers around your desk, but to support the operations of the fighting troops - people like us. But in fact, you're all far too busy feathering your own nests and preparing fictitious reports to big yourselves up that you can send back to HQ while studiously ignoring what the guys in the field here actually need.'

'What's your name soldier?' said the lieutenant. 'I'll have you up on a charge for insubordination.' There was a tremor in his voice as he said it, suggesting he was not entirely without nerves about confronting these two grizzled looking men.

'Insubordination!' shouted Macleod. 'I'll give you insubordination.' He pushed the officer in the chest with both hands, with enough force to send the man staggering back and slamming against the wall.

Several of the clerks got to their feet, unsure what to do.

Standing put a hand on Macleod's shoulder. 'Bash, we need to walk away. Now.'

Macleod was glaring at the lieutenant, who was lying on his back, shaking his head. He shook away Standing's hand and took a step towards the officer.

'Bash!' hissed Standing.

Macleod blinked several times, then looked over at Standing as if only just realising he was there. He grimaced. 'Sorry.'

Standing put an arm around his shoulder and guided him out of the office. As they strode away across the compound, Standing glared at Macleod. 'What happened to counting to ten? The deep breathing exercises? You can't go around assaulting officers. If the Colonel finds out, you'll be RTU'd.'

'That Rupert doesn't know who we are,' said Macleod. 'It's not as if we have our names on our fatigues, is it?'

'That's not the point, Bash. You have to get this under control. You can't see red and lash out like that.'

'He was being a prick, Sarge.'

'He's a Rupert, it goes with the job,' said Standing. He took a quick look over his shoulder. No one had emerged from the Intelligence Centre, and the lieutenant's only injury had been to his pride. All he'd have was a description and Macleod like most SAS troopers was fairly nondescript - average height, average build, and with no distinguishing features. 'Seriously, Bash, get a grip, all right?'

Macleod nodded. 'I will, Sarge. Sorry. But you've assaulted your fair share of Ruperts in your time.'

'That doesn't make it right, Bash.'

'I hear you, Sarge.'

'And another thing. If your name really was Go Fuck Yourself, wouldn't that be with a capital G?'

Macleod grinned. 'Fair point.'

Once they were well away from the Intelligence Centre, Standing called Colonel Davies on a secure line to request satellite surveillance footage of the Russian trench system. It arrived within the hour. 'So what are you going to do with it, now that you've got it?' Macleod said, as Standing began studying it.

'I'm going to use it to put some of the things I've learned about trench warfare over the years to the test.'

'Not more bloody training for the Ukrainians?'

'Nope, this one's just for us to have some fun with.'

'Count me in,' Macleod said. 'Anything for a bit more action.'

Coleman had been listening to them, and he frowned and shook his head. As the oldest member of the SAS team, he thought of himself as a wise counsellor, applying the brakes to some of his younger comrades' more reckless ideas. 'I don't know about that, Sarge,' he said. 'Clearing trenches is a job for assault troops like the Paras. Why would you put yourself at risk by a pretty pointless frontal attack on the enemy trenches?'

'Fair point, well made,' Standing said, 'but listen Mustard, I know you're an old man and you're probably beginning to think longingly of pipe and slippers, cricket on the village green and a pint of warm English beer in a little country pub, but the rest of us have still got a few good years left in us, and we don't necessarily want to waste them all in training other people to fight. Speaking for myself, I'm bored rigid twiddling my thumbs while the shot and shell are flying elsewhere. The Ukrainians will be watching so you can call it training if it helps, but it's going to be training by deeds rather than words.' He shot a sly glance at Coleman. 'But of course, if you'd rather sit this one out yourself, like a shy wallflower at a dance in the village hall ... '

'You cheeky bugger,' Coleman said. 'You well know it's one in, all in, and anyway, if I'm not there, who else is going to stop you from getting your fool head shot off?'

Standing slapped him on the back. 'Maybe you're not as old as you look, Mustard,' he said. 'Okay, first things first, we need to get a couple of the Ukrainian armourers to make or modify some kit for us, because our normal weaponry just isn't going to hack it in the trenches. Going on the imagery we have, I would estimate that the width of the Russian trenches is going to be about the same as the width of my shoulders, so there's no point in having any weapon longer than that because it will be almost impossible to bring it to bear and fire on a target. Any fighting is going to be just about arms-length anyway, but as I go forward along the trench, I have to be absolutely sure that everything behind me has been neutralised. It's not just a matter of killing the troops manning the firing positions in the trench, because along the main trench-line there will also be a series of little dugouts carved out of the rear face of the trench-wall. They will have reinforced roofs, making a place where the enemy troops can shelter when there are incomers, and where they can also brew up and enjoy a few home comforts when not on stag or stand-to.'

He gestured at the intel that the Colonel had sent over. 'As you can see from the satellite and air surveillance imagery, the trenches are not constructed in straight lines, they're in short sections either in a zig-zag pattern or if they are in a straight line, each section will be separated from the next by a thick buttress. Once in there I won't be able to hang about. When I'm moving along it, I've got to keep going fast, and there won't be either the time or the space to reload, so when I've emptied my AK magazine, I'll switch to pistols. As I move along the trench, I will use frag grenades to clear any dug-outs or side trenches I pass. And when it gets to the close quarter, hand to hand stuff, the best weapon will probably be an entrenching tool, followed by bayonets, or as a last resort, a pickaxe handle. If it all gets too hectic and I have to bug out, I will use Willie Pete to put down smoke to cover my withdrawal.'

Macleod was grinning and nodding now. 'Sounds like fun, Sarge.'

'I'm going to take a couple of ceramic plates from the body armour some of you use and tuck them in under my webbing to give the front and back of my chest area some protection. I suggest you do the same. And we'll need head protection as well, obviously. Much of the threat is actually likely to be from incoming air-burst artillery shells. I was going to wear one of our own helmets, but I've decided to use a Russian tank crew headpiece. It will still give me enough protection but it is much lighter than the ones we use. However, you're free to make your own minds up about which one you prefer.'

'Bloody hell, Sarge, you're like a walking Wikipedia entry on trench warfare,' Williams said. 'Where the hell did you get all this knowledge from?'

'I've studied my military history of the First World War, and this is how the Tommies plied their trade when they were in the trenches. I was hoping to get some help with my launch point into the trench from the Int guys, but as we know, as usual they're a waste of space. So we'll have to do a recce to find a likely spot and then go from there. The Ukrainians can put down another barrage with their artillery to get any remaining Russians in the AFVs to bail out of them and get into the trenches and then we can follow them in there. Should be interesting!'

Although Standing was using the plural and his patrol-mates and some of the Ukrainians would be following him into battle, the nature of the Russian trench system, and the need to avoid 'blue on blue' friendly fire incidents, meant that each of them would be targeting a different section, their own designated piece of the trench system.

He found the head armourer, who doubled as the workshop foreman, in a shed made out of four cannibalised shipping containers that had been welded together and then covered with a mound of earth to give them at least some protection from air attack, though it would do little to protect them from missile attacks or even iron bombs. The walls of the makeshift shed were lined with cupboards and cabinets containing a bewildering variety of weapons. Every space in between them contained a jumble of lengths of steel, iron, aluminium and heaps of scrap metal and the floor space was filled with an assortment of work-benches, lathes, grinders and drills. The armourer was a broad-beamed veteran of the Ukrainian army with a luxuriant grey moustache that only partly hid a scar like a sabre cut on his cheek.

He listened carefully as Standing laid out his requirements. 'I want you to measure me across the chest and then adapt an AK-47 to be slightly shorter than that measurement. Remove the stock and shorten the barrel so that it fits. I want it on a quick release harness with Velcro fastenings, so I can loosen it and fire one-handed. Also, make sure it comes with a 30-round magazine, because I won't be able to change mags one-handed. Then, I want you to make me a webbing harness similar to the ones paratroopers wear, you know what I mean? I want to be able to hang my equipment from that. I'll also need a couple of canvas bags big enough to hold about ten grenades in each one, and I'd like to borrow your grindstone to sharpen some of my other kit. Any problems?'

The armourer shook his head. 'No, if that's what you want, but why don't you use one of the modern Russian special weapons which don't require any work? We've collected quite a few of them since the frightened Russian dogs often drop their weapons as they run for their lives.' He hawked and spat on the ground for emphasis.

'No they won't do for what I want,' Standing said. 'The problem is the round. Those Russian weapons only use a 5.45, and I want the

AK-47 because the round is punchier, When I use it, I need to be sure that it will clear everything in front of me. It's a simple basic weapon that won't let me down, and that's the prime consideration because there is going to be very little room for error where I'm heading!'

He nodded to Macleod, Coleman and the others. 'If you're coming along for the ride, you can choose your own variations if you like, but I'm pretty confident my kit will do the job best.'

'If it's good enough for you, Sarge,' Macleod said, 'I'm sure it'll do for me too.'

'The one thing I'll insist on,' Standing said, 'is that no-one takes a CommsPad. This op isn't in the MoD or Hereford playbook, it's strictly off the books and we definitely don't need Hereford trying to run the show or pull the plug on it before we've barely got started. Agreed?' Everyone nodded.

'Okay,' Standing said to the armourer, 'and last of all, like I said, I need to borrow a grindstone for a while.'

The armourer gestured to one fixed to the end of a steel bench. 'Help yourself.'

While the armourer got to work on the weapons and kit Standing had requested, he spent the next couple of hours grinding the cutting edges of an entrenching tool - a short-handed spade with a V-shaped blade - until the edges were sharp enough to shave with. He did the same with a couple of standard Kalashnikov bayonets and lastly, he picked up a wooden-handled pick axe, sawed the handle in half and threw away the business end. The armourer's face showed some slight irritation at the waste of a perfectly good pickaxe. He kept watching while Standing drilled a hole through the narrow end of the remaining piece, threaded a length of para cord through it and tied a knot in it, forming a loop that slipped over his hand and onto his wrist, leaving the sawn-off handle dangling from it. He hefted it a couple of times and then winked at the armourer. 'If I run out of ammo and grenades, and then blunt or break my blade, I'll still have a club I can use.'

When the armourer had prepared the rest of his kit to Standing's satisfaction, he fixed everything onto the webbing harness, making it all secure with parachute riser cords. When his companions saw him dressed for trench war, Macleod laughed out loud, 'Bloody hell, you look like one of those one-man bands you used to see busking around Tube stations, only gone rogue. You've got more weapons on you than the Russian and Ukrainian armies put together.'

When Standing turned and saw his reflection in a mirror, he had to join in the laughter. He had the chopped down AK-47 across his chest, two bayonets and two holstered pistols at his waist, a satchel containing fragmentation grenades on his left hip, another one full of white phosphorous grenades on his right hip, the pick-handle club dangling from his wrist and the sharpened entrenching tool tucked into his waistband. There was also a small pack on his back, containing three anti-personnel mines, a variety of tools, including a wrecking bar and a pair of wire-cutters, and a couple of standard charges of PE that might be useful to deal with barbed wire or open the turrets of any tanks or AFVs that got in his way. He grinned at his reflection. He did look like something out of Mad Max.

Having the right kit was only half the battle and while the armourer got on with modifying more weapons and kit for the rest of the team, Standing began preparing himself for the particular demands of the unique form of combat he was about to undertake. He spent hours jogging and sprinting, diving, rolling and jumping until his webbing harness was completely pliable and any elasticity had already been stretched out of it, so it fitted his body like a second skin. The exercise and the wide range of movements had also got him used to the feel and weight of the harness.

Moving to the firing range area, he then spent some time taking on different sequences of targets using his wide variety of weapons. He put himself through a relentless series of punishing drills, first using frag grenade, AK, left pistol, right pistol, club, entrenching tool and WP grenade in rapid succession against a series of targets. One of his patrol mates then moved the targets and Standing attacked them again with a different sequence of weapons. He repeated those drills again and again, with every possible permutation of different weapons, sequences and reactions. Even then, he still wasn't satisfied and moved into the firing trenches, where he got his team to lay out the targets in yet more different sequences until eventually, even he was convinced that he was ready.

The others had also been breaking in their kit and putting themselves through a similarly gruelling programme of exercises and drills, so all was now in place.

The attack, chosen to be on a moonless night, was set for an hour before first light, and Standing had arranged for the Ukrainian artillery to fire a salvo ten minutes before that, both to force any Russians still occupying AFVs to get out of them and head for the trenches.

As they waited for the guns to fall silent, they put on their passive night vision goggles, smeared the exposed skin of their faces with mud or cam cream to hide its whiteness and break up their outlines. Then as the echoes of the last salvo from the guns rumbled and faded away, the SAS team began to creep across the 400 metre gap between the opposing front lines that they had to cross. They did so in total silence, inching their way forward in short bounds of no more than ten metres at a time. Standing went first, advancing a few metres and then stopping, went to ground and called the others forward. They remained upright as they moved, confident that the total darkness of the moonless, overcast night would hide them from the sight of any watching enemies.

In classic fashion, half of them moved forward while the others covered them, poised to unleash a burst of fire at any muzzle flash from the other side. Then the leaders dropped to the ground and gave cover while those in the second rank moved past them.

As they were closing on the enemy trenches, Standing was just moving through the covering line of his comrades, when he heard a faint metallic noise away to his right. Either Macleod, Perkins or Connor had caught his foot on a piece of shrapnel lying on the ground, left over from the artillery fire. It skittered away across the torn soil, making a slight scraping sound. Faint though the noise was, it was enough to alert a Russian sentry and trigger the launch of a flare from the trench ahead of Standing. He froze as the flare soared into the night sky, then burst into a harsh glare of light and slowly began to descend.

Standing had snapped his eyes shut the instant the flare went up for, seen through his PNV goggles, the glare of light would have been blinding. Every instinct of self-preservation told Standing and the others to dive for cover but he knew - and had drummed into all the others - that, paradoxical as it seemed, the best way to avoid detection in that circumstance was to remain in whatever position you were in, standing, crouching or lying down, but above all remaining absolutely motionless. A standing figure might be invisible, indistinguishable from the dark background. The only certainty was that movement meant death, while stillness gave the best chance of survival. Standing stood stock still, his flesh creeping at the thought that an enemy sniper or machine gunner might even now be sighting down the barrel of his weapon at him. There was a tremor building in his leg, for he had paused in an awkward position, with his right foot extended as he had been poised to take another step forward, but he held himself still. The flare slowly descended the last few feet to the ground, guttered and went out with a hiss as it landed in a pool of muddy water. Standing gave it two minutes to allow the sentry to relax and then began to move forward again.

There was one last obstacle for them to overcome before reaching the lip of the trench. In another echo of the Great War, a coil of barbed wire had been stretched along the ground in front of the trench. Standing lay flat, belly-crawling the last few metres to the barbed wire and then took the wire-cutters from his pack, rolled onto his back and began carefully cutting the strands. As expected, and as he had warned the others in the pre-op briefing, he spotted a single strand of plain wire, running through the heart of the coil of barbed wire - an alarm wire that would be connected to a buzzer, or even a booby-trap. Any movement of the wire would either sound an alarm or trigger an explosive device. In either case, that would draw a barrage of firing from the trench, with the sentries' weapons rapidly augmented by those of the remaining members of the garrison as they stumbled out of their dug-outs, rubbing the sleep from their eyes.

He finished cutting through the barbed wire and gently pushed the two halves of the coil a few inches apart. One barb snagged on his hand, and as he freed it a few drops of blood dripped to the ground, appearing an eerie green in the intensified vision through his goggles. He pushed his pack through the fence first, then flattened himself to the ground, lying on his back, turned his head to the side to lower his profile and stop his PNV goggles catching on the alarm wire and then wormed his way underneath it. Free of the wire, he moved on, creeping to the lip of the trench, where he flattened himself at the foot of the low sandbag wall that formed the parapet. He waited five minutes to allow all the others to get in position on their designated sections of the trench. He knew that they would all be watching him through their own PNV googles, waiting for him to give the 'Go' signal. He held out his hand towards him and counted down on his fingers, five, four, three, two, one - then pulled the pin from a fragmentation grenade and lobbed it over the top of the sandbags. He waited for the detonation, hearing the answering sound of explosions from up and down the line as the others followed suit, then he rolled over the parapet and dropped to the floor of the trench.

He was up on his feet at once, his gaze whipping up and down the length of the trench between the buttresses. One Russian lay sprawled a few feet away, cut apart by shrapnel from the fragmentation grenade, a second one, further along, was wounded but still alive and with a warning shout to his comrades, he tried to swing up his rifle, but he was at once faced with the problem that Standing's cut-down AK-47 was designed to avoid and could not bring the long barrel to bear before Standing's shorter weapon barked once, twice. The Russian was blown backwards against the wall of the trench and slid down its face to lie in a crumpled heap in the mud at the bottom.

Standing was now moving fast along the trench, hurdling the dead Russian as he headed for the buttress that led to the next section. He slowed a fraction as he approached an opening in the rear wall of the trench, the entrance to a dug-out where off-duty soldiers could shelter and rest. A length of sacking had been hung over the door frame to keep in a little of the light and warmth from a hurricane lantern and a paraffin stove the soldiers were using. As Standing approached, one Russian soldier was struggling out past the sacking curtain, his uniform half undone and his eyes sticky with sleep. Standing double-tapped him before he knew what was happening and then put a burst from his AK through the sackcloth. He followed it with a grenade to take out any others still in there, then moved on without a backward look. As he was approaching the buttress, another soldier appeared round it, weapon at the ready, but once more a Russian conscript with a full-length AK-47 was no match for an SAS veteran with a sawn-off weapon, and a double-tap delivered from close to point blank range blew a hole in the Russian's chest that would have swallowed a football.

Standing then dropped to the trench floor and eased round the buttress at ground level. That surprised a Russian soldier, waiting with his weapon at the ready to shoot the intruder but aiming at chest height. By the time he had caught sight of Standing and realised his mistake, it was too late. Standing blew him away from point blank range, firing upwards, his rounds smashed through the man's chest, one exiting through the top of his shoulder and the other through his neck. He toppled back as blood gushed from the severed artery in his neck.

Standing emptied the rest of his AK magazine into the next dug-out, following it with another grenade. He switched to one of his pistols to deal with another soldier who came bursting out of a second dug-out. He put two shots into the percentage target, the chest, to bring the enemy down and running closer, he then finished him off with a short-range double-tap to the head.

That brought him close to the entrance to the next dug-out and three more Russian soldiers scrambled through it as he approached.

He shot the first with his pistol, but it then jammed as he went to target the next. The sharpened entrenching tool was nearer to hand than the other pistol, so he switched to that, slashing the second man with a diagonal stroke that opened him up from his ear to his kidney. He went down like a sack of coal, his screams muffled by the blood spurting from his tongue, which had been split by the lethal blade as it carved downwards across his face.

The third man brought up his AK, but the burst he fired hit empty air, for Standing had dived, forward rolled and come up so close to the man that, as he knocked his AK aside to prevent a second burst, he could smell the acrid stench of the Russian's sweat. He drove the double-edged blade of the entrenching tool into the man's gut, under his ribcage, and jerked it out again with a savage twist that spilled a torrent of blood and guts onto the tench floor.

Now drawing his other pistol, Standing gave him the coup de grace with that, and hearing a gurgling noise from the first man he had carved open, he span on his heel. Despite his massive wound, the man had just managed to haul himself up onto one elbow, and was fumbling with the pistol at his belt, but struggling to grip the butt with a hand that was slippery with his own blood. Standing put an end to his struggles with another double-tap, tossed a fragmentation grenade into the dug-out in case any other soldiers were in hiding there and moved on towards the buttress at the end.

It was also the end of his designated section agreed in the pre-op briefing. Hearing shots and explosions from beyond it and not wishing to cop any shrapnel or rounds either from the enemy or one of his own troopers, he remained where he was, keeping a wary eye on both ends of the trench in case any other enemy soldiers appeared, until the firing had died down. As the last shots from up and down the trench line faded into silence, but with his ears still ringing from the explosions and shots from his own weapons, he spoke into his throat mic. 'One - okay'. The terse message told his patrol-mates that he was unhurt and ready to exfil.

There was a rapid response from the next two, Macleod and Williams: 'Two - okay' 'Three - okay.' but only silence from the next.

'Four?' Standing said. 'Report.'

There was another silence but then he heard Connor's Black Country twang. 'Five - okay, but Four's down.' Four was Perkins. 'I've got him,' Connor said. 'Give me cover.'

'Wait out,' Standing said. 'Six?'

The others checked in. There was one fatality, one of the Ukrainians who had made the fatal error of assuming the Russian he'd just shot was dead. He moved past him and two seconds later took a burst in his back from the Russian's AK. The only other casualty was Coleman who had been hit in the forearm by a stray round.

Standing called in a casevac for Perkins at once. Connor had been using his combat lifesaver training to try to staunch his mate's wounds and when the patrol medic, Williams, took over from him, and continued to work on Perkins in the hope of keeping him alive, Connor joined the others in giving them cover.

Standing took up station beside Connor and asked him what had happened. Connor told him that he had cleared his own section and was waiting for Perkins to complete his work when he saw him get hit. The AK round that had struck him had been fired from close range by a Russian who must have left the trenches for some errand behind the lines, maybe to use the latrine, just before the attack began. When the gunfire and explosions erupted, he had crept back to the rear side of the trench and shot Perkins in the back. The angle of the shot, fired from above and to one side, had seen the round blast through Perkins's back above the fourth rib, smash two discs in the spinal column and then, tumbling from the impacts, tear its way through a kidney before exiting his body.

Connor had blown the Russian away with a burst from his own AK and then rushed to give his mate first aid until Williams could take over. They had done their best to stem the bleeding and dress his wounds, but kidney damage and spinal surgery were beyond the skill-set of any battlefield medic and all they could do now was wait for the casevac heli and pray, first, that Perkins would survive, and second, that the spinal damage wouldn't leave him paralysed.

For one half of the Black Country twins, it looked like not only his battle but his army career might be over and when, out of Connor's earshot, Standing asked Williams what Perkins's chances were, the medic's bleak expression as he turned away without speaking told its own story.

Chapter 15

The arrival of the casevac helicopter was heralded by a thunder in the skies as an air armada appeared above them. F-15 Strike Eagles and Typhoon fighters, all loaded for bear and bristling with rockets and cruise missiles were flying high above them to provide cover. They were not Ukrainian aircraft but were showing NATO markings. Their aim was not to fire their weapons but to warn the Russian defenders, not to attempt to interfere with the casevac. The message, to Russian officers on the ground, their commanders in the rear and to President Putin in Moscow was a straightforward one: Step out of line while we casevac this casualty and we will flatten you.

With the top cover protecting it, the casevac Chinook came rumbling in, went into a hover and landed alongside the SAS team. The ramp was lowered at once, revealing a box like a shipping container but with a fully self-contained medical suite inside it, staffed by a team of trauma specialist medics. Perkins was stretchered into it and as the ramp was raised again, the doors of the medical suite closed, providing a sterile sealed unit where the medics could work on Perkins's wounds.

The Chinook took off at once. 'Don't worry, mate,' Standing said to Connor. 'He's in the best possible hands now.' Connor nodded but said nothing, his face hollow with worry and grief.

The Chinook flew at low level, well below its maximum speed to minimise the vibrations that could affect the treatment of the casualty. It landed at the SAS team's base where a Globemaster was already waiting on the runway. As soon as the Chinook touched down alongside it, the medical unit was wheeled down the ramp and transferred into the Globemaster's cavernous interior while the medics inside didn't miss a beat in carrying on working on Perkins.

The Globemaster took off straight away, heading for the Medical Centre at Ramstein air base near Frankfurt in Germany, the foremost trauma centre in the world, where all NATO and especially American trauma victims, not just from combat but from accidental discharges or even suicide attempts, were taken for treatment. Even while they were still working on Perkins's wounds themselves, the medics were also relaying information and video imagery of them to Ramstein so that surgeons there could already be planning and rehearsing the surgery and treatment they would be carrying out before their patient had even reached them.

Meanwhile all Standing and his patrol mates could do was get themselves back to their base and then wait for news. The air armada flying top cover had pulled back as soon as the Chinook was safely clear of the enemy, but before exiting the trenches themselves and retiring to the Ukrainian lines, the SAS team had one last surprise for the Russians. They first moved the bodies of the dead Russians off the floor of the trench, either dragging them into the dug-outs to lie with the victims of the fragmentation grenades, or manhandling them over the sandbag parapet, so they fell on the No Man's Land side, and were invisible, hidden by the sandbag wall, from anyone in the trench. Clearly the Russian replacements would know that a contact had taken place, but the absence of visible bodies would, Standing hoped, puzzle them and heighten their curiosity, making them more vulnerable to that last surprise.

Standing crouched down and used his entrenching tool to bury one of the anti-personnel mines he was carrying in his back-pack in the entrance to each of the dug outs in his section. The rest of Standing's patrol-mates did the same in their sections. The plastic casings and minimal metal parts in the mines rendered them almost invisible to mine-detectors, and any pressure, for example by someone trying to enter a dug-out and stepping on one, would detonate it. They were not designed to kill but to maim, since in the cynical calculation of armies and arms manufacturers, badly wounded soldiers can be more damaging than dead ones, since they overload the enemy's medical and other logistical support services. So anti-personnel mines usually contained enough explosive to blow off a man's foot but not enough to kill him.

Having laid his mines, Standing checked in again with the others and then said 'Smoke on three - two - one!' Then, he pulled the pin from a WP grenade and lobbed it behind the Russian lines, throwing it far enough to ensure that its white phosphorous fragments would not reach any of his own troopers.

Its detonation was followed by the almost simultaneous explosions of another half-dozen WP grenades thrown by the rest of the SAS team. They generated a billowing cloud of white smoke, the smokescreen cover that would keep them hidden from the fire of any surviving Russians, who must now have been as angry as hornets with a shattered nest.

Under cover of the dense clouds of smoke the SAS men began to pull back, climbing out of the trench and rolling over the parapet to keep their profile below the horizon. Standing began working his way back along with his patrol-mates. At any one time, half of them were moving and the other half were in firing positions covering them. When they reached the barbed wire, they again crawled carefully beneath the alarm wire. There was no need to avoid giving the alarm - the Russians would already be well aware that their trenches had been attacked - but it was still wise to avoid brushing against the alarm wire, in case it was booby-trapped with grenades or IEDs.

Back at base, Standing led the debrief and as they were taking stock and absorbing the lessons from the op they had just carried out, they received the devastating news that despite the best efforts of medics and surgeons, Perkins had been so severely wounded that he had died on the operating table, soon after reaching Ramstein.

Connor took the news without any outward sign of having heard it, but then moved off and sat down to one side away from the others, with his eyes downcast, seeing nothing, as he replayed the op and the shooting of his best mate in his mind.

His patrol-mates left him to it. They knew that any words of theirs would not help him yet. When he was ready, they would be there for him but for now, he was best left alone.

Chapter 16

The day after the trench raid, Standing and his SAS team were pulled back from the front line to a Ukrainian army base and there he was soon in receipt of an almighty bollocking, first from Colonel Davies and then from Lieutenant Balfour, who had both flown in from Hereford to see the combat zone for themselves. Colonel Davies went first. 'I have now been briefed about the trench raid that you led with your patrol and I could hardly believe what I was hearing. You not only put yourself and your comrades at risk, with permanent consequences for one of them, but you did so for no strategic or tactical gain that I can detect, other than taking out a few Russian soldiers. As you well know, Matt, I have often cut you a lot of slack in the past. You deliver on ops, so I've been willing to turn a blind eye to quite a few indiscretions and occasions when you've gone off piste. But staging an unauthorised raid on the Russian trench-line was a step too far.'

Balfour could hold himself back no longer and added, 'And as far as I can see, the motivation for it was purely that you wanted to put your theories about trench warfare to the test under battlefield conditions.'

Standing swallowed a smile, while thinking to himself that Balfour had finally got something right. 'I was doing exactly what it says on the tin,' he said. 'Killing HMG's enemies. When did that become an issue?'

Colonel Davies frowned. 'You're skating on thin ice here, Matt, and if I were you, I'd save the smart-arse remarks for your patrol mates and accept the reprimand with good grace.'

Balfour scowled as he heard the word 'reprimand' since he now realised that the hopes he had been harbouring that Standing's latest indiscretion would lead to him being RTUed had now been well and truly dashed. Having administered the ritual bollocking and received Standing's grudging acknowledgment of it, the Colonel just said, 'Right, back to business. Your friend from Six, Agnes Day, has requested your presence for a further briefing.'

'Is that part of my punishment?' Standing said with a smile.

Colonel Davies merely rolled his eyes, leaving Balfour still fuming as Standing walked out without even glancing in his direction. Standing's own smile deepened as he was closing the door and heard the beginning of Balfour's plaintive 'Sir, I really must protest…'

Standing strolled along to the briefing room that Agnes Day had commandeered. 'Ms Day,' he said. She was wearing camouflage fatigues that appeared to have been freshly ironed, and spotless desert boots. 'The Boss says you might have another poisoned chalice for us.'

She ignored the jibe. 'I won't beat about the bush,' she said, all business, as she irritably pushed a stray lock of grey hair away from her brow. 'Ukraine's forces have achieved miracles up to now, albeit greatly aided by Russian military incompetence, but even though the Russians' casualty rates have been enormous, there hasn't been the Ukrainian breakthrough on the battlefield that we might have hoped for. However, as we feared, with the war dragging on and what looks increasingly like a stalemate on the battlefield, there seems to be a growing feeling that some of our allies, in particular the United States, and even some members of our own government, are beginning to tire of the cost - both financial and in domestic politics - of supporting Ukraine. We can't easily increase our already substantial military aid any further.' She gave him a calculating look. 'So, we're looking for a spectacular - a way to put the conflict back on the front pages - and if we can do it in a way that inflicts the maximum damage on Russia's war effort as well, so much the better.'

'So what are you thinking?' Standing said. 'A Gay Pride march through Rostov-on-Don?'

'Very amusing,' she said in a tone of voice and with a facial expression that suggested it wasn't amusing at all. 'Tell me, have you heard of Yevgeny Prigozhin?'

Standing nodded. 'Of course. He's the head of the Wagner mercenaries that have been besieging Bakhmut for months.'

'Exactly. And, we believe, carrying out atrocities and war crimes there and elsewhere in occupied Ukraine. Originally Wagner Group's men were a collection of mercenaries - former soldiers from the French Foreign Legion, veterans of white colonial armies in Africa, militiamen from Chechnya and other troubled former Soviet republics, in fact old soldiers from anywhere with a taste for killing and no education or alternative skills. However, Putin then gave Prigozhin free rein to recruit prisoners for Wagner from jails and penal colonies all over Russia and anyone was eligible, including sex offenders and murderers.'

Standing nodded. 'Yeah. I'm told the recruitment offer was straightforward, apparently: fight in the front lines in Ukraine for six months and receive a payment of 100,000 rubles and, providing you don't die, you'll get your freedom. If you do die, your relatives will get five million rubles in compensation. There was no shortage of takers, despite the risks.'

She nodded. 'An estimated 50,000 prisoners have taken up the offer.'

'We've come across some of them,' said Standing. 'They're ill-disciplined but are usually better fighters than the conscripts, not that that's saying much.'

Day nodded again. 'Prigozhin is also a former prisoner. In his youth he was a gang member in St Petersburg - Putin's home area - and served 10 years in a Russian penal colony for robbery with violence, but then he reinvented himself. He ran hot dog stalls in St Petersburg to start with, then opened a series of casinos and a number of increasingly high-end restaurants. He began catering for government dinners and receptions, including banquets for

Putin himself, and that led to contracts to supply food to schools, government workers and the military.'

'It's quite a step up from being a catering contractor to the head of an army of mercenaries,' Standing said.

'Indeed it is, but that's how close his connection with Putin has become, and it's not the only string to his bow. The Wagner Group have become a deniable Russian asset, supporting factions that the Kremlin wishes to aid in conflicts and civil wars, throughout Africa and the Middle East - including Libya, Syria, Mali, the Central African Republic and Sudan. In the process of that, Wagner has also looted a fortune in gold, diamonds and other commodities. Prigozhin is now a billionaire with a fleet of private jets and a 115-foot yacht among his trinkets. However, at heart he remains a thug and a cold-blooded killer. His men have been involved in three assassination attempts on President Zelenskiy, so far mercifully without success. Prigozhin even posted a clip online of a recaptured Wagner deserter being executed with a sledgehammer,'

'Sounds like a really charming man,' Standing said, 'but why are you telling me all this?'

'Because we believe we've found a way to drive a wedge between Putin and the Wagner Group. Prigozhin was for years a very low-profile figure, shunning the limelight, but more recently he's started to revel in his notoriety. He's very active on Telegram and hugely popular with supporters of the Russian invasion and, although he has been very careful not to criticise Putin directly, he is increasingly vocal in his criticisms of Russia's Defence Minister, Sergei Shogun, and the chief of the General Staff, Valery Gerasimov. He claims that they are failing to support his troops and starving them of ammunition and supplies, even though Wagner are doing the bulk of the fighting in the front lines, and there has been an escalating war of words about it. He's even threatened to pull his troops out of the front lines if his demands are not met.'

Standing was beginning to get the feeling he knew where all this was leading. 'So let me guess,' he said. 'You're thinking that if - heaven forbid - Prigozhin was to meet with an unfortunate accident, it would not only damage the Wagner Group, but if it appeared to have been sanctioned by his enemies in the Russian hierarchy, that would not only create disharmony and conflict among Russia's military establishment and combat troops, but might also generate political instability in Moscow as well.'

Day permitted herself a thin smile. 'You're wasting your talents in the SAS, Sergeant Standing. You should come and work for us as an analyst.'

'Ms Day,' he said with a broad smile. 'I appreciate the offer, but I'm not cut out for sitting behind a desk.'

'Then let's make use of your talents in your current area of expertise, shall we? Now Prigozhin travels everywhere by private jet. He flies in regularly for briefings and visits to senior Wagner officers which occur either in Rostov-on-Don or in the Wagner forward HQ near Luhansk. He is always accompanied by at least four bodyguards and when in-country, he travels in an armoured limousine.'

'Which makes it very distinctive,' Standing said, thinking aloud. 'But if we're going to stage this in a way that apparently implicates Russia's top brass rather than Ukraine, it needs to be done a very long way behind the lines and in a manner consistent with Russian assassinations.' He paused. 'I don't suppose you can get your hands on any Novichok, can you?'

'I hope that's your idea of a joke,' Day said, 'though it is one in very poor taste, if I may say so.'

'So that's a "No" then,' Standing said, suppressing a smile. 'In that case, we might be looking at a bomb on his private jet, something with a timer or an altitude pressure switch so it detonates when the aircraft is at altitude, ensuring there are no survivors. The alternatives are to take him out with a sniper-shot, or a close range face-to-face assault, or use a mine or an IED to target his limo, although if the vehicle is armoured, it's going to take a serious amount of PE to ensure he's liquidated when it goes off.' He thought it through in silence for a couple of minutes and then glanced back at her. 'Right. What's our timing? We can track the movements of his private jet on Flight Tracker of course, but that isn't a guarantee that Prigozhin's on board. Do you or will you have intel on when he's next likely to be dropping in on his front line commanders?'

'We will,' she said, 'because we have an asset within Prigozhin's inner circle.' She permitted herself another of her bleak smiles, which in anyone else would count as a grimace. 'The disadvantage of recruiting mercenaries is that they are by definition available to the highest bidder, and we are paying him considerably more than Prigozhin, and in Swiss francs to a numbered account in Zurich.'

'Nice work if you can get it,' Standing said. 'I don't suppose you'd consider setting up the same system for me, would you?'

Ms Day's rictus smile switched off like a light. 'Once more, I'm going to assume that you are joking. Our asset informs us that Prigozhin has been calling summits of his most trusted advisers and senior commanders with increasing frequency. When he next does so, he will almost certainly be flying in to meet with them at an airstrip just to the south-east of Luhansk. It's attached to the Luhansk aviation museum, strangely enough. It's been closed to the public since Putin's "Special Military Operation" began, but Prigozhin has permanently commandeered a meeting room there. So that will present your opportunity.'

'And how long will we have to prepare and train for the op, insert and reach the target before Prigozhin's next summit?'

'I can't tell you that. Our asset tells us that there is no set pattern to the frequency of the meetings. Sometimes weeks go by without one, sometimes he may call another one within a few days of the last one.'

Standing gave a slow shake of his head. 'You're not giving us much to go on, Ms Day, are you?'

She gave him a withering look. 'Are you saying that you can't do this, Sergeant Standing? I thought "can't" wasn't a word in the SAS vocabulary.'

'It's not and we will find a way, but you know the Five Ps, don't you?'

'Perfect Preparation Prevents Poor Performance? Yes, I'm familiar with that.'

'Correct,' Standing said. 'And if you only give us a few days - or less - notice, then given the time it will take to infiltrate to the target, it may well leave us considerably short of perfect preparation.' He gave her a cynical smile. 'Okay, well, leave it with me and I'll discuss with our Head Shed and my patrol mates and we'll see if we think it's feasible.'

'I very much hope that those deliberations will lead to the right conclusion.'

'Best keep your fingers crossed, then,' he said. He winked at her and left the room.

Chapter 17

As with any potential op following a request from an MI6 operative, the first phase of the process started with an informal discussion between Standing and Colonel Davies. Standing summarised his briefing from Agnes Day and the Colonel then said 'Okay, so as ever, the first question is whether it is worth our while to be getting involved in this. Is it going to give us a reasonable return on the investment of your time and our assets, and what will be the risks involved?'

'Well, the risks are obvious and they're pretty substantial,' Standing said. 'If the op is compromised and it all goes tits up, you'll be losing a patrol and if they take any of us alive and resist the temptation to execute us on the spot, there may be some major political ramifications too.'

'So those are the risks,' the Colonel said. 'What's in it for us and are we able to refuse if we don't think the cake is worth the candle? We'll have OPCON - Operational Control - so in theory we can pull the plug, but it's something I never like to do if it's humanly possible to avoid it. So, what's in it for Six? Why are they so keen?'

'It's pretty obvious, isn't it?' Standing said. 'There's zero risk to them but big kudos if it comes off, and you can bet they won't be slow to claim the credit if so, though you won't see them for dust if it goes wrong.'

'Careful, Matt, your prejudices are showing,' said Colonel Davies.

Standing gave a rueful grin. 'So I suppose the other question is if we do the op, will it make any difference in the long-term?'

'Possibly not. My guess would be that Putin will take out Prigozhin sooner or later anyway. The Wagner Group is becoming increasingly powerful and Prigozhin himself is getting to be more and more of a popular figure with the Russian public. You don't need to know much about Vladimir Putin to realise that both of those things will be anathema to him. He does not tolerate any potential rival so as soon as he sees Prigozhin as more of a threat than an asset, he will react.'

'So if we go ahead with the op, Six get a lot out without putting much in at all, whereas we will be in the reverse position to that: we'll be putting a great deal in and getting not a lot out for our efforts.'

Colonel Davies nodded. 'But I think we should still explore our options further, if only to prevent a diplomatic war breaking out between Six, the Control Group in the UK and ourselves out here.' He shrugged as he intercepted Standing's cynical look. 'We're a very long way from the levers of power here, Matt, so for the moment let's keep our options open.'

Standing's next move was to get his most trusted Group Leaders - Ireland, Parker, Coleman and now Macleod as well - together in an underground briefing room at the base. Connor would normally have been part of the group too, but with Perkins's recent death probably still preying on his mind, Standing opted to leave him out of the core group for the next op. The walls were covered in large scale maps of Ukraine and Russia, and there were laptops, piles of surveillance photographs, print-outs of satellite imagery, intel reports and other documents of all sorts stacked on every available surface.

Standing opened the traditional Chinese Parliament that preceded every potential SAS op. Everyone was given an equal say to explore outline ideas and options for the operation. It was an open, no-holds-barred exchange of ideas and views, in which all were able to contribute to the form of the eventual plan. Any reservations had to be expressed then and there, because once agreed, it was binding on all of them and no complaints after the event or criticisms made with the wisdom of hindsight were ever tolerated.

Nothing was ever off limits in a Chinese Parliament, it was the place where anything and everything could be said without rancour or later come-backs. However, at the start, as often happened, the group were reticent and unenthusiastic, reluctant to share ideas or do anything to advance what at least some them felt was a flawed and potentially disastrous idea.

Nonetheless, as they started to realise the implications of a successful strike against Prigozhin both for the war in Ukraine and for their own prestige and kudos among their peers were they able to carry it out, the mood music began to change. Before long the Group Leaders were advancing ideas and voicing criticisms with all their customary enthusiasm, and beginning to put the rudiments of a workable plan together, with all of the team now hoping to be a part of the action on the ground.

Few of them had any respect for Prigozhin or even the experienced fighters and mercenaries within his Wagner Group, let alone the ex-con cannon fodder he had recruited from Russian jails. The SAS men considered them to be over-rated and self-publicists who were only good battlefield troops in comparison to the raw Russian conscripts in the regular army. In the SAS men's opinion, given a rough parity in weapons and equipment, none of the Wagner Group's men would measure up against the Ukrainian ground forces.

The outline plan they formed was firstly, that the operation should be a joint British and Ukrainian task. The Patrol Commander and the Medic and Signaller would all be SAS men, but hand-picked Ukrainian troops would be invaluable for their language skills and local area knowledge, as well as their fighting abilities. The recruitment of the Ukrainian elements for the mission would be left in the hands of the British patrol commander, and they all knew who that would be.

The second decision was that the Infil and Exfil routes for the attack team should be decided by the patrol members alone. If insertion by helis did not prove to be a feasible option, then a direct route through the front lines would probably be the next best - or as Macleod put it, 'the least worst' - option.

Third, the success or otherwise of the mission would rely heavily on the quality of the latest intelligence and the external administrative support.

The fourth element of the plan was based on their assessment of the potential prospects of success of the various methods of assassinating Prigozhin that they could adopt, bearing in mind the absolute necessity of it being a completely deniable op. They had to assume first of all that Prigozhin's vehicle and any building he was using would probably be equipped with electronic counter measures. In the air he would be travelling in his private jet, also assumed to be fitted with electronic counter-measures, but unlikely to have Russian Air Force fighters flying top cover above him. When on the move on the ground, he would be travelling in a convoy and would have concentric rings of security around him.

Bearing in mind that the more complex the operation they chose, the more kit, personnel and training they would require, they began looking at a series of possible assassination methods. Each was proposed and discussed in depth, before being either discarded or added to the short-list.

'We need to decide what this guy Prigozhin's weaknesses might be,' Parker said. 'What are the chinks in his armour?'

'One definitely seems like his ego,' Standing said. 'He used to be a background figure, operating in the shadows, but it sounds as if he's now gone for the full glare of publicity, making statements, holding press conferences for tame reporters and tweeting on Twitter as if his life depended on it.'

'Maybe it does,' Macleod said, his trademark cynicism to the fore. 'I can't imagine Putin likes any of his minions to be stealing his limelight.'

Standing nodded. 'So we could target him as he's addressing his adoring public or entering or leaving a meeting with his minions, but he will then be flanked by a posse of bodyguards, as will many of his commanders. We may still be able to take him out, either by a sniper shot at long range or with some heavy-duty firepower at closer quarters. However, either of those approaches will complicate our exfil and may well lead to a full-on contact with his men. And since I've become quite attached to my skin over the years, in a perfect world I'd prefer a more covert plan of attack.'

The first and safest option they considered, an air launched missile strike, was quickly considered and dropped. In its favour, it was quick, clean and offered little risk to the attackers, but there were several disadvantages. It was seen as too indiscriminate, with a very high potential for collateral damage, and it would also be very difficult to persuade domestic Russian or international opinion that such a strike could have been carried out by Russian forces on the orders of Vladimir Putin or one of his senior officials or commanders. Ukraine would be happy to claim the credit of course, but Six's double aim was not only to eliminate the Wagner Group leader, but also to generate discord in senior Russian military and political circles by pinning the blame for Prigozhin's death on Putin.

The second option, of a ground launched missile strike, carried the same minimal risks and the same disadvantages as the first and was rapidly discarded. Macleod then voiced a third option. 'If we target his aircraft while he's at his summit meeting with his inner circle, we'll only have a pilot and a couple of guards to evade.'

'Check,' Parker said. 'I can fix a device with a timer, but since we can't predict how long Prigozhin will be in his meeting, we'd probably be better using a device with an altitude pressure switch, that'll stay dormant until the aircraft begins its climb. I could fix it to the underside of the wing where it meets the fuselage on the far side of the jet from the passenger doorway. Unless the pilot's pre-flight checks are particularly thorough, he's unlikely to spot anything wrong, and once Prigozhin is on board and the jet reaches an altitude of 10,000 feet - Bang! No one will survive that and it will take investigators several days to inspect the wreckage and check the flight data before confirming a bomb attack and by that time we'll be back here with a pie and a pint.'

'And if the pilot did spot it?' Macleod said.

'Then we'd have to take him out and go to one of the other options,' Standing said, 'like a sniper shot as Prigozhin leaves his meeting or an all guns blazing shoot-out with him and the rest of his motley crew. But that's definitely a last resort unless we've got a collective death-wish, because even if we get out of that contact alive, we'll have well and truly trodden on the hornet's nest and we'll have 140 clicks of hostile territory to cross before we're back on Ukrainian turf.'

'It's all Ukrainian turf,' Macleod said. 'It's just temporarily occupied by those Russian pricks.'

Standing grinned. 'Fair point, well made, Bash, but it doesn't alter the fact that it would be crawling with Wagner goons looking for pay-back for the loss of their beloved leader.'

At first glance, the next option, of a long-range sniper attack, appeared a much more attractive prospect. It again carried minimal risk to the attackers, since by definition, the attack team would be sited at a considerable distance from the target. Curiously it was a Ukrainian sniper who had just acquired the record for the longest recorded kill with a sniper rifle, shooting a Russian soldier from 3,800 metres away, rapidly celebrated in a few crowing posts on social media. SAS snipers did not go in for that kind of publicity, preferring to hide their light under a bushel even though the Regiment had some of the most accomplished snipers in the world. The patrol's demolitionist, Parker, was one of them, a trained and lethal sniper with the Regiment's sniping weapon of choice, the Accuracy International L96A1, with a variant for covert operations featuring an inbuilt suppressor and a folding stock. However, skilled though he was not just at firing his weapon, but also factoring in all the factors that could affect a round's trajectory and accuracy: distance, elevation, air density, wind direction and speed, Parker would never guarantee a killing shot at more than a kilometre's range and preferred to operate well within that.

Mitigating against the probability of a successful long-range kill was the fact that they had to assume that Prigozhin would be wearing the highest grade of body armour and combat helmet available, whenever he was in the battle zone. Therefore, that option would only be feasible using the very latest in sniper technology, rifles and scopes, to ensure a hit on an extremely small target area.

A short-range sniper shot offered a significantly better chance of killing the target, and didn't require the shooter to possess specialist training or weaponry, but it carried a far greater risk to the attackers by putting them in turn within range of Prigozhin's security detail.

A mine or IED was a possibility but might not guarantee a kill against a target travelling in an armoured vehicle as part of a convoy, and with Electronic Counter-Measures that might prevent remote detonation of the device. The fact that Prigozhin also often chose a vehicle at random, ignoring his bodyguards attempts to shepherd him into the armoured one they had waiting meant that accurate intel up to the very last minute would be essential to ensure a successful hit. Such a weapon was also indiscriminate and carried a very high risk of collateral damage.

A much larger explosive device, a bomb concealed in a culvert or beneath the span or arch of a bridge would have a greater chance of success if Prigozhin was actually travelling in an armoured vehicle. However, like the IED, it would also almost certainly entail collateral damage. It would require a spotter to identify the target vehicle and might well also need a command wire to trigger the device and overcome Prigozhin's ECM measures. That would put the spotter and attackers at close range and at risk from fire from the Russian's security team.

The SAS team also discussed an RPG attack on the vehicle but it would only be effective if they could guarantee a correct identification of the target vehicle. Its maximum effective range against a moving target was a maximum of 300 metres and it was normally used at a much closer range of about 50 metres, once more potentially putting the attackers in harm's way.

After a long and often heated discussion, the team agreed with Standing's personal preference for a 'white of his eyes' hit, carrying the inevitable risks of such close quarter work but offering them the 100% certainty that the aim of the operation had been achieved.

Chapter 18

Once Standing had persuaded Colonel Davies to sign off on the operation, he arranged for the Intelligence people to give the op a top secret security classification and a code name, as were the target, Prigozhin, and the Wagner Group. A limited budget was also allocated to the op, though if it proved inadequate, Standing and his patrol mates, with the active collusion of Colonel Davies, could always find ways around it. To ensure operational security he also invented a fictitious cover story that the support guys could make use of when carrying out the background tasks that would be necessary for the operation's success. With all those pieces of the puzzle in place, Standing could now start allocating tasks to the support groups. The Intelligence Corps were given the task of identifying and accessing all available open source and classified material on Prigozhin himself, and the Wagner Group. Mapping and satellite footage were to be the top priority. Colonel Davies had to liaise with the Intelligence Corps as Standing had pretty much burned his bridges with them. The supply chain guys were meanwhile put to work on sourcing possible weapons and ammunition and any other ordnance requirements.

Standing had decided to go in with a six-man team: himself, Macleod, Parker, Williams and a couple of guys from the Ukrainian armed forces. While the Intelligence Corps were fulfilling their role, one of the first steps for Standing and his patrol mates was to set about locating and recruiting suitable Ukrainians to form part of the team carrying out the op.

Standing outlined the brief to them. The criteria for selection were deliberately kept very basic, but any potential candidates had to have had recent combat experience in the front lines. They had to be able to speak fluent Russian and Ukrainian and have sufficiently good English to be able to receive and react instantly to orders in that language, especially when in the heat of battle. If they were also familiar with the hierarchies and methods of the Wagner Group, that would be a considerable bonus. They also had to be accustomed to the small arms and heavy weapons used by the Russian forces, since such a deniable operation required every item they carried, from underwear to RPGs, to be of Russian origin. One slip, even wearing something as innocuous as a pair of Marks and Spencer's underpants, might be enough to blow their cover story.

'How about Jankiv?' Williams said. 'We've been working with him for a while now, so he knows our SOPs. He speaks Ukrainian, Russian and English, and as a career soldier in Ukraine and with the Sovs before that, he's familiar with their weapons.'

'Nah,' Macleod said at once. 'All that's true, but he's just too old for this op. We need young, fit men, who can move fast over rough ground, fight hard and then fuck off out of there even faster, and I don't see any of that applying to Jankiv.'

Standing nodded. 'I agree. Whatever his other strengths, this isn't an op for him.'

'He won't like it,' Williams said.

Standing shrugged. 'I don't care whether he likes it or not. We're not here to tiptoe round Jankiv's ego or anyone else's, we're here to find the best men for the job and in this case, that isn't going to be him.'

As Williams had predicted, Jankiv was both hurt and angry when told that, although the SAS were looking for two Ukrainians to join them on a special op, they didn't feel that he fitted the bill.

'Why not?' he said. 'What is this op anyway?'

'You don't need to know my reasons,' Standing said, 'and you definitely ought to know by now not to ask questions about an op that you're not going to be involved in. The guiding rule, the way we maintain security about any op we carry out is "Need To Know". If you don't, you won't be told anything. End of.'

Jankiv's face showed his displeasure but he turned and marched off without another word.

The other Ukrainian officers were not told why Standing was looking for men for an op, but knowing what he and his SAS team had already achieved for them, they fell over themselves to accommodate him and he was given total access to a long list of possible candidates. Two names at once stood out for him, even though only one was a Ukrainian, the other being Polish but a fluent Russian speaker and both were deserters from the Wagner Group, and knew their protocols and their standard operating procedures, so not only their language skills but their knowledge of the terrain and of the Wagner Group's SOPs might prove invaluable on the op.

The Ukrainian was called Dmytro and the Pole was Tadeusz, and both had similar backgrounds, having been tearaways and petty criminals in their youth, and often in trouble with the law in their respective countries. When they grew up, both had then become involved with the same criminal gang, one of the many sub-tribes of the Russian mafia, and began smuggling goods of all kinds, from cigarettes, whisky and drugs, to luxury goods and even high-end cars across the border into Russia. However, either someone had not been given a sufficiently large bribe to look the other way or one of the other mafia gangs had decided to eliminate some of their competition, for on one of their next delivery runs, both were arrested. Tadeusz, was stopped in a lorry full of smuggled American cigarettes, while the Ukrainian, Dmytro, was caught with a van load of Chanel handbags, Dior perfume, Swiss watches and other luxury goods. The fact that most of the goods were 'knock-off' imitations of the real things did not save him.

They appeared before the courts and their trial was a formality because Russian judges were not known for their sympathy to the arguments of defence lawyers, nor for their leniency in sentencing, and both were inevitably convicted and given long jail terms. They spent several years in a series of brutal Russian prisons, the last three of which were in a penal colony, a former Stalinist gulag, inside the Arctic Circle. It was sited deep in the tundra alongside the "Road of Bones", the 2,000 kilometre highway, built by slave labour to give access to the gold and uranium mines in Siberia's far north. Estimates of the number of forced labourers who had died during its construction ranged from 250,000 to one million. It was rumoured that most were buried beneath the road, since the permafrost made digging graves alongside it too difficult.

In summer, there were clouds of mosquitoes so dense that they almost blotted out the sun. In winter, temperatures fell as low as -50C and the wooden shacks that housed the prisoners were so twisted and distorted by the permafrost that the interior temperature was often little warmer than outside. The half-starved inmates were given merciless beatings for the most trivial of offences, even including raising their eyes from the ground in the presence of a guard, and few of them lived long enough to complete their sentences.

After Tadeusz and Dmytro had spent three years in this frozen hell, one day they and all the other prisoners were rousted from their cells and marshalled in the open yard of the penal colony. There they shivered in the savage cold for over an hour until a squat, ugly figure in military fatigues and with an ill-fitting combat helmet perched on his bald head, emerged from the prison commandant's office. They had no idea who he was, nor had they ever heard of his private military company, the Wagner Group. The commandant introduced him, with much bowing and scraping, as Yevgeny Victorovitch Prigozhin, and it was obvious from the commandant's deference that he was a very powerful man. Prigozhin then made his rabble-rousing pitch, his face reddening and spit flecking his lips as he ranted about fighting against 'traitors to the Motherland' and offered every inmate, no matter what their crimes, the prospect of their freedom and a pile of rubles in exchange for six months fighting with the Wagner Group, on the front lines in Ukraine. There was no mention of the massive casualty rates among Wagner Group soldiers, and he found no shortage of takers for his offer, with three-quarters of the inmates, including Tadeusz and Dmytro, willing to accept the risks of combat in a war zone to be rid of the horrors of the penal colony and its sadistic guards. Even those with relatively short jail terms still to serve often preferred to take their chances in combat, rather than remain even one more day in the penal colony. Tadeusz and Dmytro joined the long line of men waiting to sign up for Wagner, while the remaining inmates were shoved, punched and kicked back into their cells.

A convoy of canvas-backed Russian army trucks then drove into the compound and the convicts clambered aboard. They were driven 100 miles over the rough gravel roads south of the penal colony to the nearest army base, where they were issued with combat fatigues adorned with the red and gold Wagner logo: - two crossed daggers with a five-pointed star at their heart. The fatigues were second-hand, mostly unwashed and many of them still bore the marks of the bullet or shrapnel wounds that had killed the previous owners. They were then marched out to a landing strip and shepherded aboard an Antonov transport plane for the long flight to the Wagner base in Molkino in the southern Krasnodar region, just to the east of Russian-occupied Ukraine. After a mere 24 hours of training there, they found themselves on their way to the front lines.

The discipline in the Wagner Group turned out to be even more savage than they had experienced in prison, and the officers at the top of the group were absolutely ruthless, treating the grunts worse than animals. Beatings and executions were common. Meant to instil rigid, unquestioning discipline in the ranks, they were often carried out on a whim by men who appeared to take pleasure in brutalising those under their command. By a miracle, despite being forced to take part in a succession of 'human wave' attacks against well-defended Ukrainian positions, Tadeusz and Dmytro, though both wounded, managed to survive. They were clinging to the hope of reaching the end of their six month term and going back to civilian life. However, the date came and went without the promised release or any sign of payment and they came to the belated realisation that their 'voluntary' service would only end one way. It was effectively a death sentence.

Eventually, during one particularly vicious fire-fight in which most of the other members of their patrol were killed or wounded, they saw their chance to desert. Tadeusz shot their patrol sergeant in the back and they then crawled across No Man's Land, waved a tattered white flag and surrendered to the Ukrainians. For reasons that were not only logistical but often deeply personal as well, not all Ukrainian units took prisoners, but these two deserters were lucky and after being captured and held for interrogation, they took little persuasion to change sides and begin fighting for Ukraine against the Russian invaders.

Both had learned military skills 'on the job' while fighting on the front lines around the devastated town of Bakhmut and after their experiences with Wagner Group, both were now consumed by an implacable hatred for the group in general and Yevgeny Prigozhin in particular. Now formidable fighters, heedless of their own personal safety, they spent months inflicting as much damage as was humanly possible on the 'evil organisation' that had recruited, exploited and enslaved them.

They had come out of the battle zone for a few days of R & R in the reserve areas, a safe distance from the front lines, and when Standing approached them they were more than happy to share their knowledge of the Wagner Group and its leader with Standing and his team.

'When you join Wagner Group,' Tadeusz told them, 'any passports, identity cards or other documents you might have, and any mobile phones or tablets are confiscated, not that many of us had anything like that since most of us had just come straight from jails or penal colonies. You are also absolutely forbidden to communicate with anyone outside the unit or reveal your location to anyone, no matter whether you're within Russia, Ukraine or anywhere else in the world where they operate. All you are issued with in return are dog-tags with no name on them, just a number, and that's all you are to them: a statistic.'

Dmytro nodded. 'When they think they're not being overheard, Prigozhin and his senior officers call the ex-convict recruits like us "bait". We were all identified by a "K" on our camouflage fatigues, showing we were ex-con "volunteers" while professional mercenaries had an "A" on theirs. Poorly armed and under-trained - just like us when we joined - the Ks are all sent into battle in human waves to be mown down by machine guns or blown apart by shells. They die in droves - casualty rates run as high as eighty or ninety percent - with the sole apparent aim of luring Ukrainian units out of cover so that they are more vulnerable to attacks from the more experienced Wagner units and professional mercenaries or the Wagner artillery. The only option is to advance and attack because Wagner commanders have a policy they call "zeroing out"; anyone who tries to retreat or go to ground under heavy fire will be shot by his own side. You overhear it all the time in radio comms between the Wagner commanders and the junior officers and NCOs in the front lines: "Anyone who takes a backward step, zero them out." The death rate is so high that when a new batch of ex-cons arrives, nobody even bothers to learn their names or their call-signs. They show up, last a day or two, not much more, and then they are killed and some more take their place. It's like one of those conveyor belts they have in a crematorium; everyone who passes along it is just fuel for the flames.'

'All Wagner's professional soldiers are killers,' Tadeusz said, 'but some are even worse. There's a group within the organisation called "Task Force Rusic". They operate as a sabotage and reconnaissance unit, but all of the members are Nazis or neo-fascists; they even have a swastika symbol on their logos.'

Both Tadeusz and Dmytro had formed the same opinion of the Wagner Group, having fought with them and against them. 'In his tweets and interviews, Prigozhin is always banging the drum about how good his men are,' Tadeusz said, 'but he greatly overstates how well they perform. While we were with them, whenever they were in combat against the Ukrainian forces, they almost always came off second best. The ex-cons and other conscripts aren't properly trained or equipped and their morale is at rock-bottom even before their officers and NCOs start abusing them, and even the mercenaries are very over-rated. The conscripts and the ex-convict "volunteers" in the group are all looking for an escape route all the time, either hoping to be released for being brave in battle, or by deserting, or by getting wounded. Some guys hold their arms up above the parapet of their trench, hoping a Ukrainian sniper will put a bullet through it, and there are quite a few self-inflicted wounds as well, though it's not a very wise move, because if Prigozhin or his officers think you've wounded yourself deliberately, you won't be getting casevaced to hospital, you'll be getting a bullet in the back of the head.'

'Okay,' Standing said. 'We've got a fair idea about the Wagner Group in general now, but what about Prigozhin himself? Did you have any encounters with him or hear anything about him that we can use?'

'Plenty,' Tadeusz said. 'He recruited us personally when he came to the penal colony where we were being held, and Prigozhin is all his commanders and officers ever talk about. Some love him, plenty more hate him, but they're all equally obsessed with him and what he's doing and saying.'

'We all hate our commanding officers,' Macleod said, with feeling, and the other troopers nodded in agreement. 'It goes with the turf, so the question is not whether Prigozhin's officers and men hate him, but how loyal they would be to him.'

Dmytro gave a cynical smile. 'If he ordered the Wagner Group to march on Moscow they would, but it would not be out of loyalty to him, nor because they know the regular Russian Army is in such a bad state that it would not be able to put up much of a fight against them. No, they would do it just because it would be getting them away from the fighting on the front lines and their chances of surviving anywhere else are far better than in Eastern Ukraine.'

'Prigozhin's also got a massive ego,' Dmytro said, 'and he seems to have this idea that he's indestructible. He takes risks and no one is brave or foolhardy enough to try and stop him doing so, and he is also more volatile than anyone I've ever seen. You never know which side of him you're going to get. He always travels around with a treasure chest full of money and gold coins as if he was the Tsar of all the Russias, touring the provinces, and he gives out handfuls of notes and coins to troops that he thinks have done particularly well. But his mood can change from second to second, and when he is not happy about something, watch out! No one wants to catch his eye because, as we have both seen for ourselves, he carries out summary executions of Wagner soldiers and even officers for the slightest of reasons.'

Tadeusz nodded. 'You don't know if he is going to pat you on the cheek or put a bullet in your head'.

'Well maybe it's time someone put a bullet in his head instead,' Macleod said with a grim smile.

'Tell us about how he travels,' Standing said. 'Any detail, however slight, will help us to build up the picture.'

'Well, whenever he's been seen anywhere near the front lines,' Tadeusz said, 'he was always wearing the latest in high-spec body armour, with a combat helmet and camouflage fatigues.'

Dmytro again took up the tale. 'If he flies anywhere, it's always by private jet, apparently.'

Macleod challenged him at once. 'How do you know that?'

Dmytro shrugged. 'It's common knowledge and anyway we've overheard the officers talking about him often enough. Only his most trusted lieutenants are allowed to fly with him and often he flies alone. If he's not using it himself, his private jet has occasionally been used to fly in reinforcement troops who come straight from prison to the front line without even the rudimentary training we were given.'

'He has a security detail too, obviously,' Tadeusz added. 'All hard-bitten mercenaries or thugs that he recruited when he was running scams and gangs in St Petersburg, but he often ignores their advice. When he was travelling by road from which ever airfield he'd flown in to, his security team would usually have an armoured limousine or even an Armoured Fighting Vehicle for him to travel in, but Prigozhin often seemed quite happy to set off in anything, whatever was first in the queue.'

'Yeah, he'd sometimes jump in the first one that came along,' Dmytro said, 'ignoring the armoured one that had been allocated to him.' He laughed. 'His security detail would piss themselves when that happened.'

Standing nodded, turning to the others. 'That might be a bit of a two-edged sword for us, mightn't it? It could give us an opportunity to get at him in an unprotected vehicle, but at the same time, as we know from our own experience, erratic behaviour like that makes a target's actions very hard to predict and therefore he could be an even more difficult man to take out.'

He glanced back at the two former Wagner men. 'Okay, thanks, guys, that's been really helpful. Get yourself some food and a beer or two, you've earned them. But you need to remain in our section of the base until the op begins, if we do decide to go ahead.' Both men frowned and narrowed their eyes, clearly not happy with what they had heard. 'I'm not singling you out, they are the same restrictions that apply to all of us, one of our Standard Operating Procedures,' Standing told them. 'As soon as we're "warned off", as we call it, for an op, we go into complete isolation from everyone else and only those involved in the op with a need to know, will be told anything about it. That clear?'

They nodded, but it was clear from their faces that they still weren't happy. After they had filed out, Standing turned to Macleod. 'Make sure someone is detailed to keep them under surveillance at all times, will you?' he said.

Macleod raised an eyebrow. 'Are you sure that's necessary? They seem pretty motivated to give the Wagner Group any pain they can.'

'Maybe so,' Standing said, 'but they've deserted once and if they've done it once, they could do it again. Prigozhin would certainly pay handsomely from his treasure chest of money and gold, for any intel about an attempt to assassinate him.'

'Fair enough,' Macleod said, and slipped out after the two men.

Having milked Tadeusz and Dmytro for all the information they had, the SAS team turned back to the method of insertion into southern Russia for the op. After further, often heated, debate, the consensus reached was that a helicopter insertion would not be the way to go. Even flying at extreme low-level they would be vulnerable to fire from the thousands of ground troops in the front lines and reserve areas. Any intel reaching Prigozhin's ears that a hostile heli or enemy forces had been spotted close to the Wagner base or anywhere else that he was planning to use to meet his commanders would also almost certainly see him abort his plans and get back in his private jet for a flight to the safety of his HQ in St Petersburg. So the consensus was to use ground transport or to go on foot directly through the front lines. There were the official routes across the new de facto border that the Russian invasion had created, put in place in the early days of the war. Those routes, mainly using existing tracks and roads, and gap-crossing bridges for tanks and vehicles, were known to the authorities on both sides, but there were also the unofficial routes known only to the men on the front line. Those unofficial routes included old peasant tracks used to get livestock to and from their summer grazing, and the tracks, often through deep forest, swampland and marshes, that were used by hunters and smugglers, the sort of people who did not recognise borders or the authority of governments and armies on either side.

Standing kept his options open on whether to use ground transport or insert through the front lines on foot and made preparations for both eventualities, so that a decision could be left until the very last minute. Even if they eventually opted to use vehicles, they could still abandon them and switch to an insertion on foot if the situation required it.

Chapter 19

Now that the outline plan for the op was beginning to solidify into a workable option, Standing had a further briefing with Colonel Davies to update him on progress. By the time he did so, he had already raised the team's PERSEC (Personal Security) to the highest threat level, believing that the likelihood of a first strike by Russian Forces was a distinct possibility. The Colonel had commandeered a portacabin with a metal desk and two plastic chairs as a makeshift office. He was sprawled in his chair behind the desk, but Standing stayed on his feet as he briefed him. 'Okay Boss,' he said, 'we're well on the way to making this happen. PERSEC's already top level and even though I've already got our two deep-throats, Tadeusz and Dmytro in protective custody so they can't blab, we're involving so many people in different aspects of the preparation for the op that I'm far from confident that we're leak-proof.'

'And do you need your deep throats for the op itself or are they just providing intel and background?' asked the Colonel.

'Both. When we go ahead, we can use them as guides to get us to the target area and they also know the Wagner SOPs which may prove handy.'

'Okay,' said the Colonel. 'What else? Insertion method?'

'I have three Russian vehicles being modified by the local mechanics in the workshops, two UAZ jeeps and a Gaz 66 load carrier. The mechanics are making the hulls waterproof, adding extended range fuel tanks, converting them to permanent four-wheel drive and fitting weapon mounts. If we do go by vehicle, they will get us there. If I decide to go for the sniper option, I can get the latest rifles from the UK on the C-17's from Brize and there are three flights a day coming in, so there won't be any delays. The latest weapons come with barrels, ammo and scopes which give me long-range and short-range options, and there are normal or silenced versions. All we need to do is zero the scopes to the barrels on the range and we are good to go.'

The Colonel nodded. 'Okay. That'll work.'

'The Intelligence guys are flying drones constantly for us, monitoring possible routes to and through the front line and then to the target area. They have already confirmed what we were told by the deep throats, that there are numerous unofficial routes in use. They are also monitoring private jet flights to the target airfields using open source Flight Tracker info. There are a surprising number of flights, and they can ID the aircraft that Prigozhin has used previously but of course they cannot verify who the passengers are on any particular flight. Our target folders are up to speed, but we are still lacking vital intelligence. Our procurement team have put together enough of the latest weapons, mines, explosives and support devices to cover any option I choose. We can overcome the latest Russian ECM suppression systems and beat their IED and mine detection systems to hit any target we want. We have remote initiation sets for mines and IEDs and enough explosive devices to isolate and kill Prigozhin a hundred times over, as well as wipe out the whole of his command structure.'

The Colonel was listening intently, occasionally nodding.

'As you can guess, this is all well and good, but none of it tells us where Prigozhin is going to be at any particular moment and it does not cut down on our time on target at all,' said Standing. 'And obviously, the longer we are there in the target area, the greater the risk of us being compromised. The whole country is a military deployment area, every wood and every copse of trees is hiding their troops and armour from aircraft and drones. So we must get in and do the job in the shortest possible time. We can guess where Prigozhin might be, should be and could be, but we don't know where he actually is. So before we can launch our mission, we must have that information and the only source of that intelligence is going to be Six in the UK, but as usual, they're dragging their feet. With their intercept capability at GCHQ, they must know exactly where he is at any given second. Sorry for this Boss, but I and the team have taken this as far as we can, so it is now up to you to stir them up. We are ready to launch as soon as they give us the final pieces of the jigsaw.'

The Colonel gave a heavy sigh. 'The words "blood" and "stone" spring to mind, but I'll get it out of them one way or another,' he said.

As Standing started to walk back across the base, he paused to watch Ukrainian soldiers who were opening a series of large cardboard containers that they had just unloaded from a Ukrainian army truck. Curious, he strolled over for a closer look. He stared at the contents of one of them, baffled, for a few moments, trying to work out what the military application of a few bits of cardboard a couple of metres in length could possibly be, then gave up the attempt and turned to the Ukrainian army officer who was supervising his men. 'Cardboard containers full of cardboard?' he said. 'What's the story with these?'

The officer smiled. 'They're drones.'

'Cardboard drones?' said Standing scornfully. 'Get out of here.'

'I'm serious. An Australian company makes them. They're cheap, about 4,000 Euros each, so they're about a fifth the cost of any others we can buy. They're slow, but they have a range of about 150 kilometres, can carry a payload of six kilos, and even better, they're almost invisible to radar. Only the battery that powers one of these will show up on a radar screen, and that is so small that it would not necessarily be spotted by a radar operator or read as a threat even if it was.'

'But it's made of cardboard,' Standing said. 'Do you have to get a weather forecast before you launch and what happens if it starts raining?'

The officer laughed. 'It's waxed cardboard, so it's waterproof and do you know the best of it? If you damage one, you can repair it with a hot glue gun, a bit more cardboard and some paint to waterproof it.'

As soon as the Ukrainians had checked and assembled each drone, they were loaded on the back of a truck or a jeep and driven away to be dispersed to a series of scattered launch sites, so any Russian attempts to target them with missiles or artillery before they were launched would never destroy more than a small number.

Macleod had wandered over while Standing was talking to the Ukrainian officer. 'Have you seen these?' Standing said. 'Cardboard drones. What's next? Rifles powered by rubber bands and firing paper clips?'

'Not a bad idea,' Macleod said with a grin. 'I'll get working on it.'

They were both less amused that night when they heard the sound of Russian drones overhead. Invisible in the darkness, their relentless low buzzing noise, like a swarm of drowsy bees, could be heard several kilometres away and had an unsettling effect on anyone who heard it. Even experienced soldiers could be affected, since they could never be sure whether it was an observation drone or if the sound would suddenly end in a bomb or a missile strike. Larger and much more expensive than the cardboard ones Standing had been looking at earlier, the ones filling the night with their noise now were almost certainly Iranian made Shahed kamikaze drones and although the Ukrainians had had considerable success in intercepting and destroying them, the Russians launched them in such numbers that a few always seemed to get through.

Ireland and Connor had been on stag and woke their sleeping comrades as soon as they heard the first notes of the approaching drones, and they all retreated to a bunker roofed with corrugated iron covered by a layer of sandbags that would absorb shrapnel and anything but a direct hit from a bomb or missile.

As they settled themselves in the bunker, Tadeusz groaned. 'Where are all these drones coming from?' he said. 'I'd never heard of drone warfare before. Now they seem to be everywhere.'

'You can blame the Israeli Defence Force for that, if you like,' Standing said. 'Do you remember when the Israelis were fighting Hezbollah in Lebanon?'

'You'll have to be more specific,' Macleod said with a grin. 'They're always doing that.'

'Yeah, true, but I mean the last big war there. Israel is used to having total air superiority in any conflict, but Hezbollah, aided by their backers Iran and Russia, had installed so many anti-aircraft defences - gun batteries, missiles and the rest - in the Bekaa Valley in Lebanon, that Israel was losing aircraft and pilots hand over fist. So they began pouring money and effort into developing unmanned aircraft - drones. When unarmed they could be used for surveillance and intel gathering, and when fitted with bombs or missiles they could carry out attacks on Hezbollah positions without any risk to the Israeli jets and their pilots. The Iranians are never slow to catch on and, seeing Israel's success with them, they began to ramp up their own development and production of drones, hence the ones they're supplying to Russia.'

'But, if the Ukraine government can be believed, at least nine out of ten drones are getting shot down,' Dmytro said. 'If they're that good, how is that happening?'

'It's partly because Ukraine has learned from the West about layering their air defences.' Standing clocked Tadeusz's blank expression. 'You divide the air-space horizontally and vertically into layers and you have a weapon or weapons to cover each one of those layers, from small arms at the lowest level, through anti-aircraft guns and hand-held SAMs, right up to Patriot missiles covering medium to high air defence right at the edge of space. The best defence against drones, though, are anti-aircraft guns, particularly the self-propelled ZU-23-4 Donets. Do you know of it? It's a Ukrainian version of the Russian "Shilka", a self-propelled four-barrelled, auto-cannon that puts up such a blizzard of fire that it's a devastating weapon against low-flying fighter jets and attack helicopters, never mind those unmanned "kamikaze" drones the Russians keep sending over.' He grinned. 'So I reckon that's why those drones have such a high failure rate,' Standing said. 'Electronic counter measures - jamming devices - prevent many drones from reaching their intended targets at all, anti-aircraft guns account for a lot more and a few more get shot down by heavy machine guns and even AKs as well - but if you're launching them in sufficient numbers, a few are always going to get through, and with a 30 to 50 kilo warhead, they pack enough punch to cause some serious damage.'

The sound of the drones was much louder now and the beams of searchlights were probing up into the night sky, trying to highlight the drones, and their noise began to be counter-pointed by the sound of the Ukrainian counter-measures. The fire from the ZU-23s anti-aircraft guns was the dominant noise, a rattling, chattering sound that had led soldiers in Afghanistan to call them 'the sewing machines', but it was punctuated by the occasional 'Whoosh!' as a hand-held SAM was launched, the thundering bass notes of heavy machine guns and the whip-crack noise of small arms like AK rifles.

There were a series of bangs and flashes as drones exploded in mid-air, showering down fragments of shrapnel that peppered the ground like hail. The ground fire was knocking out most of the incoming drones, but there were also a couple of concussive blasts from ground level as the drones that had got through the counter-fire detonated around the base. One struck a jeep that erupted in flames and another killed a Ukrainian soldier who was still aiming his weapon at the sky.

There was a brief period of silence, broken only by the crackle of flames from the burning jeep, and then there was a sudden blinding flash from elsewhere on the base, followed by the sound of a 'Whoosh!' and a massive blast right on its heels.

'That was no drone,' Macleod said as the noise of the blast gave way to the thunderous roar of flames and a series of smaller explosions.

'No,' Standing said. 'That was a cruise missile.' Flying at supersonic speed, the missile had evaded the air defence missiles fired at it and hit its target, detonating before the noise of its approach had even been heard.

They waited in the bunker for an hour before emerging; the Russians often fired another missile to arrive a few minutes after the first one, catching out any exposed rescuers, fire and ambulance crews who had arrived to help the wounded and extinguish the flames from the first blast.

When they did climb out of the bunker, they saw the havoc the cruise missile had wrought. The workshops where the mechanics had been working on the vehicles for the op had been completely obliterated. Only a smoking crater, a column of oily black smoke and the twisted and blackened metal superstructure of the workshops showed where they had once stood. Within them was the still burning wreckage of everything the workshops had contained, with the petrol, diesel and chemicals stored there continuing to feed the flames. Even worse, the four mechanics, who all slept in a lean-to shed attached to the workshop, had all been killed in the blast.

'Poor bastards,' Standing muttered, as Ukrainian army medics began carrying out the few body parts of the mechanics that they were able to find. 'There doesn't look to be enough to fill one bodybag, never mind four.'

'Yeah,' Macleod said, 'and you know what? It looks like we'll be crossing the front line on foot now, unless you want to wait a few more weeks for some new vehicles and some fresh mechanics to work on them.'

'That's not happening,' Standing said. 'The op won't wait that long, so if we have to insert on foot, we will.'

'And what about that cruise missile strike?' Parker said. 'It's lucky the Ukrainians had moved those cardboard drones off site straight away, because they'd have gone up like Roman Candles if they'd still been kept here.' He paused. 'So, was the strike just a coincidence or have we been compromised?'

'Not sure,' Standing said. 'I don't really believe in coincidences, but it is possible the Russians just picked up on an increase in base activity, either from satellite or drone surveillance or one of their spies, and decided to target the base on general principles. Anyway, let's take it as a warning to us, to finish our preparations and work-ups, and get out of here as quick as possible before the Russians send another cruise missile over. I'll take my chances against ground troops any day rather than trying to dodge bombs and missiles. And if we have to sit out in the woods somewhere for a few more days until Six give us the intel we need, it won't be the first time we've had to do that. Right, where is everybody? Are there any casualties other than those poor bloody mechanics?'

They ran through the roll call of team members. Everyone answered or was accounted for apart from Jankiv. 'Where's Jankiv?' Standing said. 'Anybody seen him?'

There were blank looks and shakes of the head all around.

'He wasn't on stag,' Tadeusz said, 'and he's not in his dug-out, so I don't know where the hell he is.'

They were casting around for some trace of him, still keeping a wary eye on the sky and an ear cocked in case the Russians sent over more drones, when Jankiv reappeared at the base.

'Where were you?' Standing said.

Jankiv gave a weak smile. 'I couldn't sleep, so I got up and went for a run. Then I heard drones so I just hit the ground. Then I heard a missile as well, so I stayed where I was until I was sure the Russkies weren't sending anything else over.'

Standing frowned. There was something not right about the way Jankiv spoke and the way his gaze shifted away as soon as his eyes met Standing's. Standing was almost certain that the Ukrainian was lying. 'Lucky, you went for a run then,' he said. 'That missile scored a direct hit on the mechanics' workshop and wiped them all out, and a drone that got through the counter fire killed one of your comrades.'

'Shit, that's not good,' Jankiv said. 'Were any of you hurt?'

Standing shook his head. 'No, we're all okay. Like you, we hit the dirt as soon as the attack started.'

Jankiv nodded and walked off towards his dug-out, leaving Standing staring thoughtfully after him.

'Penny for your thoughts?' Macleod said, seeing Standing's pre-occupied expression.

'I don't know, something about Jankiv's story didn't quite add up, though I can't put my finger on it.'

'We got rid of one snitch in Sukut,' Macleod said, 'Surely we haven't got another?'

'Maybe I'm just being paranoid,' Standing said, 'but my instincts were right with Sukut, I just didn't act on them and I don't want to make that mistake again.' He shrugged. 'Let's keep a very close watch on Jankiv from now on. If he has been tipping the Russians off, he'll have told them we're planning something though luckily as he isn't part of the team for the op, he doesn't know what.'

'And if he had set up the missile strike, that would explain why he'd made himself scarce before it struck,' Macleod said.

'If he did set up that strike, he'll need to tell his handler that it didn't hit its prime target: us. Let's keep a discreet eye out for the rest of tonight for a start. 'I'll take the first watch and you relieve me in two hours.'

Macleod nodded and lay down in the tent to grab a couple of hours kip. Like most soldiers, he had the knack of falling asleep almost anywhere at any time, and the faint bass rumble of his snores soon reached Standing's ears. He had stationed himself just inside the entrance to the tent, lying flat in a position where he could see the entrance to Jankiv's dug-out. About an hour later, with the base now completely quiet, he saw a movement in the dug-out and the Ukrainian slipped out of the entrance and took a cautious look around, including a few moments where he was staring directly at Standing's tent. He knew he was invisible in the darkness of the tent, but Standing still kept himself absolutely motionless until Jankiv looked away. Having finished his survey of the base, he then turned and walked off in the opposite direction to the main gate where a sentry was always on duty, night and day. Instead, he went down the side of a sand-bagged portacabin being used as a store and disappeared behind it.

Standing was on the move at once, making no sound as he slipped from shadow to shadow, tracking Jankiv's movements. He eased his head round the end of the portacabin and saw Jankiv with his back to him, standing next to the perimeter fence, with his shoulders hunched and his head bowed, staring down at the object he was holding in his hand. A moment later Standing saw the glow of a mobile phone screen.

He pulled back as Jankiv slipped the phone back into his pocket. He had not spoken into the phone, so Standing knew that he must have been sending a text. As Jankiv turned away from the fence and began walking back, Standing moved swiftly along the side of the portacabin and was back in his tent before Jankiv once more emerged cautiously into the open and went back to his dug-out.

Standing woke Macleod. 'We need to pay Jankiv a social call,' he whispered.

Macleod sniffed and rubbed his nose with the back of his hand as he sat up. 'Why? What's happened? Did you see something?'

'Yeah, something that treacherous bastard didn't want us to.'

Macleod took his pistol from its holster, checked its magazine and then nodded. 'Right, ready when you are.'

Standing led the way across the open space between the tent and the dug-out and without needing to speak, he moved to one side of the entrance, while Macleod took the other. Standing counted down on his fingers, then stepped into the entrance of the dug-out with his pistol gripped in his hand and a torch beam sighted along it, lighting up the prone figure of Jankiv, whose eyes were closed and who was faking sleep as the torchlight illuminated his face, even though he had only lain down a couple of minutes before. Macleod flanked Standing, his pistol also trained on Jankiv, ready to put a double tap into him if he even so much as twitched.

'Stop pretending you're asleep and show me your hands, now,' Standing hissed, watching for any movement that might show Jankiv had a gun hidden beneath his blanket.

'What? What's happening?' Jankiv said

'We need to talk. But first you need to show me your hands and if you don't do that in the next two seconds it'll be a one-sided conversation, because you'll be dead.'

'What the hell's the matter with you?' Jankiv said, but he pushed the blanket aside and showed his hands, palms out.

'It's what's the matter with you that interests me. This is an ultra-secure site and every man here has gone through sanitisation, removing everything of non-Russian origin, and giving up all their personal items, even photos of loved ones, and that includes mobile phones.'

In the light from his torch, he could see the colour drain from Jankiv's features. He started to babble some explanation, but Standing held up a hand. 'Think carefully before you say anything else. Trust me, your life depends on it. Now sit up and no sudden moves.'

He waited until Jankiv was sitting on the edge of his bed, then sat opposite him on an upturned crate, keeping the torch beam focussed on his face, and his own eyes fixed on Jankiv's, searching for the truth or otherwise in his responses, but also alert for any flicker of movement, that might be the trigger for an attempt to attack or escape.

Standing let the silence build for a couple of minutes, noting the faint tremor in Jankiv's hands and the bead of sweat trickling down his forehead despite the cool of the night. 'You have a mobile phone,' Standing said at last. 'Don't bother to try and deny it.'

Jankiv bowed his head. 'I do,' he said. 'I'm sorry. I know it's wrong, but my daughter is very ill - she has cancer - and I could not bear to be out of touch with her. I may never see her again, her doctors say she does not have long to live, but at least I have been able to talk to her.'

'And yet you were not talking to her tonight, were you? You were just sending a text.'

Jankiv's pallor deepened even more. 'I didn't dare make any noise in case I was overheard.' His voice was trembling now and his eyes darted between Standing and Macleod.

'He's lying, Sarge,' said Macleod. He took a step towards the Ukrainian and the man flinched. 'Let me beat the truth out of him.'

'Bash, stand down.'

'He's a fucking traitor, Sarge. He wants us dead.' He raised his gun, threatening to slam it against the man's head. 'Where's the fucking phone?'

Standing put a hand on Macleod's shoulder. Macleod turned to glare at him, but then gave him a sly wink. Standing realised that Macleod was faking the anger so he released his grip on his shoulder. Macleod took another step towards Jankiv. 'Give me the fucking phone!'

The Ukrainian nodded and his hand moved to the chest pocket of his fatigues. Using his thumb and fingertips, he pulled out a slim mobile phone and handed it over. Macleod grinned at Standing.

'Where did you get it?' asked Standing.

'I bought it in Poland before we crossed the border.'

Standing examined it while Macleod kept Jankiv covered. 'It's Russian-made,' said Standing.

'They also have those in Poland,' Jankiv said. 'They're much cheaper than Western ones. It doesn't mean anything. It's just a phone.'

'Security code?' Standing said, tapping the phone to bring it to life.

Jankiv hesitated again but then told him and Standing scrolled through the call history. 'Curious,' he said, scanning down the column of calls made. 'Nothing but texts, and all of them to the same number. What does this last one say?'

He held up the screen so Jankiv could read it.

'It just says "Hope you are all right, will try to speak soon",' Jankiv said, though the flicker of his eyes betrayed his nervousness.

'Right,' Standing said. 'Last chance: are you sticking to that story?'

Jankiv nodded. 'It's the truth.'

Standing held out the phone to Macleod, still keeping his gaze locked on Jankiv's eyes. 'Wake up Dmytro or Tadeusz, Bash,' he said, 'and get them to translate that last message.'

Macleod took the phone and headed out of the dug-out.

Jankiv's eyes showed that he now knew the game was up, but Standing still bided his time.

'I'm sorry,' Jankiv said, with a catch in his voice. 'I know I've been an absolute fool.' He threw his arms wide, then whipped his right hand down towards his belt. It never reached it. Standing's pistol barked once, twice. Fired at such close range that powder burns speckled what was left of Jankiv's face, the double-tap bored twin holes through his forehead, so close together that they merged into one, and the rounds, tumbling after impacting the front of the skull, took most of his brains and half of the back of the skull with them as they exited, before burying themselves in the dug-out wall, the impact marked with a corona of blood and brains.

Macleod had sprinted back at the sound of the shots and gave a nod of grim satisfaction as he saw Jankiv sprawled across the floor of the dug-out. 'You could have waited for me,' he said.

Standing reached down and took the Makarov pistol from the dead man's belt. 'Old and slow he may have been,' he said, 'but I wasn't going to give him time to reach it.'

Parker, Williams, Tadeusz and Dmytro also arrived in rapid succession, woken by the shooting. Macleod handed the mobile phone to Dmytro. 'Tell us what the text message says,' he said.

Dmytro read it and then hawked and spat on Jankiv's corpse. 'He called in that missile strike. It says "Vehicles hit but all targets missed".' For emphasis, he gave the body a savage boot and they heard the sound of breaking ribs.

'That's enough,' Standing said. 'Save your anger for the Russians. Now, strip the body of any identifying marks and then dump it in the forest.'

While Dmytro and Tadeusz dragged the body of the traitorous Jankiv away, Standing sat back and went over the events of the last few weeks in his mind, not so much - or so he told himself - to recriminate with himself for having failed to spot Jankiv as a wrong 'un, as to learn the lessons for the future.

He realised that, suspecting him from the start, he had been so fixated on Sukut as the sole traitor that it had blinded him to other possibilities, not least that he might not have been the only traitor within the group. He groaned aloud as he thought of Jankiv's guileless expression, his friendly manner and engaging, self-deprecating smile, and the hesitant way he had shared his supposed concerns about Sukut with Standing. What could have been more disarming and what better way to disguise the calculation and treachery concealed beneath that bland exterior? And Standing, the man whose fighting instincts had never previously let him down, realised that he had fallen for it, hook, line and sinker.

Chapter 20

Standing knew that the sudden cessation of contact from their spy in the SAS camp would tip off the Russians that Jankiv had been compromised, in which case they might well launch another missile strike in the hope of neutralising the SAS patrol before they moved elsewhere. He had to get things moving before the shit hit the fan. He called Agnes Day on an ultra-secure video link. Despite the high level of security, she was giving nothing away that would have helped an eavesdropper identify the target or the location. 'Our asset tells us that the target is preparing for the meeting at the place we discussed,' she said, choosing her words carefully.

'When?' Standing said.

'In 72 hours-' She broke off and checked her watch. 'Make that 71 hours from now.'

'Bloody hell,' he said. 'I'm not sure we can guarantee being in position by then. Our transport's all been destroyed by a Russian cruise missile strike and it's a pretty long walk. Is there likely to be another window if we miss this one?'

Her lips compressed into a thin line. 'I would strongly suggest you don't miss this one, Sergeant Standing. HMG's vital interests are at stake.'

'Aren't they always, Ms Day?' he said. 'Aren't they always? Look, we'll give it our best shot and rest assured that if we can't get there in time and do the job, then no one else would have been able to either.'

'I do not find that particularly reassuring, Sergeant.'

He shrugged. 'Sorry to hear that Ms Day but it wasn't really meant to be and anyway, I'm afraid it's the best I can offer you. To reduce the risk of compromise, we'll keep comms to a minimum, but we'll send a "Standing by" burst transmission when we're on site, and request a "Go/No Go" authorisation when the target is sighted. And now, if there's nothing else, it sounds like we have a considerable need for speed, so I'll save the small talk for the next time we talk... if there is a next time.'

He called the others together at once and briefed them. 'Jesus, she's not asking much, is she?' Macleod said. 'At least we got twenty hours to do a 40-mile Long Drag on Selection. If we're going to make the target location in time, we're going to have to cover 60 miles in the same time and then do it again the next day as well.'

'True,' Standing said, 'but on the other hand, the Long Drag's over the Brecon Beacons, whereas this one will be over reasonably level terrain.'

'Yeah,' Parker said, 'but we weren't having to cross enemy lines on the way and we were only packing 55 pounds in our Bergens on Selection. How much are we going to be hefting, when we're tabbing across Ukraine?'

Tabbing stood for 'tactical approach to battle', and it involved approaching combat at high speed, in a combination of fast walking, jogging and running, while wearing full kit and with a heavy-loaded Bergen on your back. Standing grinned. 'As much as we can carry, and as usual it'll be maximum ammo, and minimum everything else. Now let's get to it, fast!'

Standing and the others completed their preparations at top speed and after briefly checking in with Hereford in case of any further updates, they were ready to move out that evening. A commandeered Ukrainian army truck drove them part of the way, getting them as close as its driver dared to the front line in the sector they had chosen, but even driving as fast as the rough road surfaces and the potholes and shell craters would allow, it was well past midnight before he ran out of road. They then jumped down and were moving off even before the driver had completed his three-point turn and begun heading back the way he had come.

As Standing had warned them, each member of the six man patrol was carrying maximum ammunition and minimum food and water. Their Bergens were heavy enough to make them stagger a little as they picked them up and loaded them onto their shoulders, but their whole training was designed to enable them to cover ground fast while carrying such burdens.

Tadeusz and Dmytro were slightly less heavily loaded, since they had not had SAS training, and although both were clearly feeling the strain they carried their own loads without audible complaint. The only food they all had with them were belt rations and each man only had a single water bottle since refilling them in a land crossed by hundreds of streams and rivers was unlikely to be a problem.

They had all opted to take AK-47s, knowing that, if needed, additional ammo could easily be found on the bodies of dead Russians, and there would definitely be no shortage of those on either side of the front line.

Williams and Dmytro carried drum-fed RPK light machine-guns which could fire 600 rounds a minute and used the same 7.62mm ammunition as the AKs. Parker and Tadeusz were armed with Russian RPG-7s. Each man also carried RGN-86 offensive grenades, an improved version of the old Russian RGD-5 with a pre-fragmented aluminium body, and they also had white phosphorous grenades that were primarily used to create smokescreens. Everyone was armed with a side-arm, a Makarov pistol, and a razor-edged combat knife for use in close quarters combat if it came to that.

They tabbed their way eastwards, passing a succession of Ukrainian tanks and artillery and mortar positions, heavily camouflaged and using every scrap of cover that the war-ravaged land offered. They were avoiding the most heavily contested areas of the front lines, like Bakhmut, where extensive networks of trenches had now been constructed, blocking previous access routes. Almost all the bridges had also been blown up by one side or the other but elsewhere in the borderlands, particularly where swamps or rivers formed difficult natural obstacles, the enemy's defences were much less hard to penetrate and Standing had selected an unofficial route crossing one of those regions as the best way to break through the Russian lines. Even those areas were far from free of the scars of war, however, and having picked their way through a stretch of marshland, crossing the worst sections using a precarious pathway of semi-submerged logs that smugglers had made, they reached an area just in front of the Russian front line.

It had recently been a battlefield and was still strewn with the bodies of a few Ukrainian defenders, though they were far outnumbered by the corpses of the Russian dead, the detritus left behind after yet another human wave, frontal assault had ended in slaughter and failure. It seemed that, even three-quarters of a century after the 'Great Patriotic War' the Russian Generals were still so wedded to its tactics, that they could not conceive of any other way to fight than mass attacks.

As the pre-dawn light was beginning to illuminate the eastern horizon, Standing and his patrol reached their pre-planned starting positions for the attempt to cross the Russian lines. Standing double-checked their location using his GPS device and the entire patrol then went to ground in the most protected cover they could find while he sent a burst transmission that was the signal for an artillery barrage to begin on this sector of the Russian trench system.

They did not have long to wait before the first salvos of shells from the Ukrainian artillery began whistling overhead and detonating around the Russian positions. The shells were exploding very close at hand to the patrol's starting position, but the guns had been carefully ranged and co-ordinated to avoid them. However, accidents and misfires could still happen and Standing and his team kept their heads well down as the barrage of shells continued, each one throwing up a cloud of black earth and shattered rock. The aim of the shelling was less to kill Russians, although that would have been a very welcome bonus, than to persuade them to keep their heads down below the parapet of their trenches and emplacements, allowing the patrol to pass through the lines without risking too much of a fire-fight on the way.

The explosions were abruptly cut off and the unseen Ukrainian artillery fell silent, but after a couple of long minutes in which the ringing of their ears from the din was only just beginning to die down, the thunder of the shells resumed. That happened twice more, the aim of such unpredictability being to discourage the Russians from emerging from their hidey-holes too quickly. When the last barrage had ended and knowing that there would be no more shells coming over, Standing and the team came out of cover and begin advancing at once, before the enemy troops had a chance to recover their nerve.

With years of training, active service and combat experience behind them, the SAS men made almost instinctive use of every piece of natural cover and dead ground as they moved forward. However, Tadeusz and Dmytro kept pausing as they were picking their way over the shell-torn ground and, reaching down, they started using their combat knives to cut the ears off several of the Russian corpses. As Dmytro began threading them on to a piece of wire, Tadeusz kept harvesting a few more ears and handing them to him.

'Bloody hell,' Macleod said. 'Now I've seen everything.'

'What the fuck do you two think you're doing?' Standing hissed.

Dmytro gave a bleak smile. 'Take it easy, Sergeant, I know what I'm doing. These may come in useful if any of the Russians poke their heads out again before we're through their lines.'

'Why? Are you going to throw them at the enemy?'

Dmytro just smiled. 'You'll see,' he said.

As they crept towards the Russian front line, they could see that while most of the firing positions were still empty, with their occupants presumably still face down and arse up in their dug outs in case the shelling resumed, one soldier had re-emerged. They spotted the top of his helmet and a few inches of the barrel of his rifle showing above the sandbagged emplacement he was stationed behind.

Dmytro turned to Standing and whispered, 'You take up firing positions while we get him to show a little bit more of himself.'

Standing wasn't used to taking orders from anyone, least of all men who weren't in the regiment, but he shrugged and nodded. He and Macleod lay flat and wormed their way forward until both had their weapons trained on the Russian's steel helmet.

Behind them, the two former Wagner men then got to their feet and walked slowly towards the Russian lines, holding their weapons in one hand away from their sides, to show they posed no threat. As they approached his position, the sentry raised his head a little and challenged them, only partly reassured by the Wagner uniform with the red and gold badge that he could see they were wearing.

'Halt,' he said in Russian. 'Who are you? What unit?'

'Relax tovarisch,' Dmytro said in Russian. 'We've just been out collecting a few souvenirs that those Ukrainian filth won't be needing any more.' He held up the garland of ears. 'We thought these would make a good present for Comrade Yevgeny Victorovitch Prigozhin the next time he comes to inspect us.'

The sentry peered at them, then did a double-take and laughed as he realised what Dmytro was holding in his hand. 'You're right, comrade,' he said, 'Prigozhin will love those. He likes to see proof that we've been doing our work well. I've been collecting a few souvenirs myself, but I won't be passing them on to him. Those Ukrainians have a lot of gold teeth,' he said, producing a pair of pliers from the top pocket of his camouflage jacket and brandishing it at them. 'I've got enough now to make a necklace as a homecoming present for my wife when they finally let me get out of this shit-hole.'

While Tadeusz had been talking to the Wagner sentry, keeping him distracted, Standing had been sighting on his forehead, now clearly visible in the gap between the rim of his helmet and the top edge of the sandbag wall in front of him. The sentry was still smiling broadly at the sight of the garland of ears, when a single shot from Standing's suppressed AK drilled a hole in his forehead and blew his head apart.

Tadeusz and Dmytro ran at a crouch to the edge of the Russian defensive line and covered the dug-out entrance while Standing and the rest moved up to join them. Had any of the dead sentry's comrades heard him fall, they were evidently not in any hurry to investigate why, and the raiders moved on across the Russian line and into the rear areas without seeing a single other soldier.

'Bloody hell,' Williams said, 'if we'd known it was going to be this easy to get across, we could have brought the whole Ukrainian army with us. They'd have retaken Sevastopol by sunset tomorrow!'

'Yeah, I'm not sure it would have been quite as straightforward with tens of thousands of men and columns of tanks and AFVs rumbling along behind us,' Standing said. 'It's a happy thought though.'

They moved on cautiously, knowing that the areas behind the front lines were densely populated with troops, tanks, mortar pits and artillery emplacements concealed beneath the spreading tree canopies. Even though the light was strengthening now, Standing urged them on. It was in breach of their normal SOPs to be crossing hostile territory in daylight, but they were all dressed in Russian camouflage fatigues and helmets and carrying Russian weapons, and Standing was willing to chance the risk of compromise by an enemy patrol in return for the extra miles they would cover.

They passed close to a number of Russian gun emplacements and forward bases without being challenged and by now were well behind the Russian lines, but they did not begin to look for a lying up place where they could snatch two or three hours rest until the early afternoon. Once they had found a suitable site, they could wait out most of the remaining daylight hours without being detected or disturbed. They found what they were looking for another mile further on. They were following an east-north-east compass bearing, moving through the fields roughly parallel to a road when they came across the ruins of a cowshed in the corner of a field. It had been struck by a shell during some of the recent fighting, but it still had two standing walls, while the wreckage of the roof had collapsed across the space between them, leaving a triangular shaped space like a rough lean-to. It would not only conceal them from the sight of passers-by but also give them some shelter from the rain that was now falling.

Parker wrinkled his nose as they hunkered down inside. There was a thick layer of animal droppings covering the ground but they had been there sometime and were dry to the touch. 'You should feel right at home here, Cowpat,' he said. 'The bloody place is full of shit.'

'Lovely,' Williams said with a grin. 'It smells just like home.'

Tadeusz and Dmytro were too exhausted to speak and the SAS men let them try to snatch some sleep while they took it in turns to rest, but two men always remained on stag in case any enemy soldiers or curious civilians approached too close. However, they remained undisturbed by any of the Russian soldiers and AFVs they saw passing along the road about a hundred metres away, and as dusk approached, they ate a couple of mouthfuls of their rations, drank some water and got ready to move on.

As night was falling, they set out once more. They tabbed all night, twice having to go to ground in a hurry as their route took them dangerously close to well-concealed Russian positions, but each time they managed to box around the obstruction and move on again.

An hour before dawn, sweat-soaked and weary, but boosted by the adrenalin surge that always came before an impending contact with the enemy, they at last reached the abandoned aviation museum, built alongside an airstrip that bore some signs of recent use. A black Zil limousine with smoked glass windows was parked on the hard standing next to the runway. It was sitting so low on its springs that it must have been armoured, but there was no sign of any movement around it. Standing immediately sent a burst transmission. 'In position. Stand by'.

They split into three groupings. Williams and Dmytro took the light machine guns and set up firing positions from where they could give cover to the others as they moved in to closer range.

Standing and Macleod found a position with a clear sight-line to the entrance to the museum through which Prigozhin would have to pass, and Parker and Tadeusz worked their way round to the other side, from where the Wagner Group leader and his bodyguards would be exposed to a withering cross-fire. Both pairs had an RPG in addition to their AKs, which could be used to devastating effect against groups of men standing together, or the jet, or the entrance to the building in the unlikely event that any of their targets had managed to reach them unharmed after the ambush was sprung.

They watched the sun rise and soon afterwards they were encouraged to see a flurry of activity around the museum, as officers with Wagner Group insignia on their cleaned and pressed combat fatigues stood around smoking and talking with each other, while minions hurried in and out, carrying trays of food and cases of champagne and vodka.

'What is this?' Macleod said. 'A briefing or a cocktail party?'

'A bit of both, maybe' Standing said. 'Shame we can't help ourselves to some of it, the booze looks like the good stuff.' He stiffened as he heard the noise of a jet engine in the sky to the north-east and soon afterwards an Embraer Legacy 600 private jet swept in and landed on the runway.

The jet braked then swung round and taxied over to the hard standing where the armoured limousine was parked. Standing watched and waited as the engines wound down and the door was opened and four hulking figures, all wearing bullet-proof vests and toting AK-74s, came down the steps and fanned out around the aircraft. Another bulky figure then emerged from the limousine and held open the rear door. It was on the opposite side from Standing and in any case was not within their weapons' guaranteed killing range so the attack would need to wait until their target reached the entrance to the museum.

A moment later the bald, stocky figure of Prigozhin emerged from the aircraft, also wearing protective armour and with an oversized combat helmet on his head. He walked down the steps and was hustled across to the limousine by his bodyguards. They jogged alongside it, US Presidential Secret Service style, as the limousine made the short drive from the edge of the runway to the concrete apron in front of the museum.

Once more the bodyguards fanned out in all-round defensive stance, as the driver of the limousine opened the rear door. Prigozhin stepped out and struck a pose while the commanders who had been slouching against the museum railings minutes before smoking and chatting, marched forward in step and formed up in a welcoming committee to greet him. They were rapidly joined by the remaining officers who had now all emerged from the museum.

Standing was looking through his sights at Prigozhin, whose bulbous nose almost filled the scope and he knew that the other members of the team would also have acquired their targets. His next burst transmission: 'Target acquired. Go?' had been sent as soon as he had spotted Prigozhin emerging from the aircraft, but there had been an unusually long delay before he received a reply and it was only now that the response finally came through: 'No Go.'

Standing stared at his comms device in disbelief. By now Prigozhin had been engulfed by the welcoming committee, and was exchanging salutes and greetings with the group of Wagner officers, but he still presented a clear target and Standing was absolutely confident of achieving a kill.

'Repeat.' He sent another burst transmission through his comms device, still scarcely able to believe the previous one.

'Repeat: No Go.'

He kept staring at the screen of his comms in fury for a few more moments before breaking the link and shoving the device back into the top pocket of his fatigues.

'It's a No Go,' he said.

'What? Why?' Macleod said, disbelief and anger fighting for control of his features. 'We've come this far and risked this much for that?'

'Orders are orders, Bash.'

'Fuck that!' shouted Macleod. 'We're here, let's do it. We might never get another chance.'

'We stand down.'

'This is fucking ridiculous,' snapped Macleod. 'It's like we're fighting with one hand tied behind our back. We're here, the target is there, we should be the ones making the call.'

There was a wild look in Macleod's eyes and he began grinding his teeth as they watched Prigozhin disappear into the museum and remained in position until he re-emerged forty minutes later.

As Prigozhin was standing around outside, still talking to his senior officers, Standing sent another burst transmission. 'Target reacquired. Go/No Go?'

'Still No Go. Pull out.'

Burning with frustration, they watched, unable to intervene as, still flanked by his massive bodyguards, Prigozhin clambered back into his limousine and made the short drive to the edge of the runway where his private jet was still waiting. His bodyguards were once more running interference for him and mounting all round defence as he boarded the aircraft and then they followed him up the steps. The door closed and within two minutes the jet was on its take-off run and climbing into the sky. It swung away to the north-east and rapidly disappeared from view, heading back towards Russia and out of the patrol's reach.

As the Wagner commanders got into their own vehicles and drove off, the patrol slipped back into deep cover and began to retrace their steps away from the aviation museum.

Without even thinking about it, they adopted the standard patrol formation: Standing, the patrol leader in the centre, Parker as point man, Williams and Macleod guarding the flanks to either side and Tadeusz and Dmytro bringing up the rear as the tail-end Charlies.

There was little of the usual banter between the patrol as they made their way back towards the Ukrainian lines. Even Parker's normally sunny disposition had been temporarily altered by the bitter disappointment of the aborted mission and he walked on in silence like the others. They found a lying-up place fairly quickly and with the need for speed now removed, they remained there through the rest of the day, only emerging after sunset to resume their journey. With none of the urgency they had felt during their approach to the target, they moved on at a steady four mile an hour pace, still fast for civilians but well within the SAS men's capabilities.

As they approached the front line, Standing could have paused, gone to ground and called in another artillery strike to keep the Russian heads down before advancing any further, but he chose not to do so. He called the patrol together as they lay up in dead ground, before beginning the move up to the front line trench. 'We don't need a barrage this time. Fan out, take out a sentry each, numbering from the left. Toss a grenade in every dug-out entrance and then make smoke with the WP grenades and we'll be back on the Ukrainian side before the Russians even know what hit them.

'And make sure you're showing your recognition signs,' he said, a reference to the luminous patches they had under the collar of their jackets in the Ukrainian colours of blue and yellow. Turning the collar up exposed the patches to anyone facing them, while still being hidden from any troops to the rear. In theory any Ukrainian soldiers manning their own front lines would see the patches and hold their fire, though the system was not entirely foolproof and wise soldiers approaching their own lines from the wrong side of No Man's Land, always did so with great care.

The patrol members fanned out then held position, glancing along the line to Standing in the middle, who held up three fingers, then two and then one. In the next instant they launched their simultaneous attack.

Standing heard the phttt! phttt! of suppressed shots to either side of him as he rose from cover, launched himself over the back of the trench and drove his shoulder into the back of his chosen sentry. As the man buckled, Standing's arm snaked around his neck, choking off the cry he was about to make. The only sound then was the snapping of bone as Standing gave the sentry's neck a vicious jerk. The man's eyes rolled up into his head, and he had taken his last breath even as he slumped to the ground. Without any apparent haste, Standing then pulled a grenade from his webbing and tossed it into the nearby dug out.

The sound of explosions triggered shouts from soldiers in the area behind them, but they would arrive too late. Standing pulled the pin from a WP grenade and rolled it along the trench away from him. As it detonated, dense clouds of white smoke began to fill the air. More followed as his comrades did the same and as one, they climbed over the sand-bagged parapet of the trench and, disappearing like wraiths into the smoke, they moved across No Man's Land towards the Ukrainian lines. They were fifty metres from the front line, with their fluorescent recognition patches clearly visible, but ready to drop to the ground in an instant if the Ukrainian centres failed to recognise the patches and opened fire. Standing shouted to the Ukrainian troops, giving the code word agreed before they set out five days before. One of the sentries showed himself and beckoned to them, and within thirty seconds they were through the frontline trench and heading back past the rear areas.

Standing summoned a truck to carry them back to base and wasted no time in demanding answers, first from Colonel Davies, although he had none to give. 'I'm afraid I don't know why the No Go order was given,' said the Colonel. 'But I can assure you that it wasn't my decision. It came from further up the line, but I think we can assume that it was courtesy of Six, so it's Ms Day you need to be talking to.'

'I plan on doing just that,' said Standing.

'You might want to calm down first,' said the Colonel.

'I'm calm,' said Standing through gritted teeth.

'Then maybe you're operating under a different definition of the word calm than the one that I use, Sergeant. If I were you, I'd take a few deep breaths before I gave her a piece of my mind.'

Standing realised that he was clenching his fists so tightly that his knuckles had turned white. He nodded. The Colonel was right.

Chapter 21

Standing went for a walk through the camp, then drank a mug of coffee before calling Agnes Day on the ultra-secure video link. The caffeine possibly wasn't a great idea, but he sipped it slowly and went through what he planned to say to her. She had her hair clipped up and she was smiling, but he could see the apprehension in her eyes. He opened his mouth to speak, but she pre-empted him. 'I understand your frustration,' she said. 'But it's because you're not seeing the bigger picture, Sergeant.'

Standing gritted his teeth and swallowed the tirade of abuse that he wanted to send her way. He took a deep breath and forced himself to keep smiling. 'We spent days preparing for that op and then, at considerable risk to our lives, we inserted through Russian lines and tabbed at top speed, carrying maximum ammunition, across a hundred miles of Russian-occupied territory in order to meet the deadline for the op that you had imposed. We set up an OP and firing positions in the target area, waited for Prigozhin to roll up and walk into the trap, and at the moment when he finally arrived, and the cross-hairs of my sights were locked on to the bridge of his nose, you decided to pull the plug. So I think you owe me an explanation and it had better be a good one.'

Agnes Day bridled at the suggestion. 'I don't owe you anything, Sergeant Standing, and please don't threaten me.'

'I wasn't threatening you, Ms Day. If I was, you'd know it.' He felt the anger start to flare but he forced himself to take a deep breath. 'But yes, I would appreciate an explanation.'

'Thank you,' she said. 'The simple fact is that situations are fluid. Things change. Nothing is written in stone. Only a fool would fail to reconsider and, if necessary, amend a previously agreed plan, if the circumstances surrounding it were to change. I hope that we can at least agree on that.' She paused, waiting for some acknowledgement of that, but Standing, his expression set like concrete, merely said, 'Go on.'

'While you were in the latter stages of your approach to the target area, we were in receipt of a tip-off from an asset of ours within Prigozhin's inner circle. It appeared frankly unbelievable at first. His claim was that a group of Wagner officers close to the front lines near Bakhmut had been targeted by a salvo of rockets fired from behind their own lines. Friendly fire incidents occur of course, but on this occasion, the Russian military denied any knowledge of it. That was not the unbelievable part of our asset's report, though. He claimed that as a result of it, Prigozhin was about to launch a mutiny, a rebellion against his own side. We would have discounted it without any corroboration from a different source, but GCHQ then began to pick up a vastly increased amount of comms traffic between Wagner bases and command HQs, and Ukrainian infantry facing Bakhmut reported that Wagner troops were pulling back from the front lines. The summit meeting with his commanders that you were targeting, had evidently been called by Prigozhin to finalise plans for the mutiny.' She paused again. 'Need I go on?'

Standing frowned. 'So you decided that Prigozhin alive was more of a threat to the Putin regime, than Prigozhin dead, and called us off.'

'Exactly. And so it proved, or at least so it did in the short-term. I'm not sure how much of this you are aware of since you were making your way back through hostile territory at the time, but Prigozhin and his Wagner troops entered Rostov-on-Don, the HQ of Russia's Southern military district, without opposition. After pausing for television interviews in which he launched a fresh tirade at the Defence Minister and the General Staff, for the first time he also included a coded criticism of Putin. "The happy grandpa thinks he's happy," he said, "but what is the country to do if it turns out that grandpa is a complete asshole?". It was clear that he was referring to the Russian president.'

'That was bold of him,' said Standing.

'Very bold.'

'And foolish. I can't see Putin taking abuse like that without retaliating.'

She gave one of her trademark thin smiles. 'Well Prigozhin's forces then went even further and began to advance towards Moscow, shooting down an Ilyushin command control aircraft and a number of attack helicopters as they did so. However, Prigozhin then paused the advance and soon afterwards he called off his rebellion altogether, possibly as a result of the actions of a previously close ally of his among Russia's senior generals, who had now publicly criticised him and refused to back him. A face-saving deal has now been brokered by President Lukashenko of Belarus in which Prigozhin has been given an amnesty by Putin and will confine Wagner's future activities to Africa, while his troops in Ukraine will now be co-opted into the regular Russian forces.'

Standing gave a cynical smile. 'And does anyone really believe that Putin will stick to his side of the agreement?'

'Almost certainly not. However, of more pressing concern to us is that Prigozhin's value as a source of trouble for the Kremlin has now been almost completely dissipated.'

Standing shrugged. 'So you're saying that our work here is done and we can be on our way back to Hereford then?'

'Not exactly,' she said. 'Having planned but eventually called off an attack on one of Putin's top commanders, the thoughts among senior figures in my organisation and in yours, have turned to the possibility of an even more daring operation and one which you and your colleagues are uniquely well-placed to carry out.'

'Why do I get a sinking feeling when you say that?' Standing said.

She ignored his sarcasm. 'It has been decided that we need to find a way to shorten this conflict. Continued Western support cannot be guaranteed, least of all if Donald Trump is returned to the White House. But even in Europe, the cost, coupled with the lack of progress from the Ukrainian offensive, is leading politicians to question whether they can continue to back Ukraine. Sooner or later they will have to face their electorates, and being seen to support an unpopular war always carries the risk of leading to the termination of political careers.'

'So?' said Standing, wishing that she would just get to the point.

'So it has been decided that something new is now necessary to concentrate Putin's mind and to make Western governments and their electorates feel that progress is being made towards an eventual Ukrainian victory, which is definitely not the case at the moment. For a very brief while, it seemed as if Putin was going to be toppled, but now he again seems to think he is immune and his position has even been strengthened by the failed mutiny against him. He has seen off Wagner Group and Prigozhin, cracked down on any whisper of dissent among critics like Navalny, castrated the media and continues to cow the oligarchs and the Russian elite with the threat of stripping them of their yachts and wealth if they interfere in domestic politics.'

'I get the feeling there's a "But" coming,' Standing said.

She inclined her head. 'As you say. But despite all this, we are still picking up rumblings of discontent from some in the military, and from potential rivals among the handful of politicians who have managed to tread the delicate path of avoiding antagonising Putin, without having to follow his party line so slavishly that they lose all credibility outside the Kremlin walls. There is nothing overt as yet obviously - anyone foolish enough to put their head above the parapet prematurely is likely to get it cut off - but if they sense Putin's grip is weakening, rivals will rapidly emerge. However, they first need to be absolutely sure that he won't recover again and be in a position to take his revenge on them.'

'So you're hoping that someone senior in the Russian military or the FSB may already be plotting against him?'

'They undoubtedly are so despite surviving the mutiny against him, Putin is more vulnerable than he has ever been before and if he is toppled, a new leader will eventually emerge.'

'And if Russia descends into chaos and civil war as a result?'

She gave a cynical smile. 'No Western politician, with the probable exception of Donald Trump, is going to lose much sleep over that. Anyway, we've decided that we need to send Putin a message, ideally a fatal one.'

Standing's jaw dropped. 'That's some sort of sick joke, right? Kill Putin? Even if it were possible, aren't you worried that assassinating him would simply push the world to the brink of nuclear war?'

'Not if it looked like the work of a rival or the trigger for an attempted coup...'

Standing shook his head in disbelief. 'I didn't take you for a person who likes a bet, Ms Day, and that seems like a hell of a gamble to take and anyway, even if HMG and the White House can handle the political fall-out, how do you hope to achieve it? He's one of the world's most heavily-defended individuals, in one of the world's most closed and rigidly controlled police states. We can't just waltz up to the Kremlin, armed to the teeth, and ask the way to Putin's office.'

'No, that is quite correct. In Moscow there's a ring of steel around him and bunkers where he can wait out a nuclear winter if necessary. So we don't see any realistic possibility of targeting him in Moscow, but his palace on the Black Sea coast may be another matter. He loves the place and although he pretends that it belongs to an oligarch, everyone knows it really belongs to Putin. The workers there all point to the ceiling when they are talking about the owner and as I'm sure you know, that is the universal symbol for Putin in Russia. I must warn you though, that it looks pretty impregnable. We were able to obtain plans of the building even while it was still under construction. The architect is Italian, and has worked for a number of Russian oligarchs, but the security of his offices doesn't match that of the buildings he designs for his clients. So we have studied the plans and coupled with intel from other sources we can give you a complete briefing on the place, including lay-out, floor plans, and right down to the furniture, fixtures and fittings. I can tell you that the palace is a monument to self-indulgence on a grand scale. It has a full-size ice-hockey pitch in a separate building under a domed roof, so that he can indulge his passion for the sport, no matter what the cost might be, and that is certainly substantial because it is apparently kept frozen and ready for use at a moment's notice, even in the heat of the Black Sea summer. Outside the main building there is also an arboretum, a huge winery, an orchid-house, a helipad, a guest house, a Russian Orthodox church with a red panelled roof, an amphitheatre where Western singing stars willing to turn a blind eye to Putin's excesses have performed for his guests in return for lavish fees.' She gave another of her thin smiles. 'Naturally, all of them are extensively debriefed on their return to the US or UK.'

'And you think Putin is reachable in his palace?'

'Everybody is reachable, Sergeant Standing. But yes, some are more reachable than others. There is a "Prohibited Special Use Airspace" or in plain English, a no-fly zone, extending for fifty miles around the palace, and among the other defences it is policed from an air-base that is home to a squadron of Mig-29 Fulcrum fighters. There are anti-aircraft gun and missile batteries to further guard against attack from the air, and destroyers, fast patrol boats and anti-submarine nets offshore to deal with naval threats from above or below the waves. Two escape tunnels have also been built into the palace, one leading to a dock for access to the sea, the other to a bunker with concrete walls fifteen feet thick, and both the tunnel to it and the bunker are buried deep in the solid rock. Even a nuclear weapon might not be enough to penetrate that. There is an air purification system, so you can not attack it using gas and there is also a tank regiment and a garrison of Spetsnaz troops stationed nearby, so a frontal assault probably would not work either.'

'Sounds like an absolute walk in the park then,' Standing said.

Agnes Day gave her standard, brief, humourless smile at his sarcasm. 'Nonetheless, we have absolute confidence that if anyone can find a way to penetrate the palace, it is you and your team. Obviously it is a false flag operation. Your tracks must be well enough hidden to avoid even the least suspicion of Western involvement. All the clues - and they need to be subtle ones - have to point unmistakably towards this being an attack from within Russia by those opposed to him. Wagner Group would be the obvious suspects given recent events. So I don't for a moment underplay the difficulty of the task we are setting you, but any and all of our considerable resources are at your disposal to bring it to a successful conclusion, though I must also warn you that the operation-'

'- is completely deniable,' Standing said, finishing her sentence for her. 'I hear you,' said Standing. 'I'm assuming you are able to give us a window of time during which Putin will be in residence in his palace and ready to receive visitors like us.'

She nodded. 'With the invasion of Ukraine going so badly for the Russians, and the shock waves of Prigozhin's mutiny only now ebbing away, Putin has called his senior commanders and advisers to a council of war at his palace on the Black Sea. That will give you the opportunity to carry out the task.'

'Even though all his senior commanders will also have substantial personal security details of their own?'

'Indeed they will,' said the MI6 officer. 'But tyrants like Putin do not take even the slightest risk with their own personal security, so no bodyguards other than Putin's own Presidential Security Service and his even more loyal personal bodyguards are allowed within the palace and no one but them is permitted to carry any weapon within the palace precincts. Even his most senior generals have to hand in their personal weapons before entering the palace, let alone being admitted to Putin's office or the presence of Putin himself. Only two things are required of his protectors: absolute loyalty and a willingness to carry out any order he issues, no matter how illegal or repugnant, without question. And he ensures their total loyalty by lavishly rewarding them. Three of his former protectors have not only acquired vast estates at negligible or sometimes no cost at all to themselves, but they also now fill some of the most senior positions in the Russian state, which give them almost limitless opportunities for further corruption.'

'So we'll not expect any help from them in knocking Putin off then,' Standing said, though once more his attempt at humour fell on stony ground. 'At this point I expect to hear the theme from Mission Impossible.'

She flashed him a cold smile. 'You're no Tom Cruise, Sergeant Standing,' she said.

Chapter 22

As soon as Standing had brought his SAS team and the pick of the Ukrainian fighters available to him up to speed about the task they had been given, they began to put together an improvised plan to attack the palace complex. The group still included Tadeusz and Dmytro, but after his experience first with Sukut and then Jankiv, all the non-SAS men were put into complete isolation as soon as the planning began. 'You're a vital part of the team,' Standing told them. 'And I'm not for a moment accusing any of you of treachery like those traitors Sukut and Jankiv, but until we launch, I cannot allow any possibility of careless talk, so everyone is in complete lockdown and a total comms black-out.'

As he began to throw ideas around with his patrol-mates, Mustard Coleman was the most pessimistic about their chances. 'It's a bloody impossible task,' he said, 'and it will probably just get everybody killed and achieve nothing at all.'

'Bloody hell,' Macleod said. 'Way to piss on our parade, Mustard. Why not tell us what you really think?'

'I hear what you're saying, Mustard, and I'm not suggesting it will be easy,' Standing said, 'but apart from anything else, maybe you're forgetting how incompetent, lazy and arrogant the flunkies around people in power can be. They're the same the world over. It's a false flag operation so we need to make sure that any smoking guns are pointing in the general direction of a Russian faction, and that almost certainly means the Wagner Group. Agnes Day was banging on about the need to make the clues to that subtle, but I don't think we need to be worrying too much about that. The last word you'd think of in relation to the Wagner Group's bunch of criminals, murderers and psychopaths is "subtle" so I think some Wagner badges on our Russian-issue battledress and a couple of aerosol cans of spray paint in our kit should do the job. We can splatter the Wagner logo on the walls and doors of Putin's Palace and that should be more than enough to pin the blame on the Group and steer any backlash from Putin's loyalists in that direction.'

'I'll bring some spray paint cans,' said Williams. 'I've always fancied myself as a bit of a Banksy.'

Standing grinned. 'Some kind of artist, that's for sure. Okay, insertion. I think after the Prigozhin op cock up, we've not only all had more than enough of tabbing to the target area, but the distances involved make that a non-starter anyway, so I'm thinking a heli insertion at absolute minimum height, either by sea or land, but we'll let the heli pilots work that one out for us. Once we're at the landing zone, we'll be fast roping down and dealing with whatever obstacles there might be between us and the target.' He gave a broad smile. 'So…a piece of piss, right?'

Over a series of intense and sometimes acrimonious sessions, they formed a workable plan, first in sketchy outline but gradually taking firmer shape as they raised and solved problems and objections, and continually fine-tuned it. And fierce though the arguments often were, no grudges were ever carried forward from the process. All of them understood that it was a necessary part of the planning and preparation that would lead to the operation having the highest possible percentage chance of success. When they finally had something they could all sign up to, Standing called a briefing for the entire team, including the group of Ukrainian forces who would be acting as support troops. They would have a vital role in securing a broad perimeter around the street area to give the assault team led by Standing enough time to penetrate the palace's defences and identify and kill their principal target.

Standing made sure not to mention Putin by name, though it would not take any great intellectual capacity to guess who the principal target was likely to be in a palace that was exclusively reserved for the use of the Russian President.

'We obviously need a strong fighting group to secure such a large and well-defended area,' he said. 'But we'll be separating you into independent fighting patrols, probably led by some of our SAS comrades, and acting on your own initiative when in contact with the enemy. And we'll break the terrain surrounding the palace into patrol areas of operations and set tight boundaries of exploitation to prevent any "blue on blue" contacts. The palace is surrounded by thousands of square miles of forest and swamp, the stuff they call 'No Man's Land'. Well, that is where you are going to operate, so make it your own. If the Russian defenders want to take you on, they are going to have to leave the comfort of their dachas and base camps, with all their facilities, and get down and dirty in the boondocks to mix it with you. Just be sure you are ready for them when that happens. Concentrate initially on the supply lines, get them pissed off and make them feel under siege. Use the surveillance and attack drones that you have carefully, you don't need to mix it, keep your distance but keep the bad guys on the back foot and defensive. The SAS team obviously know the ropes of this kind of op and will be taking the lead roles, but it will only be successful if everyone plays their part. So keep your eyes on the professionals, and look and learn from them, and one day you'll be telling your grandkids about this or boring your mates to death in the pub about it. Oh, and by the way, keep away from the palace, because that's where I'll be and if I get company, I'll be shooting first and asking who it is afterwards!'

After weighing up his options and discussing it with the troopers, Standing had decided that a single eight-man assault team would be the way to go. It was the maximum number that could be carried in a single Hind heli and after her decisive intervention in the battle with the Russian paratroops, Standing had asked for Lisa to fly the mission.

Once within the palace they would split into two-man or four-man teams and as a result, he felt that he needed two Russian-speaking

Ukrainians in the team. As well as their fighting skills, they might be needed to relay commands to any servants or other Russian civilians who had to be moved out of the firing line or kept prisoner while the assault team cleared each area. The Ukrainians would also be able to interrogate any prisoners, even though Standing was not planning to take any, some might be needed to reveal the target's location within the palace. That decision left him with the awkward choice of which of his seven remaining SAS patrol mates would have to be asked to stand down from the op, but while he was pondering that, it was taken out of his hands.

'Sarge, I need a word,' Connor said, as they were finishing their meal that evening.

Standing looked up, surprised, but then nodded and led him away from the others. 'Okay, what's on your mind?' he said.

Connor hesitated for a few moments. 'I need you to stand me down from the op.'

Standing did a double-take but said, 'Okay Connor, I can understand that. Perkins was a really close mate of yours and it's natural that it would take a bit of time for you to process his death.'

'No,' Connor said. 'It's more than that. I just-' Again he hesitated. 'I just don't think I've got it in me any more.'

'Well, we all have times when we wonder that,' Standing said, 'but I know you almost as well as you know yourself, and I would put my life in your hands without giving it a second thought, so I've no doubts on that score and nor should you.'

Connor shook his head. 'You're still not getting it, Sarge. Of course, Perkins not beating the clock was a blow, but we've all lost close mates before and carried on. But now it feels different and that feeling had been building for quite a while, even before Perkins died. The last few ops we've been on, I've been bricking it big time. I've not slept, or if I have, I've woken up streaming with cold sweat.' He paused again. 'You know I'm not a coward. We've been in some hairy situations together and fought our way out of them, and I never gave them a backward look until now.'

Standing held up his hand. 'Mate, I hear what you're saying but I'm sure that all you need is a good break to recharge your batteries. Sure, I'll stand you down from his op,' he said, although he couldn't resist adding, 'but you'll be missing a real treat! However, I'll talk to the Boss, and a month's R and R back in Blighty with a pint in one hand and a Hereford beauty in the other, and you'll soon be as right as rain again.'

Connor shook his head. 'You still don't get it. This isn't something that a few beers and a bit of time off will fix. I've lost it and I'm done. I'm going home, back to the Black Country.'

'And what'll you do there? Come on, I know you, you'll be bored shitless inside a few weeks and desperate to come back.'

'Not this time I won't.' Connor locked his gaze on Standing. 'Don't make it any harder for me, Sarge. Trust me, my mind's made up.'

Standing studied him in silence a while longer and then shrugged his shoulders. 'All right Dum, if you're sure that's what you want. Say your goodbyes to the others and I'll sort some transport for you. There'll be the usual Globemaster or C5 flying back empty tomorrow morning, so I'll make sure you're on it.' He held out his hand. 'You're one of the best, Dum, another of the 'old and bold' we'll be talking about round the fire in a few years' time. We'll keep the door open for you just in case you have a change of heart, but if not, then go well, and I'll see you down the road.'

Having broken the news of Connor's departure to the rest of the team, Standing still had to choose two Ukrainian special forces soldiers to take into Putin's Palace with them. Tadeusz and Dmytro had been expecting to be chosen and showed their bitter disappointment when Standing told them that they would not be part of this op, but he sat them down away from the others and talked them through the reason why he had to disappoint them. 'This is no reflection on your fighting qualities at all,' he said. 'You've already shown yourselves to be brave and resourceful soldiers and in other circumstances - if we were going to knock over a platoon of Russian infantry or storm an enemy gun position - you'd be the first names I'd be calling out, but this is not like the ops we've done so far. For this one I need men with Close Quarter Battle skills and that is not something you've ever trained to do, whereas it is meat and drink to special forces. Don't worry, you'll still be taking part in the op but only as part of the independent fighting patrols clearing the areas around the target, and engaging any enemy troops who try to break through your positions. It's still vital work - the op won't succeed if you fail - but you won't be taking part on the assault on the Palace itself, I'm afraid.' He paused, measuring the impact of his words on them. 'I hope you understand.'

Both men shrugged and gave grudging nods, though Standing could tell from the look in their eyes that they didn't agree with him and resented him for leaving them out of the assault group.

The two men he'd eventually chosen, Malko and Pawluk, were Ukrainian Spetsnaz troops. Normally SAS men regarded the Spetsnaz as special forces in name only and often little more than glorified infantry, but these men had been part of the contingent sent to England for additional training in the early stages of the conflict and their skills, in particular in Close Quarter Battle, had been honed over weeks of live fire drills in the Killing House at Hereford and exercises out on the ranges. The Killing House was laid out like a normal house with rooms that included a kitchen and even toilets, the only difference being that normal houses don't have thick rubber sheets hanging over the walls to prevent ricochets wounding or killing the men training there. Watched over by SAS instructors, the Ukrainians had learned to burst through the doors of darkened rooms, instantly identify the threats among a range of targets and take them out with rapid double taps, while avoiding shooting any innocent bystanders or hostages among them. Furthermore, they learned to fire accurately while avoiding return fire by diving and rolling across the floor, and even to change magazines while doing so. When firing their weapons, whatever the circumstances, they also had to have achieved an accuracy rate of 99 per cent in situations where one missed shot could compromise the whole operation.

Like the SAS men themselves, Pawluk, Malko and the rest of the Ukrainian contingent, including the still disgruntled Tadeusz and Dmytro, had now been placed in complete isolation from everyone not directly involved in the mission. A comms blackout was imposed on them and all mobile phones and other communications devices were taken from them. Just as before the aborted Prigozhin op, every item of kit and clothing they were taking also had to be carefully screened and sanitised. That applied not just to their weapons, clothes and underclothes, all of which had to be Russian-made, but even to apparently insignificant items. If anyone was carrying a pen or pencil, for example, it had to be of Russian make or if it had been made in China, or somewhere else, it had to be of a kind that was widely available in Russia.

All of them were issued with kit marked with Wagner Group logos, badges and identifying patches, and as they were making their final preparations for the op, Colonel Davies had news for Standing that made the attempt to false-flag it as a Wagner attack much more likely to be believed.

'I've just had a rather interesting conversation with Agnes Day,' the Colonel said. 'The private jet that Yevgeny Prigozhin was using to fly to St Petersburg this morning, blew up in mid-air and everyone on board was killed, either immediately or when the aircraft impacted the ground.'

'So Putin got his revenge?' Standing said. 'I guess the only surprise is why it took him so long to do so.'

'True that,' said the Colonel, 'but Putin's nothing if not methodical. He would first have needed to reassure himself that Wagner's heavy weapons had been transferred to regular Russian army units and Wagner's senior commanders sweetened or eliminated before he acted against Prigozhin. And you can also bet that before he gave the order to take him out, his men had already compiled an inventory of all Prigozhin's assets, and identified his closest allies within the Wagner Group and their principal contacts in the countries where it operates.'

'A pause might also have been designed to lull Prigozhin into a bit of a false sense of security,' Standing said. 'Whatever else he was, it didn't sound like he was naive, so he knew what Putin was capable of, but he must somehow have imagined that the face-saving deal they had concocted, with him handing over control of Wagner to the state and relocating to Belarus, would have been enough to keep him off the Putin kill list.' He gave a grim smile. 'Bad idea. So do you know how they got him?'

'It's not completely clear as yet, but according to Six, there was apparently no trace of a missile strike visible on the satellite surveillance, so the most likely explanation would have been a bomb on board. The fact that the aircraft went into an immediate death spiral, strongly suggests that it had lost a wing, and that definitely points towards a bomb.'

Standing nodded. 'It's the way we'd have done it if we'd been tasked with it. They wouldn't even have needed access to the interior of the jet because a device placed externally at the point where the wing meets the fuselage would have blown it clean off. But it's interesting that Putin chose such a public way to dispose of Prigozhin.'

'Well,' the Colonel said, 'either Putin is starting to run out of Novichok, or more likely, he just wanted to make sure the message was received loud and clear by anyone else in Russia who might have been toying with the idea of challenging him.'

Standing paused, staring unseeing at the wall, while he thought through the implications for their own op. 'Well, I really don't see how it's going to make that much difference to us. Security may be a bit tighter, but that shouldn't present any obstacles we can't overcome, and it may even be that, with Prigozhin out of the picture, Putin's guards turn out to be a little less alert.' He shrugged. 'We'll find out soon enough, anyway.'

'One other thing,' Standing said. 'As you know, we're using Ukrainian Special Forces as independent fighting patrols around the target area, but with no disrespect to them, although they're tough fighters, I'm very doubtful that they have the full SF skill-set. So...' He paused, giving the Colonel a calculating look. 'I need you to spare me a few more men from our squadron to lead each patrol.'

The Colonel thought about it for a few moments. 'We're already pretty hard-pressed with other ops but, given the importance of this one, I'll see what I can do. What's the least number of men you need?'

Standing shrugged. 'Eight, two to lead each independent patrol and coordinate actions with each other if and when necessary.'

The Colonel nodded. 'Okay, eight men it is. Don't worry, I'll find them from somewhere.'

Chapter 23

With the assault team members in place, they began the intensive work-up training for the op. Using the blueprints of Putin's Palace that MI6 had covertly obtained, they laid out tape and tent pegs in the centre of the training area in an exact replica of the floor plan of the entrance and the main corridor on the ground. A set of display screens commandeered from a bankrupt exhibition company's warehouse in Kyiv, were set up to form rudimentary walls, with curtains draped across the entrances in place of doors. They then practised the assault on the building and their progress through it, clearing each room as they came to it, doing it over and over again, trying to anticipate and form an effective means of dealing with every conceivable eventuality.

Although it would be daylight when the assault began, they had to assume that the rooms they were targeting might be windowless or darkened so they carried out their training exercises during the night, disturbing the slumbers of the troops in the parts of the base neighbouring their own fenced off area with an endless succession of shots and explosions. The two Ukrainians, Pawluk and Marko, performed well in the training, setting Standing's mind at rest about the wisdom of his choices. Eventually they were all satisfied and they sat back to await the signal to go.

When the most up to date intel was received from Six, just prior to the launch of the op, it concluded that the assassination of Prigozhin had not affected arrangements for Putin's council of war with his senior commanders and advisers about the 'special military operation', otherwise known as the war in Ukraine.

Standing led the final briefing for the team. 'The Palace will be surrounded by several rings of security,' he said. 'There will be armed patrols in the grounds, and all entrances will be manned by the Palace Security Team. They will be there to make sure that nobody and I mean nobody, is allowed into the Palace with a weapon. This will cause queues to form, because none of the self-entitled VIPs and generals will want their security teams to be unarmed. They are scared shitless without them but the only people allowed in the Palace with weapons are the President's own Close Escort. They will therefore be the main threat to us but they will also be attempting to move the target out of harm's way, so once inside the building we need to move fast.'

He was giving the briefing to all of them, but the SAS men all knew their SOPs inside out and backwards, and he was really mainly addressing the two Ukrainians, Malko and Pawluk. 'When we are in the Palace, you two,' he said, nodding to Macleod and Pawluk, 'will be working together. I'll be with Malko, and we will leapfrog each other along the corridors, you two taking one room, us taking the next.' Standing looked over at Parker. 'Banger will have standard charges with him and as we clear an area and move deeper into the palace he will set charges that will block the corridors behind us, preventing access by any of Putin's troops who've managed to react fast enough - and avoid our independent fighting patrols - to reach the Palace while we're still working our way through it. Once the job is done we will exfil by means of the escape tunnel that leads to the dock at sea level, and there with any luck, the US cavalry, in the shape of our good friend Lisa, will be riding to our assistance.' He looked over at Williams. 'Did you get the paint, Cowpat?'

Williams grinned and held up a carrier bag full of spray cans. 'I managed to get black, red and yellow, the Wagner colours,' he said. He gave the bag to Malko.

Standing nodded at Malko and Pawluk. 'It's our job to make sure the blame for the target's death doesn't point in the direction of the West in general and the US and UK in particular. Nor should it even point towards Ukraine, although,' he winked at Pawluk, 'I'm sure your President would be very happy to take the credit for it. So we need it to seem as if it was an assassination carried out by dissidents from within Russia itself and luckily Putin's own recent actions have given us some very plausible scapegoats, which is why all the Russian uniforms we'll be wearing have Wagner Group insignia on them. Right, any questions? No? Then let's get to it and we'll be back here for tea and medals, or preferably some of that firewater you call vodka, before you know it.'

Chapter 24

The additional SAS men who would be leading the Ukrainian special forces in the independent fighting patrols flew in by Chinook to the Forward Operating Base, where Standing greeted them and gave them a briefing on their roles. He knew them all from rubbing shoulders with them around the Squadron and had worked with several on previous ops, but although the others were unknown quantities in terms of their skill-sets and combat experience, he knew that the Colonel would only have sent him battle-hardened men for an op of this importance.

The independent fighting patrols were inserted by heli into the wider region around Putin's Palace. Four Hind helis carrying no markings and each holding an eight-man patrol, took off an hour after sunset. They flew at extreme low level, hedge-hopping a few feet above the rich, black earth that had made Ukraine the granary of the Soviet Union.

The helis crossed the Russian border, appearing and disappearing past a succession of enemy gun positions before their crews managed to get off even one shot at them, although there was a pretty low risk of that anyway. Since their helis were Russian-made Hinds, most of the gun crews would simply have assumed that they were carrying Russian troops, or on a mission too secret to have been notified to gunners on their lowly pay grade.

The fighting patrols were set down in their dropping zones, and as the helis disappeared into the night, the patrols moved out to cover the remaining distance to their separate designated operating areas on foot. Their DZs had been 40 kilometres from Putin's

Palace, far enough away that they were outside the exclusion zone surrounding the Palace and even if they were compromised there, it would not automatically trigger a full-scale security alert. They had been inserted 24 hours before the assault group would go in, purely so they would have time to reach their operating areas and be in position when Standing and his team fast-roped down and began the attack.

Just twenty four hours later, the fighting patrols had all reached their operational areas without being compromised, and were lying up in cover waiting for zero hour, when they would begin attempting to interdict any supply or troop convoys or armoured fighting vehicles making for the Palace, and fight off any counter-attacks.

Meanwhile scores of Russian officials and generals, their chests groaning under the weight of multiple decorations and medal ribbons, were now arriving for the council of war at the Palace on the Black Sea. The flight paths into the airfield were busy with military and private jets and helicopters, each carrying one of the self-entitled delegates. Emphasising his personal importance, each one had brought with him a deputy and each deputy in turn had brought an assistant, and all were determined to get their share of the crumbs falling from Putin's table.

The chaotic scenes on the ground, as the aircraft jockeyed for space on the taxiways and concrete hard standing, were replicated in the air. Since the collapse of communism in 1989, Russian investment in infrastructure had been almost non-existent and as a result, the Air Traffic Control system around the Palace was a very long way from state of the art, and the controllers were struggling to keep up with the demands that were being made upon them.

As it began its approach, the pilot of each aircraft was ordered to give his 'squawk number', a four-figure identity code which showed up on the radar in the control tower as an on-screen number, allowing the operator to prioritise landing slots and parking areas, but the occasional breakdowns of the system were causing increasing anxiety in the tower. Numbers were wrongly allocated to some aircraft, others were already on their final approach before their numbers even appeared on screen, and a few had been circling so long while waiting for a landing slot that they were short of fuel and were bombarding the tower with pleas to be allowed to touch down. Meanwhile the pilots of the aircraft that were carrying the Defence Minister and other very senior officials and army officers, were pulling rank and demanding to be given priority and immediate clearance to land.

The eight-man SAS attack team was inserting in the Hind helicopter gunship piloted by Lisa, but this time Earl was not accompanying her as gunner. The weight of the SAS men and all their gear was already close to the maximum load for the heli, even before taking on the additional fuel that was necessary for a such a long flight, so to his visible displeasure, Earl had been left at base, kicking his heels.

After snatching a few hours' sleep, the assault team assembled for a final briefing at four in the morning, although there was little to say, for all foreseeable eventualities had already been assessed, discussed and catered for in their preparations. They knew that, in the famous forces' saying, "No plan ever survives contact with the enemy", but if anything unexpected did crop up, as usual they would wing it and no other group of soldiers was better prepared than the SAS to deal with whatever surprises were thrown at them. They ate bacon rolls for breakfast washed down with coffee and were all out on the hard standing and ready to board the Hind well before the scheduled take off time of 0500 hours. Unusually for a behind the lines op, the insertion would take place in daylight, rather than during the hours of darkness and the false dawn was already lightening the eastern sky, as Lisa wound up the engines to a scream. Although it was work-worn the heli was still perfectly serviceable, and it had also been taken apart and put back together again by the ground crew with even greater care than usual, to ensure it was in the best possible condition for the op.

Opening the throttles to reach the operating RPM, Lisa pulled up the collective and as the pitch increased, she pressed the left pedal. When the Hind began to lift off the concrete, straining under the heavy load of men and equipment, she adjusted the cyclic to level the heli and then eased it away from her to set it moving forward. As it transitioned from vertical to forward motion, the heli shuddered and the nose began to pull up, but she adjusted the cyclic again to maintain the forward momentum and the Hind picked up speed.

Once clear of the airfield, she swung the heli away towards the south-east, out over the Black Sea. Its heavy payload meant that it was flying well below its top speed of 200 miles an hour, but what was important on this op was not speed, but undetectability. When the Hind was far enough out at sea to be invisible and virtually inaudible to any watchers on the coast, she swung it around onto an easterly heading, and dropped to extreme low level. They were now flying just a few feet above the water.

Lisa kept the Hind flying parallel to the Black Sea coast, still at wave-top height, and skirted Crimea at some distance, keeping well clear of the Russian defences there. She flew on past what was now the de facto border after the Russian invasion and then past the actual, internationally recognised border as well. Any Russian aircraft, shore patrol or anti-aircraft gun battery spotting them, could now shoot them down without hesitation or repercussion, but only if they had satisfied themselves that the heli was a hostile aircraft. Lisa and her passengers were counting on the fact that battered looking Hinds were such a common sight criss-crossing the skies on both sides of the border that they were unlikely to be challenged or recognised as intruders, even assuming they were spotted at all on their covert approach to the target.

Twenty kilometres beyond the border she turned the heli inland, still keeping it at ultra low level, skimming trees and hedgerows and startling a herd of cattle into a panicked stampede. She then brought the heli round in a broad arc, keeping well clear of the fifty-mile radius 'Prohibited Special Use Airspace' - the air defence zone around Putin's Palace, that bristled with radar installations, missiles, anti-aircraft gun batteries and the base that housed the squadron of Mig-29 Fulcrum fighters. Two of the Migs were always on Quick Reaction Alert, inside their concrete Hardened Aircraft Shelters, designed to withstand a direct hit from anything up to and including a tactical nuclear device. Working in relays, the Russian pilots sat in their cockpits 24/7. They read comics and twiddled their thumbs as they waited for an alert that would send them streaking down the runway and into the air to shoot down any intruder with the temerity to stray into the forbidden zone around the palace.

The SAS team's target, the palace, stood within a 180 acre site on Cape Idokopas, a promontory projecting from the coast into the Black Sea near the village of Praskoveyvka. An offshore reef made seaborne access difficult, adding to the Palace's security, and the headland was flanked by steep, rocky cliffs and screes, though the top of the promontory was flat and thickly forested with Turkish pine trees.

Lisa finally brought the Hind to a hover and set it down on the ground just over fifty miles to the north-east of the palace, directly under the flight path of any aircraft approaching the airfield next to the palace from the direction of Moscow. With the engines still idling, she remained seated in her cockpit, to outward appearances still utterly calm despite being a hundred miles inside hostile territory.

While Parker, Macleod, Ireland, Williams, Coleman, Pawluk and Malko were jammed together in the passenger compartment, Standing had been seated in Earl's normal seat in the gunner's cockpit during the flight, ready to let rip with the Hind's formidable weaponry if they came under attack. However, he had now had to abandon the cockpit and squeeze into the back with the rest of the team, so that as soon as they were over the target, they could make a swift exit, fast-roping down.

The men surrounding Standing were all going through their little, semi-subconscious, pre-combat rituals. Williams was positively zen-like, eyes closed, and thumb and second finger touching, silently murmuring his meditation mantra to himself. Macleod was the opposite, a coiled spring, fingertips drumming out an accelerating tattoo on his thighs, his gaze fixed on the floor of the heli. Ireland and Coleman sat back, silent and staring into space. Parker's fingers were almost caressing the grenades on his harness, touching each in turn in a superstitious ritual.

The two Ukrainians sat close together muttering terse comments to each other. Malko was either relaxed about the op to come, or hiding it well, but Pawluk's pale face and the bead of sweat on his forehead suggested nerves that Standing had noted but hoped would evaporate as soon as the call to action came. They could not afford any weak links or hesitations once they were on the ground and moving through the palace.

Sensing the mounting tension and impatience among some of her passengers, Lisa thumbed the intercom switch and said, 'You guys back there, just try to sit back and relax. We'll be on the move again shortly.'

Standing flashed her a thumbs up. 'Okay then, Lisa, well once we're up and running, just keep an eye on the signal from my Personal Locator Beacon. As soon as you see that it's clear of the palace, come and get us as fast as you like, but if it doesn't show us as being outside of the palace at all when you reach Zero Hour plus ten, turn tail and head for home, because if that's the case, you can be sure that we won't ever be coming back.'

'Roger that,' she said, 'although let's be honest, we all know that's never going to happen, right?'

Even though she had been swapping a little banter with the patrol, Lisa was also keeping one ear firmly fixed on the transmissions from Air Traffic Control in the tower at the airfield. Suddenly, stock still and listening intently, but still speaking to them very calmly, she said, 'All right, this next one will do us nicely, hold on to your hats because here we go.'

Standing could hear the noise of another helicopter's rotors above the beat of their own, and squinting upwards, he caught a glimpse of a VIP Hip helicopter passing above them. On her headset, tuned to the Air Traffic Control's frequency, Lisa heard the controller repeating the Hip's 'squawk number': its four-digit identity code. She at once tapped in the same squawk number as the Hip into her comms, wound up the engines till they were screaming and took off vertically, tucking the Hind in, almost within touching distance of the rear of the Hip flying in front of it. Although heli pilots sometimes used mirrors when carrying underslung loads, their aircraft were not normally fitted with rear view mirrors, so the pilot of the Hip was unlikely even to have noticed the new arrival behind him. Even if he had, he would almost certainly just have assumed it was another in the endless column of aircraft coming in with yet another official, officer or dignitary on his way to President Putin's council of war, albeit an aircraft that was flying considerably closer to him than the normal protocols of air traffic movement would have allowed.

On the ground, on top of all his other problems, the air traffic controller would have seen the same squawk number showing twice on the screen for a couple of seconds, but by then it would have been too late. When both the Hip and the Hind on its tail were close to the semi-organised chaos of the Landing Zone, Lisa pressed the firing button and let loose a burst of 30mm cannon fire at point blank range into the rear of the Hip. Raked with armour-piercing rounds from end to end, the Hip immediately went into a death spiral and, trailing black smoke behind it, it was sent crashing down to the ground, where it erupted in a ball of flame.

The Air Traffic Controller had not had time even to take in this catastrophe on his watch, before his life was brought to a sudden, savage end as Lisa followed up with another prolonged burst of fire, raking the top of the Control Tower from one side to the other. Everyone inside was killed or badly wounded and the ATC screens went blank, causing further chaos among the arriving and circling aircraft, those trying to land and those trying to taxi on the ground.

Lisa turned the Hind around and put the gunship in a hover, aligned on the massive front doors of the palace, beyond the wrought iron gates that were surmounted with a gold double-headed eagle, the emblem of the Tsars that had been adopted by the Russian president.

In the long traditions of Russian bureaucracy, a cluster of officials and security guards stood at the doors of the palace and were taking an age to check the credentials of all the arriving officers and officials against the official list. The visitors' sense of self-importance and impatience with the delays cut no ice with men who knew that there was only one person they needed to defer to and hurry through security, and he was already installed inside his palace.

'Okay guys,' Lisa said. 'You wanted a guaranteed entry to the palace, you're about to get a guaranteed entry.'

Flicking a series of switches in rapid succession she selected Ranging - Automatic; Sight - On; Weapons - Off/Missile On; Master Arm - On; Sight Glass - Unlock, Move and Re-Lock. A cross appeared on her head-up display and she moved it on to her chosen target, the palace doors. She then manoeuvred the helicopter until the circle in the centre of her vision that she used to position the helicopter was precisely overlaid on the targeting cross. A tone sounded, showing the target was locked on, and she then pushed and held the weapon release button, until the Ataka missile she had selected blasted away from the pylon that had been holding it. It was a Russian made, guided, high explosive anti-tank missile, known by Nato as the AT-9 Spiral-2, similar to the American helicopter- or drone-launched Hellfire missile.

The missile struck home with a blast that not only reduced the massive wooden doors to matchwood but also wiped out most of the officials and guards who had been stationed around it and the queue of visiting VIPs, generals and senior Kremlin officials who would now have no further need for impatience, since they had all simultaneously reached their lives' ultimate destination.

Lisa brought the Hind back to a brief hover closer to the burning entrance doors. 'The doors are open and the way is clear, since the welcoming party seems to have disappeared. Go get 'em. Happy landings, bring me back a souvenir and I'll see you on the other side.'

Standing and his team were already fast-roping down, the first ones hitting the ground and going into all-round defence for the couple of seconds it took for the rest of the assault team to join them. The Hind swung around and disappeared from view, with Lisa making good her escape, flying low level and by a circuitous route past the air defence zone, hoping to throw off any pursuit. She then made an abrupt course change and headed due south, crossing the coast past a resort where a few early-season Russian holidaymakers were sitting on the sands or sprawling on sun-loungers. She had brief glimpses of their upturned faces as they watched the Hind flash overhead and disappear out to sea. Skimming the waves, she was heading for an area offshore that she had decided was the optimum point from which she hoped to be doing nothing more than simply watching and waiting for Standing's signal, well before the Russian air defences finally got round to working out who and what had been responsible for the carnage that had engulfed the palace.

Chapter 25

Led by Standing and with the others in echelon formation, giving everyone a clear field of fire against threats from the front, the patrol sprinted across the manicured lawns and immaculate gravel paths towards the palace. The entrance was flanked on either side by double Corinthian columns as if it was a Roman temple rather than a Russian dictator's palace. The immaculate grey facade of the building appeared almost white in the bright sunshine. The tall, arched ground floor windows had been fitted with bulletproof glass, according to the architect's drawings that MI6 had obtained, while wings extended to either side of the main building, and to the rear, where they surrounded a central courtyard. That would force the attackers either to split their teams to advance down either side of it, or cross the open space, potentially under fire from defenders using the cover of the rooms on either side.

Flames were still flickering from the smouldering doors, with one hanging from its hinges, while the other had been blown clear of the doorway altogether. Many of the guards and visiting dignitaries who had been gathered around the door were already dead, but there was the whip-crack sound of rapid double taps as Standing and Macleod each gave the coup de grace to the two security guards who, despite their massive wounds, still appeared capable of firing a weapon. Standing and his men entered the palace, their Kalashnikovs at the ready. As they advanced along the corridor inside the door, they were stepping over more bodies sprawled on the floor and finishing off any that they could not be certain were already dead with double-taps or head shots from their suppressed AKs.

There was a guardroom a few yards from the main entrance where any off-duty soldiers were likely to have gathered. The noise of the suppressed fire as the SAS team disposed of the wounded survivors among the guards who had been stationed at the main doors had not triggered any response from the guardroom but Standing was taking no chances. As they moved forward he and Malko, who was alongside him, kept their sights trained on the guardroom doorway, while the next two in the formation, Macleod and Pawluk, covered the empty corridor ahead of them.

On a training exercise, Standing would have tossed a flash-bang into the guardroom and taken out the startled occupants with a double-tap a fraction of a second later, but this wasn't a training exercise and he needed minimum risk and maximum damage. He paused before the open doorway, pulled the pin on a fragmentation grenade and tossed it into the room. There was a flash as the grenade detonated and the tinny rattle of shrapnel against the wall of the corridor facing the door. The next instant, Standing moved into the doorway, his gun at the ready but there was no need for him to fire. The Russian guards who had been lounging at a table in the middle of the room when the grenade went off were all dead.

A door led off the main guard room but Standing left the following pairs to mop up any other guards while he and Malko, and Macleod and Pawluk advanced along the corridor. It was dangerous territory, closed off by double doors at the far end, but long, broad and straight, without a scrap of cover and with nothing to prevent ricochets from the concrete walls and marble floors if enemy troops appeared and began firing.

By now alarms would have been going off in every Russian base within 500 miles, but Standing's only concern was to penetrate to the heart of the building, eliminate their target and then be out again before the garrison from the nearest base could arrive and deploy. Any other troops and guards already stationed within the palace would just have to be eliminated as the SAS and their Ukrainian counterparts fought their way on through the building.

To reach the state rooms beyond they first had to negotiate the remainder of the main corridor. They were no more than about one third of the way along it when one of the doors at the far end swung open and a uniformed figure appeared in the gap. He was armed with an AK but was clearly not responding to the destruction of the main doors and the guardroom, because his weapon was held loosely in his left hand and was pointing down at the floor, not at the approaching SAS assault team. He was not given any time to correct that error, a double-tap from Standing punched twin holes in the man's chest and blew him backwards through the half-open doorway in a spray of arterial blood.

There was a momentary pause and then Standing saw the barrel of another man's AK poking around the edge of the door. Like his comrade, the unseen soldier did not manage to get a single shot off before rounds from Standing, Malko, Macleod and Pawluk stitched a pattern into the woodwork of the door. Bursting out of the other side, they showered the enemy fighter with rounds that ripped through his body at the same time that needle sharp wooden splinters were tearing at his flesh.

As soon as he had fired, Standing had dived to the ground, and changed magazines as he was rolling across the floor. He then sprang up again at once and moved rapidly forward with Malko while the other two covered them. The thick walls of the palace and the size of the rooms, meant that the sounds of combat were unlikely to travel far enough from the source of it to trigger a general alert, but the SAS team now had to assume that any element of surprise had been lost and that they could come under immediate fire from any soldiers and guards within the maze of rooms further into the building. More alarming from Standing's point of view was the prospect that Putin's Presidential Guard would hear the gunfire and immediately begin hustling their principal away to a safe area, beyond the reach of his would-be assassins.

Tossing a grenade through the gap of the half-open door, Standing and Malko barrelled through it, one after the other, both men diving as they did so, while bursts of fire from two Russian soldiers crouching behind an upturned chaise longue, ripped through the empty air above them. Standing was already returning fire, punching holes through the upholstery and showering the left-hand Russian with kapok fibres, while the rounds found their mark in his body. Malko was a beat slower to fire and, forgetting the principles of numbering off targets left to right, had then put two rounds into the same Russian soldier. By the time he had realised his error, it was too late. Standing put a double-tap into the other one too, but the man had fired a fraction of a second before that and although much of the burst of semi-automatic fire from the Russian's AK had gone high and wide, three rounds had stitched a line across Malko's torso from his stomach to his lungs. One glance was all it took Standing to realise that the Ukrainian had fought his last battle and paid the ultimate price for his error.

Macleod and Pawluk had followed them through the doorway and Pawluk froze as he saw the body of his friend. Still covering the ground ahead of them in case fresh threats emerged, Standing took in the Ukrainian's reaction and made an instant decision. 'Macleod, Pawluk, you're with me now,' he said. He waited for Pawluk's nod before advancing again as the other four moved through the doorway after them. Within a few paces they had reached the point where the main corridor running north-south intersected with the one connecting with the east and west wings, where the guest suites were located.

Standing had memorised the lay-out from the plans MI6 had given them and did not hesitate for an instant. 'Bash, Pawluk and me will clear the rooms off the right corridor. Cowpat, you and Paddy work through the left hand side. Banger and Mustard, hold this area and cover the corridor ahead. Banger, fix a couple of standard charges on the main entrance side of the doorway here. If there's any sign of movement or activity from the corridor beyond it, you know what to do. RV back here in five minutes from now. Anyone not here by then will be assumed not to have made it. Let's go.'

Standing began moving fast along the right hand corridor, pausing at each door and then while Pawluk covered the rest of the corridor, Macleod stood poised facing the doorway with his Kalashnikov in one hand and a grenade in the other. Standing turned the handle and opened the door with his left. To avoid triggering a knee-jerk reaction from anyone inside, he didn't throw it back but pushed it gently open. Inside was an officer with the badges of rank of a Russian general. He was sitting on the edge of a bed, while an orderly with corporal's stripes knelt before him tying the General's shoelaces. Macleod's Kalashnikov spat twice and the General toppled over onto the bed, his blood soaking into the Egyptian cotton sheets. Standing double-tapped the orderly as well, then quietly closed the door and they moved onto the next room.

Standing killed a Chechen officer in the next room, a man who looked more like an eighteenth century pirate with wild, unwashed hair and beard, and a black patch over one eye. Disarmed by Putin's guards on his way into the palace, he was powerless to defend himself as Standing's double-tap blew holes in his chest.

Most of the other delegates to Putin's conference had either not yet arrived or had already moved on to another part of the palace, because the only other occupants they found on the corridor were four Syrian servants tidying and bed-making in the guest rooms, probably sent to work in Russia as a quid pro quo for Putin's support for President Assad. Standing gave each of them the finger to the lips sign that was intelligible in any language, closed the door and moved on without harming them.

Having cleared the corridor of potential threats they returned to Parker and Coleman at the intersection, and were joined a few moments later by Ireland and Williams. 'All good?' Standing said. Ireland nodded and gave him a thumbs up. 'Okay,' Standing said. 'Banger, let's close the door behind us. Set a two minute fuse and we'll be through the next set of doors before it goes off.'

Parker pushed a detonator into the standard charges he'd placed on the far side of the double doors, fixed to the post where the wall met the ceiling on either side, so the blast would demolish the walls, bring down the ceiling and block the doorway with rubble. They moved on again deeper into the palace towards the main state rooms and Putin's presidential suite, and as a sign that they were nearing the holy of holies, the marble floor that they had been walking on gave way to a carpet with such a deep pile that it felt almost like they were walking on air. Baroque sofas, chairs and tables stood against the walls, there were crystal chandeliers overhead and the ornate plasterwork of the ceiling was lavishly gilded. 'Bloody hell,' Macleod whispered as they advanced along the corridor, 'it's an oligarch's wet dream made real, isn't it?'

Standing nodded. 'Dictator chic: a perfect combination of limitless wealth and absolutely zero good taste. Pity that all that money's been wasted though,' he added as they heard the muffled blast of the standard charges going off behind them. The heavy doors had absorbed some, but not all of the blast, and they were now hanging open but, as Parker had intended, the corridor beyond them was completely blocked by fallen rubble. Any Russian pursuit of them from outside the palace would be delayed by several minutes while they struggled to clear the blockage.

They were now into the heart of the palace where the decor became even more over the top. They were advancing in two teams on either side of the broad main corridor, pausing to clear each room as they went. The first room they came to was a theatre and cinema. Lavishly embroidered velvet curtains hid a stage under a golden proscenium arch and there was another gilded ceiling surrounding yet another massive crystal chandelier. The room was empty and they moved on.

Next to it was a bar which was marble floored, huge and entirely devoid of furniture except for four gold and red plush bar stools lined up facing the bar at once side of the room, behind which were mahogany shelves displaying rare brandies, whiskies, vodkas and magnums of vintage champagne, the price of any one of them enough to feed an ordinary Russian family for a year. Once more the room was empty but Pawluk put a burst of rounds through the display, scattering shards of glass and liquor in all directions before closing the door. This was obviously the entertainment complex within the building, catering to every whim of Putin and his guests, because the next room was a casino with green baize roulette, poker and chemin-de-fer tables and an arcade full of one armed bandits and video games consoles.

Beyond that was Putin's own private strip club. It was lined with purple velvet and dimly lit, the only natural light being filtered through a stained glass panel set in the ceiling. The leather and velvet banquettes around the edge of the room faced onto a small circular stage. At its heart, its metal catching the light, was a shiny steel pole for the strippers and pole-dancers to entertain Putin's cronies. A row of cubicles off the main room each contained a bed draped with black or cream satin sheets.

A dozen beautiful and minimally dressed young women, their pale faces suggesting that it had been some time since any of them had seen the sun or even daylight, were sitting around the room. They leapt to their feet as Standing opened the door, and they were already assuming professional smiles, though their eyes remained blank, until they realised that the men in the doorway were not what they were expecting. Rather than elderly Generals and Russian apparatchiks they saw a group of young, roughly dressed and heavily armed soldiers staring back at them. 'Tell them to stay quiet and they'll not be harmed,' Standing said to Pawluk. 'If they hear bangs and crashes after we've gone, they need to get down on the floor and stay there until well after the last shots or explosions.' He waited until the message had been relayed and then shut the door and moved on again.

For the most part, the rooms they had passed so far had been empty of threats or targets, but that all changed as they reached the next corridor and immediately came under fire from a group of Russian marines who were guarding the entrance to a suite of rooms with another double-headed golden eagle above the doors. If Standing had not already known from his study of the plans that they had reached Putin's master suite, the eagle would have been a dead giveaway. Standing's hair-trigger fighting instincts had already kicked in as the firing began and he had dived and rolled across the carpet, returning fire as he went. He took out one of the marines, the Russian's head erupting in a spray of blood that half-blinded the man next to him, who was soon adding his own lifeblood to the mix as a double-tap from Macleod felled him. Two men remained. Rounds from Parker's suppressed AK took care of one of them and although the other man dropped his weapon and raised his hands as he tried to surrender, Pawluk, still burning with rage at the death of his friend Marko, put a burst into him.

The SAS team were already sprinting up the corridor and bursting through the double doors with Standing once more in the lead, giving any remaining defenders inside minimal time to prepare for the threat. However, this time there were no targets to engage and Putin's own personal master suite was deserted. Moving quickly, they searched the lounge area and the vast bedroom with a canopied bed that would not have been out of place at the Palace of Versailles, and checked the marbled bathroom with an ornate bathtub that was surmounted by yet another canopy, but that room too was empty.

Retracing their steps, they headed down towards the last remaining state room in this part of the complex, the conference room, off which was Putin's own personal office. If the Russian President was to be found anywhere, it would surely be here.

Rounding a bend in the corridor, they found their way once more blocked, this time by four soldiers from the Kremlin Regiment. All of them were over six feet tall and all were dressed in full ceremonial regalia. They were guarding another huge double door.

Standing double-tapped one of the soldiers, poleaxing him to the ground while the others simultaneously took out the other three. Moving quickly, they formed up on either side of the doors, Kalashnikovs and grenades at the ready. Standing gave the usual silent three - two - one signal with his fingers and then pushed the door open and dived through it, taking in the disposition of every person within the room in a single glance. Inside the room there was an armed bodyguard in each corner, two bodyguards by the door and a further four bodyguards around a man in the centre of the room. Standing had seen enough news coverage of Russia to know that he was looking at Vladimir Putin. As the Russian President dived behind his desk, a gun battle erupted with a succession of precise double taps from the attackers, answered by wilder bursts of semi-automatic fire from the rapidly diminishing number of bodyguards who were still upright and capable of firing their weapons.

The Ukrainian, Pawluk, was wounded as a round shattered his forearm, sending blood spraying in all directions. Williams dragged him out of the direct firing line behind a sofa and although he had to stay flat to the floor himself to avoid the enemy fire, he managed to clamp a tourniquet round Pawluk's upper arm and jammed a field dressing on to the wound to slow the bleeding.

Standing ducked behind a sofa but he knew that it would offer little protection from a bullet. He bobbed up but as he did so Macleod shouted a warning. A hail of bullets tore through the sofa as Standing dropped to the floor. 'Stay down, Sarge!' shouted Macleod.

Standing rolled on to his back. Macleod was ignoring his own advice and was standing upright, sighting down his carbine, making no attempt to take cover.

'Bash!' shouted Standing, but Macleod ignored him.

Macleod had a slight smile on his face as he continued to fire at the remaining bodyguards.

'Get down, Bash!' yelled Standing, but Macleod continue to fire double taps. Then there was a loud click and Standing realised that Macleod's Kalashnikov had jammed.

Macleod swore and he looked across at Standing. He flashed him a tight smile and Standing instinctively knew that he was thinking - unlike the new carbine that they had been testing at PATA, Kalashnikovs never jammed. Until they did.

As Macleod locked eyes with Standing, the AK of one of the bodyguards spat fire and Macleod convulsed as he was hurled backwards by the force of the rounds.

Standing rolled over again, got up on his knees and double-tapped the shooter, then dived and rolled to duck the incoming fire from another and then took him out too. A third man made a fatal hesitation as he tried to pick a target and he too was cut apart in a hail of fire from Standing and Coleman. Only one bodyguard was now still capable of fighting and as Standing heard the rattle of double-taps from Parker and Ireland's weapons that signalled that man's end as well, he dropped to his knees and leaned over Macleod.

One glance at the three craters punched through Macleod's chest by the close range burst of AK fire, showed Standing that this was one battle that Macleod would not be able to survive. As he met his gaze, Macleod, still conscious, opened his mouth to speak but before he could say anything he convulsed and went still.

Looking down at the lifeless body of his friend, Standing felt a momentary feeling of utter helplessness and despair, but pushed it away swiftly. This was not a time for any weakness, regrets or what might have beens. The job was not yet finished and they were far from safe. His responsibility was to look after the living, not grieve for the dead. In one swift glance around the room, he made sure that all the threats had been eliminated and then turned his attention to the figure who was now crouching behind his over-sized, throne-like chair and casting around desperately for some means of escape. There was none.

'Don't even think about it you bastard,' Standing said. 'We've come a long way to find you and your time's up now. If you hadn't invaded Ukraine, a hell of a lot of people would still be alive who are dead now, including my mate there.' He gestured towards Macleod's body. 'And I wouldn't be standing here in front of you with a gun in my hand. You're going to pay the price for all that now and I just wish your people could see you now, hiding behind a chair like the snivelling coward and pathetic little bully you are.'

Putin said something in Russian.

'What did he say?' Standing said to Pawluk.

He said, 'I am not who you think I am.'

'What the fuck does that mean?' Standing shrugged and pulled the trigger, twice. Both shots hit the man in the chest, not his face, so it remained untouched and would be instantly recognisable to the first Russians to reach his corpse.

'Pawluk,' Standing said, 'use your good arm to spray a few slogans on the walls to make sure the surviving Russians get the message we want them to have. While you're doing that, Banger can be preparing a little senseless destruction and then we need to get out of here.'

Pawluk produced the cans of spray paint and sprayed in Russian cyrillic script on the walls of the room and the corridor outside. Standing had brought a miniature camera with him just for this purpose and took pictures of the corpse of Putin and the slogans on the walls. MI6 could then leak these to the world's media via anonymous sources, ensuring that if the Russians tried to cover up Putin's death it would still be revealed.

The fire-fight had been so intense that the team were now short of ammo, and they helped themselves to the weapons and ammunition Putin's bodyguards had been carrying. Standing then took one more look around the room, still astounded by the level of opulence, the gold chandeliers and wall lights, the priceless works of art, porcelain ornaments, ancient tapestries and the thick, thick carpets.

Before leaving, there was one last distasteful task to perform. They could not take Macleod's body with them, since they would still have to fight their way out of the palace past Putin's remaining guards and troops, and although none of them were carrying any identification of any sort, the absolute deniability of the op meant that they could not risk Macleod's face being recognised, or his fingerprints taken, or his teeth being compared with dental records. So, hating himself for doing it, but knowing that it was necessary, Standing waited until the others had exited the conference room, then placed a white phosphorous grenade against Macleod's face. 'Sorry, mate,' said Standing. He pulled the pin from the grenade and ducked out of the conference room, slamming the door behind him just before it detonated.

The others were waiting in defensive firing positions but before they could begin moving off, they heard noises from the direction of the entrance corridor as the makeshift rubble barricade that Parker's charges had created was breached and within seconds Russians troops came into view. They were met with a hail of fire that scythed down the front row of men. With characteristic indifference to losses, the Russian officers, unseen behind their men, merely urged the next rank of soldiers forward and when they too fell, cut apart by the SAS men's relentlessly accurate fire, the next rank after that were sent forward in their place.

Even though they were reaping a terrible harvest among the Russians, the SAS men were now hard-pressed with the enemy inching ever closer to them and even using the bodies of their dead comrades as cover while they fired from behind them. The SAS team began to give ground, 'pepper-potting' their way back, with half retreating through the corridor of the palace while the other half covered them and then dropped back behind them in turn. They passed the entrances to other side corridors and more rooms, but the aim of the op, the elimination of their principal target, had now been achieved and Standing could see no useful purpose in clearing those areas as well, particularly when they were coming under such heavy pressure themselves. So they simply tossed grenades down the side corridors to deter any pursuit from that direction and then moved on again.

'Buy me a few more seconds,' Parker shouted to Standing, as he prepped more standard charges and inserted fuses into them, and set them with a minimum delay, purely to block off any possibility of pursuit. When they detonated, they would be as dangerous to the SAS men behind them as the Russians in front, unless they had made good their retreat by then. On Parker's 'Ready' signal, Standing lobbed his last WP grenade as far up the corridor as he could throw it and the instant it exploded and the familiar choking pall of white smoke spread through the corridor as a blizzard of white phosphorous fragments filled the air, the SAS team rose as one man and ran back along the corridor behind them. Parker, having triggered the fuses, followed them. They all threw themselves down on his shout of 'NOW!', opening their mouths and blocking their ears to avoid perforated ear drums in the blast that followed a heartbeat later.

They didn't wait to discover if the fresh blast had blocked the corridor, but hurried on before any remaining Russians could resume their pursuit. The wound Pawluk had sustained in the shoot-out in the conference room was now bleeding heavily again and with his fingers slippery with blood he was struggling to hold his weapon, so he went ahead of the others as they continued to pepper-pot their way back, still fighting a rearguard action against the persistent but diminishing number of Russians on their tails.

Parker had one last set of charges and laid them at the end of the corridor just before it opened into the area housing the covered swimming pool, flanked by yet more Corinthian columns. As they moved along the edge of the pool, they heard the muffled explosions of the charges that he had laid.

Ahead of them was the narrow opening of the escape tunnel, a long, artificially lit and concrete lined passageway burrowing down through the earth at a 45 degree angle. About 800 metres in length, its bottom end opened directly on to the boat dock at the edge of the Black Sea.

Standing told Pawluk to drop back behind them while he and Parker led the way forward, with Ireland, Coleman and Williams in close support. The SAS men flattened themselves to the tunnel floor and wormed their way forward, weapons extended in front of them, ready to engage any target. In the entrance to the tunnel, they could see two dark figures outlined against the bright sunlight. They were facing out towards the sea, not up the tunnel, seeming to confirm that whatever alarms had been raised had yet to reach these men.

Standing could simply have shot them or rolled a grenade down the slope at them, but that would have alerted any other guards, standing unseen on the dock at either side of the entrance. Instead, he drew his combat knife, waited while Parker did the same, then both men crept forward, getting to their knees and then their feet while behind them Ireland and Coleman each lined up one of the two men, ready to drill them with double taps if they should turn and see the two SAS men bearing down on them.

With painful slowness, each footfall measured and deliberate, Standing and Parker closed on the two men. A metre short of his target, Standing paused again for an instant and glanced sideways at Parker to make sure he was also poised and ready. Then once more he gave the three- two- one countdown on his fingers and both SAS men sprang forward, each covering the gap to their target in a single stride. Standing's left arm snaked around his man's neck and jerked savagely tight, choking off any shout or cry he might have made, while the razor-edged combat knife cut through flesh, windpipe and jugular vein in one stroke.

As a gout of blood spurted out of the man's severed throat, Standing glanced across to make sure Parker had also dealt with his target, then both men lowered their victims silently to the ground and as the others moved up to them, they advanced to the tunnel mouth. They paused again there for a couple of minutes, allowing their eyesight to become accustomed to the bright sunlight after the gloom of the tunnel, then on Standing's signal, the SAS men burst out into the open.

To their left were a group of four Russian Marines clustered around an officer who had a radio receiver clamped to his head. Standing and Parker raked them with gunfire and they fell to the ground without firing a single shot.

A smaller group of men on the other side of the dock had no better luck under the withering fire of Ireland, Coleman and Williams, and within seconds the dock was covered with lifeless Russian bodies. As Ireland and Coleman began pushing them off the dock, they had the enthusiastic assistance of the wounded Pawluk, who had now emerged from cover in the tunnel.

'What now?' Parker said to Standing, as they scanned the sea and checked the tunnel for any continuing threats.

'Now?' Standing said, pointing to the butt of his AK, where his Personal Locator Beacon was concealed. 'We wait for the cavalry and hope she's not far away.'

Chapter 26

As they waited with mounting impatience for Lisa's heli to show up, scanning the sea for the first sight or sound of the heli, there were increasingly ominous warnings from behind them. Gunfire was now coming from Russians moving down the tunnel, and although the SAS men were of course returning fire, they were now in a vulnerable position, outlined against the bright sunlight but directing fire into a darkened tunnel with only the muzzle flashes from the enemy weapons to guide their own shots. An RPG round was then fired down the tunnel. It flashed past Standing close enough for him to feel the searing heat from the rocket propelling it, and clipped the edge of the dock, sending fragments of concrete flying like shrapnel before the grenade buried itself in the sea and exploded in a water spout. It had caused no casualties but the warning signs were there. They needed to get the hell out of Dodge.

Equally threatening, if not more so, more troops were now firing down on them from among the trees lining the cliff tops high above them. Those Russians were in good cover, whereas the open dock offered the SAS men almost no protection at all, and despite having liberated those spare magazines from the dead soldiers in the conference room, they were once again running short of ammunition.

To Standing's huge relief, the Hind at last appeared offshore, a black speck skimming the waves, and growing rapidly in size as it headed in towards them. But he could also now hear the ominous sound of rotors coming from the land side, out of sight for the moment behind the cliff edge above them but getting louder as a Russian heli approached.

Trapped at the water's edge and with enemy fire now so heavy that to remain where they were would be suicide, there was only one decision that Standing could make. 'We'll have to swim for it!' he shouted, just making himself heard above the crack and rattle of enemy rounds and their own return fire. 'Loose off every round and grenade you've got and then drop everything and dive for it. Lisa'll pick us up.'

There was a final tremendous fusillade of fire, shredding the foliage at the cliff edge above them and sending torrents of rounds whining and ricocheting up the tunnel, and then the others dived off the dock. Standing covered them for a few more seconds, then threw his last grenade into the tunnel mouth and fired his last few rounds at the enemy on the cliff edge, before following his patrol mates and diving off the dock into the sea.

The SAS men were all good swimmers and although hampered by their boots and clothes, they were swimming steadily away from the dock, but with a wounded arm, Pawluk was struggling behind them. Standing swam over to him, took a grip on his collar and, kicking hard with his legs, propelled them both along. As he did so, the Ukrainian reached inside his jacket with his one good hand and held something up out of the water above his head.

'What the hell are you doing?' Standing said, swallowing a mouthful of sea water.

'Don't worry, we'll be safe, it's an icon of our patron saint, St Olga of Kyiv, she'll protect us! I took it from the wall of Putin's office.'

'That won't save us,' Standing said. 'Only one thing will do that, and it's the heli, not some superstition. And meanwhile you need to use that good arm to help me by keeping swimming yourself, not using it to wave your toys at invisible saints.'

Pawluk didn't say anything in reply and did begin to splash the water in a ragged stroke with his arm, though he still kept a firm grip on the icon in his hand.

By now they were about a hundred metres off shore, which was not a centimetre too far because rounds fired by the Russian soldiers who were now spilling out of the tunnel on to the dock, were adding to those from the men on the top of the cliff, and whipping up the water around them like hailstones. However, Lisa had now brought the Hind to within reach of them.

The Russian heli appeared above the cliffs. Lisa launched a missile within seconds of the Russian Hind coming into view and though its pilot made frantic attempts to evade it, almost standing the heli on its tail rotors as he threw it around, the missile struck home and the Russian Hind disappeared inside a cloud of fire, smoke and metal fragments.

With small arms rounds bouncing off her own heli's armour plating, and an RPG round streaking past her nose, Lisa fired a burst of cannon to suppress any further fire from the Russians on the dock and then brought the Hind into a hover with its hull resting on the water alongside the SAS team.

A few centimetres lower and the Hind would have filled with water but by making constant minute adjustments of the triple flight controls - cyclic, collective and pedals - Lisa held it steady as the surviving members of the SAS team scrambled aboard. Parker, Ireland, Coleman, Williams and Pawluk were in the back, but Standing had used the footholds in the fuselage to clamber into the gunner's cockpit, forward and below the pilot's. He settled himself in the seat and took the gun controls while sea water puddled around his feet. Quickly donning the comms headset, he said to Lisa, 'You'll have your hands well full getting us out of here, so I'll take over the weapons. You just get us into the air!'

Suddenly the sea erupted around the Hind, as a couple of Russian Navy gunboats from the Black Sea fleet, assigned as guard ships to the palace, sped into view and at once opened fire on the helicopter as it hovered with its fuselage still kissing the water. Standing swung the 12.7mm chain gun and gave each of the gunboats a long burst. The sailors quickly hit the deck with the rest of their cannon fire going high over the top of the heli.

Lisa increased revs until the Hind was shuddering and hydroplaning across the water at a high rate of knots then suddenly shot a couple of hundred feet into the air. She quickly brought the heli back down to wave-top level before swinging around and heading for home.

Standing followed up his bursts with the chain gun with the launch of a missile from the pylon fixed to the fuselage alongside the cockpit. The missile was radio guided with five VHS frequency bands and two codes to prevent the enemy jamming it, but the gunner had to keep the cross-hairs of the laser sight on the target until impact. As Lisa threw the heli around, Standing struggled to keep the target - the lead Russian gunboat - in the cross-hairs, but each time the Hind's swoops and lurches and corkscrewing turns threw his aim off, he locked on again and the radio signal, slaved to the sights, corrected the missile's course. There was a blinding flash as the missile finally struck home and when it cleared, the gunboat had disappeared. Torn apart as its magazine erupted, it sank in a heartbeat.

Standing loosed off a final burst at the other Russian gunboat, now a rapidly diminishing target astern of them as Lisa steered the Hind onwards at maximum power, with the airframe juddering from the strain on the twin engines.

'What do you reckon Lisa?' he said over the intercom. 'Are we going to make it back?'

'Yeah, we should be okay now. The Ukrainians will soon be flying top cover and their forces are on the ground most of the way once we cross the coast, so if we can get across the rest of sea without meeting any more Russian gunboats, or any Mig-29s scrambled to intercept us, with a bit of luck we should make it.'

'Why do I not find that reassuring?' he said.

She laughed. 'Maybe because you're a natural pessimist. Me, I'm one of life's optimists and anyway, let's face it, I've probably encountered as many shit-storms in mid-air as you have on the ground and since we're both still here, we must be doing something right.'

'Okay I'm convinced,' Standing said. 'I'll just sit back and enjoy the ride.'

'And that's the first sensible thing you've said.'

They passed well wide of another Russian warship patrolling the Black Sea, but either its crew were not at full alert or the Hind's distinctive profile fooled them into thinking it was a Russian Air Force heli, and they passed it without any incoming fire.

They crossed the Ukrainian coastline soon afterwards and the remainder of the flight passed without incident save for a burst of badly aimed ground-fire from a trigger-happy Ukrainian army patrol which left the Hind undamaged. As the heli came to a hover over the SAS Forward Operating Base, its top cover escort of Ukrainian jets waggled their wings and then flew on towards their own base, while Lisa set it down on the ground.

Standing hurried to make his report to Colonel Davies. Despite their losses, the op had been a blinding success, and the Colonel was cock-a-hoop as he congratulated Standing and then hurried to pass the good news up the chain of command to his superiors via the ultra-secure scrambled comms.

'He'll already be mentally measuring himself for a general's uniform,' Parker said, with a grin. 'Ready for a celebration beer yourself?' he said gesturing towards the Mess tent. 'We've only got Ukrainian beer but it'll do the job.'

'Get them in,' Standing said, 'but I must have a quick word with Lisa first, before she disappears into the wide blue yonder.'

Parker cocked an eye at him, but said nothing.

By the time Standing strode back across the helicopter landing pad, Lisa had already finished checking over the Hind and was leaning against the fuselage, chatting to Earl, who had rejoined her as soon as the heli touched down.

She looked up and smiled as she saw Standing. 'I wasn't sure if I'd be seeing you again, Sergeant Standing,' she said.

'After you risked your neck again for us, both to get us in there and then, even more importantly, to get us out again afterwards, I'd have to be a complete arsehole not to at least say "Thanks".'

'It's been my pleasure,' she said, the sound of her Southern drawl sending tingles down his spine. 'And I'll say this for you, Sergeant, there's never a dull moment when you're around. Flying

CIA taxi runs is going to seem even more ho hum than usual after all the excitement of the last few weeks.' She paused and gave him a calculating look. 'And speaking of excitement, as Mae West used to say, "is that a pistol in your pocket, or are you just pleased to see me?".'

Standing laughed. 'It's a pistol, but I am pleased to see you as well.'

'And do you ever mix business with pleasure, Sergeant?'

'Well, technically the business is finished now. It's job done here for us and we'll be heading back to the UK tomorrow.'

'All the more reason to take your pleasures while you have the chance.' She gave him another sly smile. 'You quite sure that's a pistol in your pocket?'

'Well, I guess there's only one way to find out.'

'Now you're talking.' She glanced at her gunner. 'Earl, you wanna take a stroll around the base?'

'Way ahead of you,' he said, with a wink to Standing. 'I'll be finding myself a beer and a burger somewhere and I won't be hurrying back any time soon.'

'Banger's got a cold beer waiting for me,' Standing said. 'Why not have that one on me, because it looks like I may be a while.'

'So, Sergeant,' Lisa said, as Earl walked away. 'You ever made out in the back of a helicopter before?'

'No, that'll be a first. Should I buckle up for a bumpy ride?'

'Hell no, it'll be as smooth as silk with just the right amount of danger.' She moved towards him, moistening her lips with the tip of her tongue, but paused just out of reach. 'Just don't be getting any ideas about true love and happy ever after though,' she said.

Standing smiled as he reached for her. 'Lisa, you took the words right out of my mouth.'

Chapter 27

Twenty four hours later Standing and his team had been flown back to Britain and transferred by heli to Hereford. As soon as their feet touched the ground, the team headed for the bar in the Sergeants' Mess, as was traditional after any operation in which a comrade had been killed. At their invitation, they were also joined there by a handful of their closest friends from their troop. Any other SAS men there, knowing what was going on, tiptoed round them or went somewhere else for the night, leaving them all with plenty of room to talk things through.

Later, as Standing strolled across the base, he passed a workman who was replacing the inscribed plate on the plinth below the regimental clock. Every time a new name was to be added to the plate it was unscrewed and taken to be engraved at an old-established small family jewellers shop in the town centre. It was the sort of place where you took the trophy for winning your local pub darts league or having the biggest giant marrow at the flower show to be engraved with your name, but had also been serving the SAS ever since the Regiment had arrived at Bradbury Lines, Hereford, and the jewellers was now run by the second or third generation of the family since then.

Once the new name had been engraved on the plate it was sent back to the SAS base and refitted to the plinth. At the same time, in a tradition going back to when the idea of the memorial was first conceived in the early 1960s, the same jewellers inscribed the name in perfect calligraphy inside a bound book of remembrance which was held in the Regimental chapel. Standing stood in front of the clock in silence, head bowed, for a minute and then moved slowly away.

The following morning, Standing received an urgent message summoning him to RAF Northolt for a meeting with Agnes Day. When he came out of the ops room, he found a Puma already waiting, rotors turning, on the heli pad in the middle of what used to be the parade ground until the powers that be realised that, since SAS men didn't really go in for marching, saluting and all the other bullshit which the regular, green army delighted in, they might as well turn it over to something more useful.

Less than two hours later he was facing Agnes Day across a table in a windowless briefing room at Northolt. Three other people, all men of a certain age and wearing Savile Row suits, were in the room with them. Standing did not recognise any of them and Ms Day made no effort to introduce them. They remained silent throughout, one occasionally jotting notes on a pad, while the others listened intently as she interrogated Standing.

'First of all,' she said, 'and of course I realise you've already been debriefed on the op at some length, and in fact I have seen a summary of it, but I'd like you to talk me through the events that took place within the conference room at Putin's Palace.' She rolled her eyes. 'I'd prefer to call it something a little less tabloid, but it doesn't seem to have any other recognisable name.'

She listened carefully as he ran through the events leading up to the assassination of Putin, and only interrupted him when he had described the killing. 'You're absolutely sure it was Putin?' she said.

'I didn't see a birth certificate, but I've seen him on enough news broadcasts; it was him all right.'

'And you're certain he was dead?'

Standing was not used to having his word questioned and he could feel the familiar warning signs of anger rising inside him. 'I double-tapped him at a close enough range to leave powder burns on his chest. Why? Don't you trust me?'

'Look at this,' she said by way of reply. She opened her laptop, tapped a couple of keys and then turned it towards him. A news clip with Russian titles was running on the screen. It showed Putin with a group of his advisers and generals.

'So what?' he said.

'This was broadcast by Moscow this morning.'

Standing frowned. 'And? It's probably old footage. They'll be trying to pretend everything is normal to avoid panic or encouraging rival factions to get busy. They probably won't announce his death until a new regime has control.'

'You'd think so, wouldn't you? Except this footage includes a comment from Putin on an attack on Kyiv that only happened yesterday.'

'Are you saying I'm making it up?' Standing said.

'Not at all, not at all,' Ms Day said hastily. 'I'm sure you killed the man you thought was Vladimir Putin and I'm sure he looked just like him.' She paused. 'Do you remember how Saddam Hussein used lookalikes, doubles of himself, whose job was to sit in his car during motorcades, or appear on the balcony of the presidential palace, waving to the crowds, while Saddam kept himself safe from potential assassins by keeping out of sight or travelling in an anonymous-looking, but bullet-proof car, further back in the motorcade?'

Standing's jaw dropped and he felt a chill in his guts. 'You mean I shot a Putin lookalike?'

She nodded. 'I'm afraid that's the conclusion that we have come to. No doubt Putin was elsewhere in the palace or in his bomb-proof panic room, leaving his lookalike to smile, nod and of course, draw any fire, before he emerged to address his generals and officials once the conference actually got under way.' She gave a theatrical sigh. 'And now unfortunately, forewarned and forearmed, he will become even more wary of attack from within or outside Russia, and consequently even more difficult, if not impossible, for us to reach again.'

Having rained on Standing's victory parade, she did her best to throw him a bone. 'None of this reflects on you personally, of course. It was a good plan, and you chaps did wonders to get as far as you did. No blame attaches to you for the fact that it didn't achieve its ultimate objective.' She gave another sigh. 'It's just unfortunate that we're now going to have to work out how to deal with an even more paranoid and vengeful Russian leader. However, in addition to the spray-painted slogans you left behind yourselves, we have taken further steps to steer Putin's suspicions in other directions, safely away from any thoughts of Western involvement. A hitherto unknown group calling itself "The Sons of Prigozhin" has put out a statement on Telegram claiming that they launched an attack on Putin at his palace in revenge for the killing of Prigozhin. The attack was narrowly thwarted but, the group says, "Putin will not be so lucky the next time".'

Standing shook his head in disbelief. 'And the Kremlin has actually swallowed that?'

'Don't sound so surprised, we can be very convincing when we want. So with luck Putin will blame some of the surviving elements of Wagner Group or, failing that, the Ukrainians for the attempt on his life. However, we can be sure that someone, somewhere, is going to be made to pay for his close call with death.'

Standing gave her a dubious look. 'Well, I hope you're right, because if Putin ever finds out that we were behind the attack on him, the consequences don't bear thinking about. Now, is there anybody else you'd like me to kill at the moment or can I take a few days off?'

'No, you enjoy some rest and relaxation, Sergeant Standing,' she said with a seraphic smile, 'but just make sure you keep your sat-phone switched on.'

About the Author

Stephen Leather is one of the UK's most successful thriller writers, an ebook and *Sunday Times* bestseller and author of the critically acclaimed Dan 'Spider' Shepherd series and the Jack Nightingale supernatural detective novels. Born in Manchester, he began writing full time in 1992. Before becoming a novelist he was a journalist for more than ten years on newspapers such as *The Times*, the *Daily Mirror*, the *Glasgow Herald*, the *Daily Mail* and the *South China Morning Post* in Hong Kong. He is one of the country's most successful ebook authors and his ebooks have topped the Amazon Kindle charts in the UK and the US. In 2011 alone he sold more than 500,000 ebooks and was voted by *The Bookseller* magazine as one of the 100 most influential people in the UK publishing world.

His bestsellers have been translated into fifteen languages. He has also written for television shows such as *London's Burning*, *The Knock* and the BBC's *Murder in Mind* series and two of his books, *The Stretch* and *The Bombmaker*, were filmed for TV. In 2017 The Chinaman was filmed as The Foreigner starring Jackie Chan and Pierce Brosnan.

You can learn about Stephen Leather from his website, www.stephenleather.com, or find him on Facebook.

First Strike

MI5 analyst David White has always tried to be a good father, so when his daughters want to go to a music festival in Israel, he agrees to take them. But his world falls apart when his daughters are killed in the Hamas massacre that left 1,200 innocent civilians dead.

White is taken hostage down in the tunnels under Gaza, and Dan 'Spider' Shepherd and a crack SAS team are sent in to rescue him.

Safely back in London, White is a changed man. He wants revenge for what happened to his family and sets out to kill the men who planned and financed the Hamas attacks.

And as White embarks on a vengeance-driven killing spree, Shepherd is the only man who can stop him.

First Strike, the new Spider Shepherd book, is available on Amazon now.

Printed in Great Britain
by Amazon

270f3757-c645-412e-9bd3-eb9c05983f24R01